THE
MARTIN
BOOK
WALTER CARTER

The Martin Book
A complete history of Martin guitars
By Walter Carter

GPI Books
An imprint of Miller Freeman Books, San Francisco

Published in the UK by Balafon Books, an imprint of Outline Press Ltd,
115J Cleveland Street, London W1P 5PN, England.

First American Edition 1995
Published in the United States by Miller Freeman Books,
600 Harrison Street, San Francisco, CA 94107
Publishers of GPI Books and *Guitar Player* magazine
A member of the United Newspapers Group

ISBN 0-87930-354-9

Library of Congress Catalog Card Number 94-78805

Printed in Hong Kong

Art Director: Nigel Osborne
Design: Sally Stockwell
Editor: Tony Bacon
Typesetting by Type Technique, London
Print and origination by Regent Publishing Services

95 96 97 98 99 5 4 3 2 1

CONTENTS

THE CF MARTIN ORGANISATION
NAZARETH PENNSYLVANIA 18064

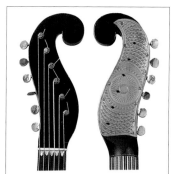

Martin
Guitars

INTRODUCTION

*Martin is the oldest and most respected name among American instrument makers –
and not just guitar makers, but makers of all instruments. In the guitar world, Martin
had been established for over 50 years when Orville Gibson started carving the tops
and backs of mandolins in the 1890s, over 100 years when Leo Fender started putting
pickups on solid guitar bodies in the 1940s. Martin has carried on steadily while such
important names as Washburn, Epiphone, Gretsch, National, Vega, Kay and Harmony
arose, flourished and perished.*

*Unlike most of the great names in the guitar world, Martin never became a big
company. From a one-man shop it grew into a small factory in a small town. Even as
the acoustic guitar market was booming in the 1960s, Martin turned out less than 20
per cent of the guitars that Gibson was producing. Now in the 1990s, with demand for
Martins exceeding production capabilities, the company plans only a small, cautious
expansion, refusing to sacrifice quality for quantity. At a trade show in 1993 dealers
were told that Martin was back-ordered for one year. Yet the store owners still bought
Martins – a testament to the quality signified by the Martin name.*

*The guitars are the stars of this book, and they deserve to be. They are pictured
prominently in color portraits – from C.F. Martin Sr.'s Stauffer-influenced creations of
the 1830s to C.F. Martin IV's innovative models for the 1990s – as the stories behind
them are told through the words and actions of those who made and played them.*

Then in a reference section, they are described in detail, model by model.

*In researching and writing this story, I discovered that everyone likes to talk about
Martin guitars, and as this book shows, the author is no exception.*

WALTER CARTER, NASHVILLE 1994

"The Martin guitar fills every place. It is used by the child taking its first lessons, by the soloist in concerts, by the young lady to accompany her voice, by the club player, by the teacher in his work."
Frank Henry Martin, *PRESIDENT OF MARTIN, 1904*

"Martins are more than the standard against which all other guitars are measured. They are the definition of the steel-string acoustic guitar."
David Bromberg, *SOLO AND SESSION ROCK GUITARIST*

"When people get with Martin, they stay here. They love their work, they love the product, they love the company. It's an attitude, a pride in the product."
Mike Longworth, *CURRENTLY CONSUMER RELATIONS MANAGER, MARTIN GUITAR CO.*

"Martin was the prestige brand of guitar. It was the guitar everyone aspired to own."
Tom Paxton, *1960s FOLK SINGER/SONGWRITER*

"Our goal is to make the perfect guitar. And while it is difficult to craft anything that is absolutely perfect, we do come closer to it with every guitar we build."
C. F. Martin IV, *CURRENTLY CHAIRMAN AND CEO, MARTIN GUITAR CO.*

"I feel safe with a Martin."
Johnny Cash, *COUNTRY SINGER*

"If a tree is going to come down, if you were to ask the tree what it wanted to be, certainly the answer would be a Martin guitar. I can't imagine being anything quite that nice."
Dick Boak, *CURRENTLY DIRECTOR OF ADVERTISING, MARTIN GUITAR CO.*

THIS PAGE, LEFT: *A beautiful example of Martin's work from the end of the 19th century, this model 2-42 was probably made in the 1890s, when the company had already been building guitars for over 50 years.*

THIS PAGE, BELOW: *The original Martin factory, started in 1859, as represented in a company brochure from 1940. Catalog covers are shown at the bottom of the page dating from 1937 and from 1941.*

OPPOSITE PAGE, TOP ROW: *C.F. Martin Sr. (left; 1796-1873), founder of the Martin company, and his son C.F. Martin Jr. (right; 1825-1888). The house on Cherry Hill (right) was the Martin family's first home in Nazareth, Pennsylvania. This photograph shows how it looked in 1994.*

OPPOSITE PAGE, BOTTOM ROW: *The sticker (left; much enlarged) was issued as part of the celebrations surrounding Martin's 125th anniversary in 1958. The members of the Martin family pictured at the bottom right of the page are Frank Henry Martin (center; 1866-1948), C.F. Martin III (top; 1894-1986), and the current CEO, Chris Martin IV (born 1955).*

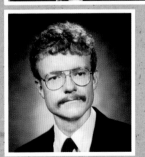

7

Martin's longevity is not so hard to explain. C.F. Martin, who founded the company in 1833, transformed the European guitar into a new, uniquely American guitar. The flat-top guitar we know today is larger, and it has steel strings rather than gut, but otherwise it's not much different from the ones Martin was making by 1850. All the Martin company had to do was keep on making guitars the same way that C.F. did. Martin was enticed at times into unfamiliar markets by the surging popularity of mandolins, banjos and electric guitars – but flat-top guitars remain the backbone of the company's fortunes.

Unlike Gibson's mandolins and archtop guitars, unlike Fender's electric solidbody guitars, Martin guitars never effected a revolutionary change in popular music. C.F. Martin's X-braced flat-tops of 1850 were well accepted... but did not start everyone playing guitar (everyone was playing banjo at that time). Martin instruments played an important role in the guitar's rise to prominence in the 1930s, but the innovations that sparked the movement should for the most part be credited to other makers. Martin guitars epitomize the folk boom of the 1960s, but the guitars themselves had been developed decades earlier. Rather than leading musical movements, Martin guitars have provided a foundation for popular music – a consistent, solid base that was always there, regardless of what style of music was the current rage.

Consistency goes a long way in explaining Martin's success, but there is more. You don't have to walk into the factory to see that Martin is a different kind of company. The factory looks more like an elementary school from the 1960s than an industrial facility – an image underscored by its location in a residential area.

Perhaps the key is a sense of humanness that comes from family ownership. In 1833, the company was founded by a man named C.F. Martin; in the 1990s, the chairman of the company is still a man named C.F. Martin. In the context of family ownership, there is today no company like Martin. Orville Gibson and Leo Fender had no children, so bloodlines were never a part of those companies' traditions. Kaman (Ovation) is in its second generation; Peavey and Taylor are still run by their founders; Gretsch has been resurrected by a descendant of the founding family after a fatal period of corporate ownership. The Martins, like any family, had their own set of problems, arguments and controversies – maybe even more emotional than those of a corporate boardroom – but after all is said and done, C.F. Martin & Co. remains a family business.

'Family' encompasses more than just a bloodline between owners. Granted, a computer-controlled router will cut the same pattern in a piece of wood regardless of whether it's owned by a corporation or a family, but the family feeling pervades the Martin workforce. Mike Longworth, Martin's historian and consumer relations manager, speaks for many employees when he says, "It's been a wonderful career. I've been here 26 years now, and there's still a lot of people here who've been here longer than I have. When people get with Martin, they stay here. They love their work, they love the product, they love the company. It's something that you might find lacking elsewhere. It's an attitude, a pride in the product."

EMBELLISHING THE ORAL HISTORY

The Martin family is obviously intertwined with the history of Martin guitars. And while written records and other documented facts can't be argued with, there is a parallel history of the company, a family history, an oral history passed down from fathers and grandfathers to sons and grandsons that casts a different, more personal light on the written facts. Chris Martin, who is C.F. Martin IV, the great-great-great-great grandson of the founder, learned the Martin story not from the company archives but from his grandfather, C.F. Martin III. Although C.F. III headed the company through the modern folk era, all the way until his death in 1986, he was a man from a different era. "So much information at that time was oral," Chris recalls, "where today it's all TV. I lived with my grandfather, and I learned so much, after work sitting in the den, just by saying, 'Well, pop, what about this?' And he'd go on for half an hour. And I'm sure his father did that to him. Today you don't. When my dad and I would hang out, we'd turn on a basketball game. My grandfather wasn't a TV watcher *per se*, and he reveled in just talking."

Chris Martin carries on that oral history in a most traditional way, admittedly embellishing it. "It's been a while since I had a chance to talk to my grandfather," Chris says in 1994, "and I've found that over time, because I tell this story so often, I'm starting to create some facts that may or may not be true."

Between the oral history and the documented history, Martin is a fascinating story – not just of a family, not just of guitars, but of American's foremost guitar family.

TO THE NEW WORLD

Christian Friedrich Martin arrived in America in 1833. To him, as to millions of immigrants, America represented freedom – in his case the freedom to make guitars without interference from violin makers.

C.F. was born on January 31, 1796. His father, Johann Georg Martin, was noted as the chief developer of the guitar in the town of Markneukirchen in the German area of Saxony (a part of East Germany from 1945 to 1990). Markneukirchen was home to many violin and guitar makers. The Martins' work as guitar makers is documented, but Chris Martin puts a more practical, less idealistic wash over the picture, based on their membership in the cabinet makers guild: "What I understand is that my great-great-great-great-great-grandfather was basically in the furniture business. Grandfather-five [Chris sometimes refers to his forebears by the number of *greats* in front of grandfather] was a cabinet maker, and his son was apprenticed with him in the business of making furniture but took an interest in guitar.

"So my great-great-great-great grandfather as a young man learned how to work with wood from his father, but his father couldn't teach him how to build guitars, because he didn't really know. He knew how to build furniture. So he went around town and asked the violin makers, would they take him on as an apprentice. And they didn't want him to have anything to do with guitars. What I concluded was that they didn't consider the guitar to be in the same class. The violin was something else again. But he was inspired enough that somehow he finagled a job with Mr. Stauffer in Vienna."

Indeed, guitars were regarded as a lower class of instrument than the violin. This was still the dawn of the guitar era in

Europe, and they had only recently evolved from a sort of poor man's lute, with five courses or pairs of strings, to an instrument with six single strings. Johann Stauffer of Vienna, Austria, the man whose shop C.F. Martin went to, was one of the more innovative guitar makers of the period.

C.F. Martin became a foreman in Stauffer's shop, but by 1825 he quit. "He quit because his goal wasn't to work for Mr. Stauffer forever," Chris explains. "His goal was to work for Mr. Stauffer and move on. And one of the things I think is important is that by becoming the foreman he learned not only how to build guitars but how to manage a business."

By the time C.F. returned to Markneukirchen in 1826 he had a new wife, whom he'd met and married in Vienna, and a new son, C.F. Martin Jr., who had been born in Vienna on October 2, 1825. Back home again, C.F. became involved in an ongoing dispute between violin makers and guitar makers. Chris Martin picks up the story: "So he goes back to Markneukirchen and he's ready – hangs out the shingle. Well, the violin makers, they're incensed. They take him to court. And their argument was that Mr. Martin was not a member of the violin makers guild. He was a member of the cabinet makers guild. And the judge said, 'Mr. Martin, what do you have to say for yourself?' And he said, 'Your honor, I asked these darn violin makers if they would teach me how to make guitars. They wouldn't give me the time of day. I was inspired. I wanted to learn. Yes, I left Germany, I'm guilty of that. I apprenticed in Austria, but I think I know what I'm doing.' The judge ruled in his favor, said, 'I'm going to make an exception.'"

The dispute involved more than C.F. Martin. As explained in A.P. Sharpe's book, *The Story of the Spanish Guitar*, the guild of violin makers filed the first complaint against the guild of cabinet makers in 1807. They renewed the complaint in 1826, calling the guitar makers "bunglers" and "nothing more than mechanics" whose products consisted of "all kinds of articles known as furniture." They argued that they themselves were the true artists with "cultured taste" and that they should have the exclusive right to make guitars.

The court denied the complaint, but five years later, in 1831, the violin makers were back in court, claiming that the cabinet

9

10

Guitar attributed to Stauffer c1820s (right) Johann Georg Stauffer (1778-1853) was born in Vienna, Austria. He became one of that country's most notable guitar makers, and in 1824 made a special instrument for the Austrian composer Franz Schubert. Christian Friedrich Martin was a foreman at Stauffer's shop during the 1820s, leaving the business in 1825. Eight years later Martin emigrated to the United States, absorbing much of the style and influence of Stauffer's instruments into the first guitars that he built there.

Ledger 1834 (above) This records that Martin's store sold violins, tuning forks, French horns, double basses, bugles — but few guitars.

Martin Stauffer-style 1830s
(below) In his new home in the United States, Martin gradually began to sell guitars that he built in the style of his Austrian mentor Johann Stauffer. Some customers evidently had a taste for ornate decoration, as on this example made for one Theresa Rand.

Back (left) The ivory inlaid neck is seen on some early European guitars. Note the Stauffer-designed key system for adjusting the neck angle, visible at the neck/body join.

Martin Stauffer-style 1830s
(left) A splendid example of early Martin. The fingerboard is angled at the body join and raised from the body, elements which recall Stauffer's work. The curving bridge design is more typical than that seen on the large guitar (above left).

'Coffin case' (above) The severe black-painted wooden cases supplied for Martin's early guitars have since been nicknamed 'coffin' cases, thanks to the coffin-like angled shape of the body section.

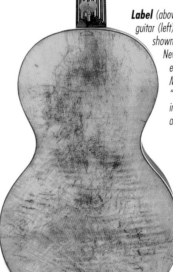

Label (above) From the Stauffer-style guitar (left). Martin's store address is shown as 196 Hudson Street, New York, and equal emphasis is given to Martin's role then as an "importer of musical instruments" and a "guitar and violin manufacturer".

11

makers already made a good living producing instrument cases for the guitars that the violin makers built (about 40 of the 120 violin makers were also guitar makers). Furthermore, the violin makers claimed that the guitar makers had stolen their guitar patterns from samples they had supplied for the construction of cases. In 1832, the court again ruled in favor of the cabinet makers, on the grounds that guitars were not mentioned in the 1677 charter of the violin makers guild.

Chris Martin's story may border on the folklorish, but an experience in Germany supported his version. Chris says that after one of his recent clinic/lectures there, a member of the audience approached him. "And he says, 'You know, that part of the story you told about the guilds, that is still the law today in Germany. I apprenticed in Belgium and I wanted to be a guitar maker in Germany, and I've got to go apprentice again with a German guitar maker.'"

One of the concerns of the violin makers was that the cabinet makers might drag the guitar industry into foreign lands. As a result of the continued harassment, that's exactly what the guitar makers did. Heinrich Schatz sailed off to America and opened shop in New York City. In September 1833, his friend C.F. Martin followed, and by the end of the year Martin had opened a music store at 196 Hudson St. (the site today is the entrance to the Holland Tunnel). There was no looking back for either man. They Americanized their names: Christian Friedrich became Fredrick or Frederick; Heinrich became Henry.

Martin's business was a full-line music store where a musician could buy a set of strings, pick up the sheet music to a popular song, try out a wind instrument, have his instrument repaired or buy a guitar made by the owner of the shop. In addition, Martin imported instruments and wholesaled them to other dealers.

Daily sales books from the 1830s are preserved in the Martin archives, and they suggest that C.F. was busier as a shop owner than as a guitar maker. He sold any kind of instrument, with flutes, violins, cellos and trumpets constituting a large part of his business. He also sold accordions and French horns, even a double bass and a piano. He took trade-ins, and he loaned

instruments on consignment to prospective salesmen. He also rented guitars at the rate of $1 per month.

In the early years Martin sold about one guitar a week. They varied in price depending on materials and ornamentation. An order for five guitars to Messrs. Nuns, Clark and Co. in 1836 illustrated the range: "1 with pegs…$7; 2 with patent screws @ $10; 1 with screws…$12; 1 with ornament…$15; 5 cases @ $3."

Other entries in the same time period include: "No. 1 guitar, got in exchange… $8; Guitar with patent screws and varnish …$18; Guitar with box and one D string…$23; Guitar and case to Mr. Frank…$28; Guitar with wood screws…$10; Sold a guitar of maple wood to the Institution of the Blind…$25."

The main pricing factor appears to have been the tuners. Guitars with wooden pegs sold for around $12 or $14, while those with metal tuners (presumably the elaborate scrolled tuner assembly of Stauffer's guitars) brought more. Violins sold in the same price range, although a cheap fiddle and bow could be had for $4. The double bass sold for $60, the piano for $70.

PENNSYLVANIA GERMAN

Early guitar labels identify Martin as an importer, and dealers in Philadelphia, Boston and other cities ordered from him. He extended credit and he also offered a 10 per cent discount for payment in cash. Four orders by J.G. Miller of Philadelphia in 1836, for example, included 11 guitars, ranging from a maple one at $9 to two with gold parts at $40. Miller's tab as of April 16, 1836 was $402.34 and ¾ of a cent.

An 1837 sales book notes that "Mr. Hartman has repaired 2 valve trumpets." This may have been a reference to another longtime associate, one of whose family members would help manage the company after C.F. Sr.'s death.

The 1834–37 sales books are written in a mix of German and English — 'with' appears on the same page as 'mit'. By 1838 the records are all in English, but despite this evidence of assimilation into American culture, the Martin family was not happy in New York. They wrote letters to friends in Germany, saying they were considering going back to the old country. They also corresponded with German friends in America who had found a place that looked just like home – the Lehigh Valley of eastern Pennsylvania. Chris Martin has visited his ancestral home in Germany, and he says, "It looked like this part of Pennsylvania. If someone would have blindfolded me and plopped me down there I would have thought I was about three miles up the road in some cornfield."

The area sounded like home, too. "A hundred and fifty years ago, people still spoke German around here," Chris says. "You know that term Pennsylvania-Dutchman? It's Pennsylvania-Deutsch Mann, in other words Pennsylvania-German."

CHERRY HILL, NAZARETH

As far away culturally as Nazareth was, geographically it was about as close as you could get to New York City and still be in Pennsylvania – today it's about 100 miles by air, but it wasn't an easy wagon ride in the 1800s. Henry Schatz had moved to the area, to the town of Millgrove, in 1835. The Martins decided once again to follow Schatz, and on May 29, 1838, Martin sold his inventory to Ludecus & Wolter, a dealer located at 320 Broadway. In 1839 they moved to Nazareth. (The association with Schatz would continue, as evidenced by guitars with a Martin & Schatz label.)

Nazareth was a hub of activity, but the town proper was owned by the Moravian church, so the Martins, not being Moravians (although they would later convert and C.F. Sr.'s grandson, Frank Henry, would become a church officer), had to settle outside of town. They bought a house in Cherry Hill, a settlement on the first hill to the north of the hill on which Nazareth was built. The Martin factory today sits at the foot of that hill.

Isolated in Nazareth, Martin maintained several business partnerships in New York as a sort of informal (and later a formal) distribution network:

- John Coupa is mentioned many times in 1830s sales books. He was a guitar teacher who had guitars made with Martin & Coupa on the label at least through 1851. During this period, Martin's 'showroom' at 385 Broadway was actually Coupa's teaching studio. As late as 1881, Coupa's name appeared in Martin advertisements as one of the "best solo players ever known" who preferred to use Martins.

- Charles Bruno of 212 Fulton St. had guitars made with a Martin & Bruno label in the 1838–39 period.
- Martin's longest New York association was with C.A. Zoebisch and Sons. Zoebisch's business at 46 Maiden Lane in New York City became the "depot" or distribution center for Martins, and they would maintain an exclusive relationship until 1898. Martin's address in print ads was the Zoebisch location, and as long as Zoebisch distributed Martins, they were stamped "New York."

With representatives in New York ready and willing to sell his guitars, C.F. Martin was free to devote all his time to building them. Business was good enough that he enlarged his facility in 1850, but he was doing more than just building and selling guitars. He was making great changes in guitar design, and by 1850 his guitars did not look like they came from the same maker as those of his New York years.

Martin's early guitars showed his Stauffer background. They were small by today's standards, with fat-waisted bodies, and upper bouts as wide as the lower bouts. Some early examples carried on a tradition of exotic materials that dated back to the Renaissance – an entire fingerboard of elephant ivory or abalone pearl, for example, or a body of highly figured 'birdseye' maple. The typical bridge had delicate pointed ends. Many guitars had a detachable neck adjustable with a clock key (one of Stauffer's innovations).

In America, a country of newcomers working hard to build a new life, there was only a limited market for ostentatious European-style instruments. Furthermore, the banjo was rising in popularity and would overshadow the guitar for the rest of the century. Consequently, C.F. Martin began adapting the European guitar to a rougher-edged, simpler American society, making his instruments plainer, more utilitarian and more competitive in price with banjos. The Stauffer-style scrolled peghead and complicated tuners were showy and expensive, so they gave way to a slotted peghead with squared-off corners. C.F. broadened the lower bout to give his guitars a deeper tone as well as a sleeker, more graceful body shape than their European antecedents. He settled on Brazilian rosewood for back and sides. Fancy ornamentation was muted down to a

13

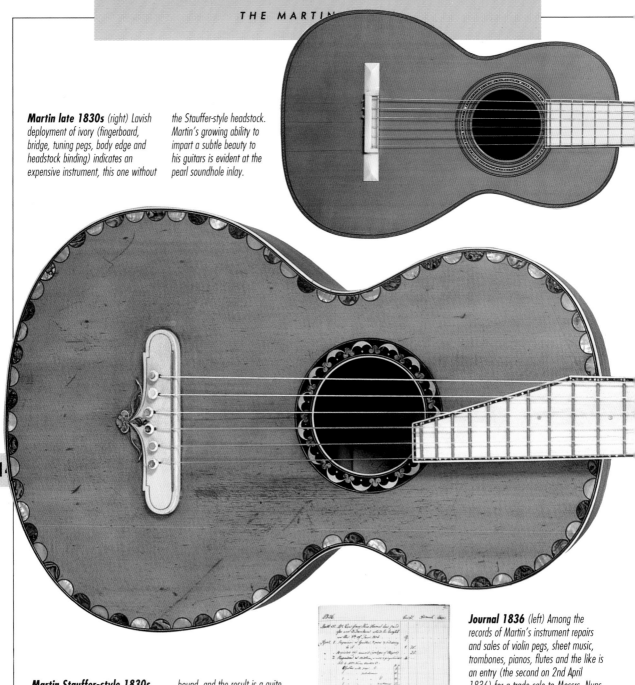

Martin late 1830s (right) Lavish deployment of ivory (fingerboard, bridge, tuning pegs, body edge and headstock binding) indicates an expensive instrument, this one without the Stauffer-style headstock. Martin's growing ability to impart a subtle beauty to his guitars is evident at the pearl soundhole inlay.

Martin Stauffer-style 1830s (above) The highly decorated body, using ivory and abalone semi-circles around the edge and a harmonizing circular theme around the soundhole, is very similar to that of the guitar on pages 10 and 11. But here the use of ivory is extended to the bridge and the fingerboard, which is also beautifully bound, and the result is a quite magnificent looking instrument. These highly decorated guitars are often referred to now as 'presentation' models, either because they were made to present the best of Martin's handiwork, or because they may have been presented to special customers and/or players.

Journal 1836 (left) Among the records of Martin's instrument repairs and sales of violin pegs, sheet music, trombones, pianos, flutes and the like is an entry (the second on 2nd April 1836) for a trade sale to Messrs. Nuns Clark & Co. of five guitars and cases. These 1830s Martins range in wholesale price from $7 for one 'with pegs' (as the example at the top of this page) to one at $15 with 'patent screws' (Stauffer type) and 'ornament'. The cases add $3 to each sale.

Martin Stauffer-style c1850s
(below) Long before Martin's famous Style 45, he was exploiting the decorative potential of abalone inlay on body and fingerboard. Around 1850 Martin also began a significant change inside the guitar: this example is internally braced in an X-shaped pattern, whereas earlier guitars had fan-shaped bracing. This 'X-bracing' came into its own many decades later on Martin's steel-string guitars.

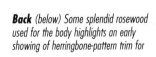

Back (below) Some splendid rosewood used for the body highlights an early showing of herringbone-pattern trim for which the Martin company would later become famous, most notably on Style 28.

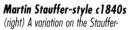

Back (right) This rear view of the guitar below reveals the beauty of the 'figured' patterns of the maple back.

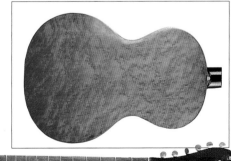

Martin Stauffer-style c1840s
(right) A variation on the Stauffer-shaped headstock is visible on this instrument, exhibiting less of a 'scroll' at the very tip. Unusually, the back and sides are all-maple; rosewood backs and sides were much more common.

strip of purfling imported from Europe, inlaid around the edge of the top, around the soundhole and down the back center seam. This 'marquetry' was typically made of pieces of colored wood in a slanted or 'half-herringbone' pattern. That was the fancy trim; plainer trim comprised several layers of wood binding with an outer layer of rosewood or ivory. The ornamental bridges of the Stauffer-style instruments gave way to a simpler rectangular shape with a pyramid at each end, sometimes with an ornamental point below the bridge.

There was still some experimentation. Some Martins from the early Nazareth era have a line of binding material around the middle of the sides, so that the sides appear to have been made of two strips rather than of a single piece of rosewood. Others have a very thin layer of spruce lining the body on the inside. Even after C.F. Sr.'s death in the 1870s, the occasional Martin would be fitted with a solid peghead and friction tuners. The clock-key neck adjustment lasted to the 1890s.

GOOD TASTE AND X-BRACING

By the 1850s, the typical Martin guitar was not fancy, not even in the understated way of later Martins with their delicate snowflake fingerboard inlays and abalone top borders. "Martin designs are notable for rich dignity and neatness," the company said. "There is only a little ornament, and this is in good taste." This statement came from a 1920s catalog, but it applied to the guitars of the 1850s. Despite their relative plainness, these guitars were elegant by virtue of their simplicity of design, the unity of their lines. To the modern eye, they are the first guitars that look like the guitars we play today. Although C.F. Martin probably didn't realize it at the time, this was a monumental achievement – the modern, American flat-top guitar.

The Martin guitar of 1850 had one innovation that has garnered C.F. Martin a permanent place in the history of guitars: X-pattern top bracing. The standard bracing of his day was a fan pattern or a simple series of lateral braces. Although he was not the only one who thought a better pattern might exist (there are a handful of surviving guitars by other makers from around 1850 with the X, including one by English makers), he was the one who managed to perfect it.

Ironically, the X turned out not to be the optimum pattern for gut-string guitars, as Chris Martin found out the hard way. He recalls: "I thought, 'Let's put X bracing on a classic guitar – that's what they did in the 1800s – and the market will open up.' They sounded horrible! I don't know what they sounded like in the 1800s, but I guess they sounded all right, because we sold them. It was a good experiment that taught me that X-bracing isn't the Holy Grail for nylon strings."

The fan pattern perfected in Spain by Antonio Torres (coincidentally by 1850) eventually was adopted by 'classical' guitar makers. C.F. Martin's X, however, was stronger than the fan, and it would find its true calling with the advent of large-bodied steel-string flat-tops in the 1930s.

C.F. Martin never knew a time when the guitar was the most popular fretted instrument in America. The banjo, played by blackface performers, was already becoming popular when he arrived, and with the invention of the minstrel show in the 1840s the banjo boomed. It continued to evolve and become more sophisticated until it was challenged by the mandolin in the last years of the 19th century. The dominance of the banjo did not mean, however, that no one played guitars. There were more than enough guitarists to support a small maker like C.F. Martin. And there were no large instrument makers in existence in the first part of the 19th century, only some general merchandisers who sold mostly European-made instruments. It would be the last quarter of the century before improved railroads and turnpikes would allow large scale distribution of instruments. In C.F. Martin's time, markets were more localized, and in that context he enjoyed a broad market with clients as far away as Philadelphia and Boston.

C.F. Martin's abilities as a guitar designer and builder are unarguable. His early guitars show a high level of skill and artistry; later, less-fancy examples show a sense of practicality and solid, lasting craftsmanship. But equally important to his success was the opposite side of the artistic persona. With his shop in New York he showed that he was a capable businessman. And with the move to Nazareth and the opening of his factory, he displayed the production knowledge he had gained back in Vienna, Austria, as a foreman in Stauffer's shop.

16

A factory expansion in 1850 makes it clear that he was no longer an individual who could handmake guitars according to custom orders. In 1852, to simplify sales and marketing as well as production, he standardized body sizes. The largest he designated Size 1, the smallest Size 3. There was a 2½ as well as a 2. Larger and smaller sizes – 0 and 5, respectively – were added in 1854. It would seem that Size 4 might have been added at the same time or even before, but there is no Size 4 guitar recorded until 1857. These smaller sizes seem tiny by today's standards, and they were not viewed as standard-size guitars even in their day. They were often called terz guitars, a name derived from the Latin *tertius*, which is the root of the English 'third'. Terz guitars were typically tuned a minor third higher than standard.

The first standardized style designations appeared about the same time: Style 17 in 1856, Styles 18 and 27 in 1857. With these style designations, every Martin acquired a two-part model name consisting of the size number and the style number, separated by a hyphen. It was a simple system that allowed Martin to offer numerous models with a minimum of confusion and explanation. Unfortunately, style specifications were not recorded by Martin in the 1800s. A good number of Martins do survive from these early years (it's likely that there are more 19th-century Martins still around than the guitars of all other makers combined). They provide evidence of early style specs, but since labels were attached to the cases – not the guitars – in those days, this evidence is not irrefutable.

Style 17, though well-known today as an all-mahogany guitar, had rosewood back and sides and a spruce top in the 1800s; its trim included colored-wood purfling around the soundhole and several layers of wood binding with rosewood on the outermost layer. Style 18, familiar today as a model with mahogany back and sides and spruce top, was also rosewood in the 1800s, and the distinctions between these early Styles 17 and 18 are not clear – perhaps more colorful purfling or an extra layer of binding. Style 27 had a pearl soundhole ring; the top edge was trimmed with colored wood inlaid in a diagonal pattern with a contrasting white outer binding of elephant ivory. (Style 27 is known today as an "out of order" style – fancier than the higher-numbered Style 28 – but the earliest examples of Style 28 would have a pearl soundhole ring and herringbone purfling, making them a bit fancier than Style 27 guitars and maintaining the order of the Style system.)

Around 1857, the Moravian church decided to sell its land, and C.F. Martin bought a piece at the corner of Main St. and North St., a few blocks north of the town square. He built a home and then built a factory behind the house in 1859. The factory would eventually be expanded until it covered the entire end of the city block.

Founding the Factory

The buildings still stand and are still owned by the Martin family. The house is a two-story brick structure (occupied by the Nazareth Visitors Bureau), although Chris Martin has some doubts about the originality of the brick. "If you go down in the basement, in the front of the house there are the remnants of a walk-in fireplace," he says. "And if you look on the outer walls there's two big windows and there's what looks like it used to be the outline of a doorway. Apparently the street level was lowered by several feet and that was actually an entranceway to the kitchen. Dirt floor, big boulders for a foundation and one of those big walk-in fireplaces – I have to believe it may have been a log cabin at one time, and then as business prospered later in the 1800s they knocked the cabin down, they kept the foundation, and they built that Victorian-style building."

Contrary to Martin lore, Chris adds, C.F. Sr. never built guitars in his kitchen, which was downstairs, musty and a center of family activity. Nor was the house connected to the factory. "There was some separation there," he says. "If you look at the old factory next to the house, there's a chimney, and to the right of the chimney it looks like what is now a window used to be a door. It seems it was filled up to window height and then a window put in. So it looks like he would go out his back door and right in."

The important aspect of the factory, Chris says, is that it was the place where they then started to make the Martin guitar in earnest, starting to hire people, starting to divide

Martin & Coupa c1840s (right)
John Coupa was a New York guitar player and teacher who from the late 1830s to the early 1850s had guitars made for him by Martin, with Martin & Coupa labels. He returned the favor by letting them use his first floor teaching studio at 385 Broadway as a 'showroom'.

Label (above) Stuck over the Martin & Coupa label is one indicating that the guitar was 'Sold by John F Nunns'. Martin & Coupa claimed "the largest assortment of guitars that can be found in the United States".

18

Back (above) The back and sides of the Martin & Coupa (right) are made of koa, a wood similar to mahogany and grown mainly in Hawaii. This is an early use of the wood for a guitar; later it became popular in the manufacture of guitars played in the Hawaiian style. Note the wood's characteristically 'streaked' appearance.

Martin & Coupa c1840s (above)
By 1839 Martin had moved his workshop from New York to Pennsylvania, and this relatively plain example of a Martin & Coupa guitar was probably made at the new location. Note also the squared-off headstock with rear-facing tuning pegs rather than the older Stauffer-influenced design.

Martin & Schatz c1830s (right) It was German guitar maker Heinrich Schatz's move to the US that prompted his friend CF Martin to follow, and this guitar is evidence of a subsequent collaboration.

Label (above) Martin & Schatz's mention of guitars "made in the best Italian style" probably refers to the models which Stauffer made for the famous Italian guitarist Luigi Legnani (1790-1877).

Headstock (above) One of the most distinctive features of many of Martin's early guitars is the scrolled peghead that copies the style established by Johann Stauffer. The tuning gears are enclosed by the decorated metal plate on the rear of the headstock, as seen on this Martin & Schatz.

Zoebisch c1900 (left) C.A. Zoebisch of New York was Martin's main distributor until a disagreement in the late 1890s about mandolin production. This guitar, very Martin-like and made after the split, bears a 'C.A. Zoebisch & Co.' mark inside almost identical to Martin's famous stamp.

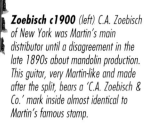

Receipt (above) An 1888 bill for a Martin guitar, showing Zoebisch's address as 46 Maiden Lane, New York – Martin's main distribution center. The partnership would continue for another ten years.

19

Key (left) Another Stauffer invention copied by Martin is this adjustable neck mechanism. Many of Martin's guitars from this period are fitted with a detachable neck, the angle of which can be adjusted by means of the key seen here which acts on a pivot inside the neck 'heel' (a curved deepening of the neck near the body joint that makes for extra strength).

up the labor. "That's probably when his ability to manage a business by working with Stauffer really started to come into it."

In 1867, C.F. Martin turned 71. He took on as partners his oldest son (he had two sons and three daughters), Christian Frederick Jr., and a nephew, Christian Frederick Hartman. An announcement of the new association, now called C.F. Martin & Co., noted that his partners had both worked for the business for over 25 years. Six years later, on February 16, 1873, the founder died. (Hartman was gone from the company by the late 1880s, although the family association would continue. Chris Martin remembers his grandfather socializing and even taking family vacations with the Hartman family.)

EASTERN COPIES

The guitar line had expanded by 1870, when a pricelist showed 11 different styles – 17, 18, 20, 21, 24, 26, 27, 28, 34, 40, and 42 – in sizes ranging from 3 to 0 (including 2½). The 20-series models sported wood purfling (except for Style 27 with its abalone soundhole ring). The 30-series (Style 30 would join the line by 1874) had the wood purfling plus an abalone soundhole ring. A 40-series number signified an abalone soundhole ring and abalone borders. Prices started at $36 for a 3-17 or 2½-17 and then went progressively up as style numbers increased. The most expensive was the 2-42 at $90, which was specified with 'screw neck,' a reference to the clock-key adjustment. Prices remained steady, increasing only slightly in 1897 and then dropping by 25 per cent the next year. After that they wouldn't escalate back to 1870 levels until 1920.

By the 1870s the five-string banjo had evolved from primitive minstrel forms to a more sophisticated construction, one result of which was a louder sound. Martin responded with a louder guitar, by way of a larger body: Size 00, introduced in 1877.

By the 1880s, the Martin name was well known and well respected enough to inspire imitators. Martin ads referred to "The Old Standard" and "The Old Reliable." They warned: "No connection with any other house of the same name," a reference to G. Robert Martin, a New York maker who advertised himself as the "manufacturer of the celebrated

Martin Guitars." G. Robert was no doubt happy that C.F.'s guitars confused the issue with their "New York" brands.

The Martin family also expanded during this period. C.F. Jr.'s first wife had died childless, but he remarried and, in 1866 at the age of 41, fathered his first child, Frank Henry Martin. In 1888, at the age of 63, C.F. Martin Jr. died, leaving the company in the hands of his 22-year-old son. Fortunately for the company, Frank Henry, like his father and grandfather, had grown up working in the guitar business.

THE SPANISH STUDENTS

Frank Henry came of age in a different world from the banjo-dominated era of his father and grandfather. In 1880, when he was 14 years old, a performing group billed simply as The Spanish Students (they were students of the University of Figaro and were famous throughout Europe as Estudiantes Figaro) hit New York with an impact that wouldn't be equaled until the arrival of The Beatles in 1964. The Spanish Students played bandurrías – small double-strung instruments that to most Americans appeared to be mandolins. Their music, their 'mandolins' and even their dandy outfits (traditional student dress) caught on quickly.

During Frank Henry Martin's teenage years, the mandolin became a national fad. By 1888, when the fortunes of the Martin company fell into his hands, the mandolin was on its way to supplanting the banjo as the most popular fretted instrument. It was an exciting musical time, enhanced by the introduction of the phonograph in the 1890s, and Frank Henry saw an opportunity for Martin to become for the first time a front-line player in the world of instrument production. He made plans to build the first Martin mandolins.

As the sole proprietor of C.F. Martin & Co., he should have had no opposition. However, Martin's exclusive distributor, C.A. Zoebisch and Sons, objected. Perhaps Zoebisch was cautious after the financial panic of 1893, which had caused a worldwide depression. It would have been futile for Martin to make any instruments that Zoebisch couldn't or wouldn't market. Frank Henry Martin, still a fearless young man in his 20s, stood up to the venerable Zoebisches and severed the relationship. As a result, Martin began distributing their instruments themselves from the factory in Nazareth (which the company still does today).

This was a bold move, considering that Martin had no experience in sales and distribution and was remotely located. Furthermore, Frank Henry had to support a complete new product line (not to mention a mother and four unmarried sisters). How the company managed the transition without a drop in business is a mystery. Chris Martin speculates that perhaps the names of buyers had been included on orders passed from Zoebisch to the factory and that Frank Henry simply copied the clients' names off those orders. "My great-grandfather might have just written a letter saying, 'We are now selling direct. Would you like to buy from us?'"

Martin mandolins debuted in 1895. Built according to the standard designs of the day, they were bowlback or 'taterbug' types, with as many as 42 ribs or bent pieces of wood forming the back. The top was a flat piece with a 'break' or bend just below the bridge. The challenge of making these instruments still amazes Chris. "They apparently were bears to make, those bowlbacks. If we had to make some of the fancy ones with the fluted back, they'd be 30, 40 thousand bucks today."

Mandolins were highly successful for Martin. Average production of bowlbacks through 1913 was almost 250 a year – slightly more than guitars. The bowlback style became passé by 1910, as most mandolinists switched to instruments with the new Gibson-style carved top and back. Martin responded with a more guitarlike (and more bandurriá-like) mandolin – still with a bent top – in 1914. Although these Martin mandolins are not especially highly respected today, they were still quite successful for Martin. Through the late 1910s and 1920s, sales averaged around 500 a year (guitar sales by this time averaged more than 1,000 a year).

Martin mandolins and the split they caused with Zoebisch had one well-known effect on the guitar line. In 1898, the brand-stamp was changed from "New York" to "Nazareth, Pa." In collectors' terminology it marks the end of the 'New York Martins,' even though Martins had not been made in New York after 1839.

By the turn of the century, the mandolin and banjo were drowning out the guitar. Guitarists needed more volume, and the easiest route to a louder instrument was to make it bigger. Martin's largest guitar at the time was the 14⅛in-wide Size 00. Next to a Size 2½, the 00 seemed huge (a full 2⅛in wider), but it was still a dwarf next to the 18in behemoths of Orville Gibson and the early Gibson company (founded in 1902). Martin's response in 1902 was a considerable push outward to a 15in-wide body (although the body depth remained the same). The new body was designated Size 000.

Though priced only about $5 more than a 00 of the same style, the 000 guitars were failures. In the first 20 years of production, sales of all 000 models came to a meager 104 guitars. (Sales did finally pick up in 1926, when the 000-18 alone sold 224.)

PUTTING ON THE PEARLS

The 000 was not the only unsuccessful idea of 1902. Frank Henry Martin may have looked to his popular mandolin line for an idea to help guitar sales and decided the key was better-looking guitars. Even the plainest Martin mandolin, with a pickguard inlaid with pearl curlicues and large engraved tuner enclosures on the front of the peghead, outshone the fanciest guitar, the pearl-bordered 00-42. Competitors such as Lyon & Healy offered guitars with all-pearl fingerboards; in the 1890s Martin's fingerboards didn't have the first piece of pearl inlay.

By 1898 Martin had inlaid the Style 42 fingerboard at three frets, beginning with a delicate six-point snowflake figure at fret five; Styles 30 and 34 received slotted diamonds at two frets and a sort of Maltese cross at the ninth fret. By 1901 pearl fingerboard inlays were beginning to spread across the line: small dots on Styles 17 and 18, slotted squares on Style 21, slotted diamonds on Style 28, two more inlays on Style 42. Then in 1902, the pearl dam broke (at least by Martin's conservative standards) when Martin put a pearl border around the sides and back of a guitar as well as the top, and inlaid the peghead with an intricate scrolled pattern. The first of these ultra-pearl models were noted in 1902 as special-ordered Style 42s. In 1904 they received their own designation: Style 45. Available in

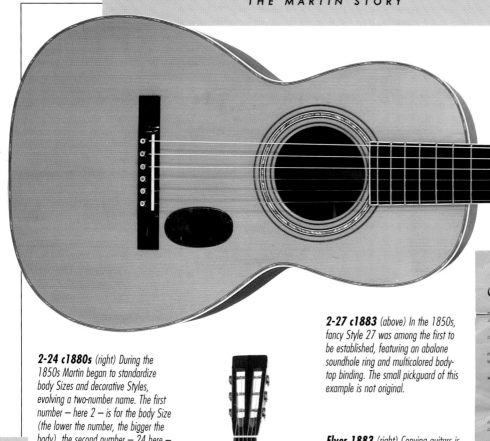

2-27 c1883 (above) In the 1850s, fancy Style 27 was among the first to be established, featuring an abalone soundhole ring and multicolored body-top binding. The small pickguard of this example is not original.

2-24 c1880s (right) During the 1850s Martin began to standardize body Sizes and decorative Styles, evolving a two-number name. The first number – here 2 – is for the body Size (the lower the number, the bigger the body), the second number – 24 here – is the Style (the higher the number, the more ornate the guitar).

22

Flyer 1883 (right) Copying guitars is not a 20th century development: Martin's 50th anniversary is marked by a warning about "inferior and unreliable" copies.

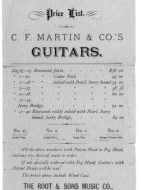

Pricelist (above) Probably from the 1870s, this lists guitars of Sizes 0, 1, 2 and 2½, and Styles 17, 21, 26, 27, 28, 34 and 40.

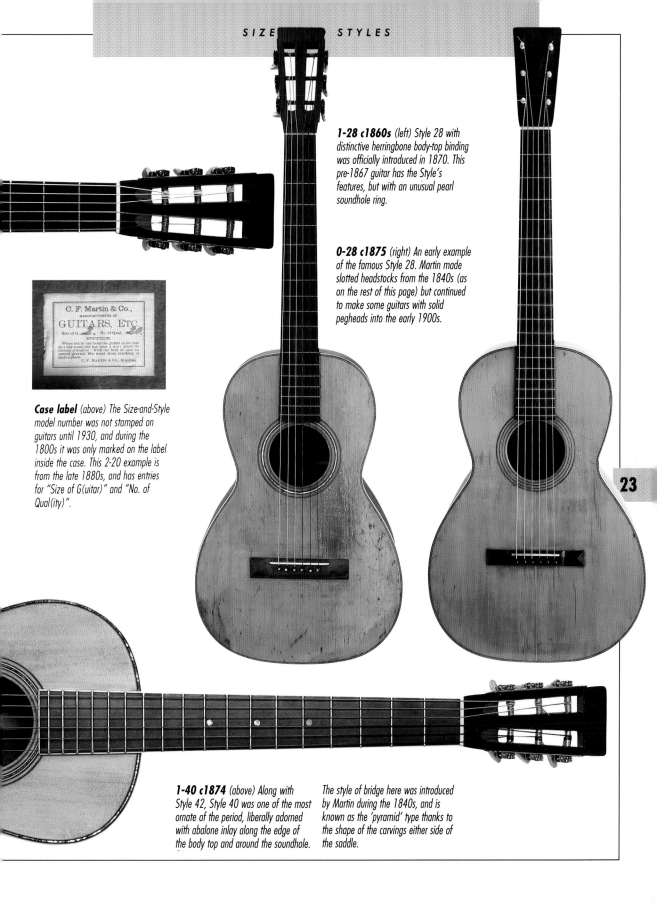

1-28 c1860s (left) Style 28 with distinctive herringbone body-top binding was officially introduced in 1870. This pre-1867 guitar has the Style's features, but with an unusual pearl soundhole ring.

0-28 c1875 (right) An early example of the famous Style 28. Martin made slotted headstocks from the 1840s (as on the rest of this page) but continued to make some guitars with solid pegheads into the early 1900s.

C. F. Martin & Co.,
MANUFACTURERS OF
GUITARS, ETC.
Size of G........ No. of Qual.........
NOTICE.
When not in use keep the guitar in its case in a dry room, but not near a fire; avoid the vicinity of heaters. With the best of care we cannot prevent the wood from cracking in such a place.
C. F. MARTIN & Co., M'd'f's.

Case label (above) The Size-and-Style model number was not stamped on guitars until 1930, and during the 1800s it was only marked on the label inside the case. This 2-20 example is from the late 1880s, and has entries for "Size of G(uitar)" and "No. of Qual(ity)".

23

1-40 c1874 (above) Along with Style 42, Style 40 was one of the most ornate of the period, liberally adorned with abalone inlay along the edge of the body top and around the soundhole.

The style of bridge here was introduced by Martin during the 1840s, and is known as the 'pyramid' type thanks to the shape of the carvings either side of the saddle.

Sizes 0, 00 and eventually 000, Style 45 was not a great success at first. Not until the opulent, carefree 1920s would sales of any Style 45 model top 10 a year.

By the end of the first decade of the 20th century, the future did not look good for Martin. Although the company had been able to catch the mandolin wave, the banjo was now making a comeback – not the old five-string minstrel or classic style but a new four-string, called tango banjo at first, then tenor or jazz banjo.

The expansions on Martin's high end – Size 000 and Style 45 – had not helped. A panic in the financial world in 1907 probably caused Frank Henry to turn his attention to the low end of the line. The plainest of C.F. Martin's 1856 styles, Style 17, had been dropped in 1898, but in 1906 it was revived in Sizes 1, 0 and 00 at the bargain prices of $20, $20 and $25, respectively. Martin also rolled back prices on Style 18 models by 20 to 30 per cent so that models 1-18, 0-18 and 00-18 were priced at $25, $25 and $30, respectively.

MARVELLOUS MAHOGANY

The lowly Style 17 of 1906 marked a major point in Martin guitar history: the first Martin with mahogany back and sides. Mahogany was viewed at the time as an inferior wood for guitar bodies; virtually all makers of quality guitars used rosewood, except for Gibson which had started with walnut and then claimed to have switched to maple (although it was really birch). Mahogany, as it turned out, was quite suitable for guitar bodies. Style 17 led the way to mahogany in 1906, but it would be the Style 18 guitars, which switched from rosewood to mahogany in 1917 (knocking Style 17 out of the line altogether), that brought respectability to mahogany.

Mahogany was also found to be better than cedar for guitar necks and was adopted on all Martins in 1916. With the advent of mahogany, a one-piece neck and peghead was possible, although the diamond-shaped volute, showing the old-time splice, was still carved into the mahogany necks on Style 28 and higher (except the modern 30-series and 60-series).

A move to modern materials occurred in 1918 when elephant ivory was dropped as a binding material, replaced by white celluloid with an ivorylike grain – a material that has commonly come to be known as ivoroid.

The end of World War I in 1918 signaled the beginning of a new cultural era in America. The Jazz Age introduced a new type of music with trumpets and later saxophones as the lead instruments. The sweet pre-war sound of the mandolin orchestra was lost in the din of horn bands, and the banjo – the tenor banjo, with metal strings, played with a plectrum – emerged as the fretted instrument best suited for the new music of the 1920s. Chris Martin saw an illustration of the state of the business in a newspaper photo from the 1910s showing the Mummers Parade, Philadelphia's New Years Day version of a Mardi Gras parade. "Today it's all banjos – banjos and glockenspiels," Chris says, "but in this picture, every other instrument was a guitar, and they were all small-bodied, like 0-17s and 00s. I guess they just realized if you want punch you've got to have a banjo. Walking around the street with a guitar just doesn't do it. So there was a guitar orchestra that eventually segued to just banjos."

Martin had been able to move easily into mandolin production, but banjos, with their drum-like bodies and numerous metal parts, were a different story. Martin got into the banjo business in 1923 and got right back out in 1926. The banjos were made with parts supplied by Walter Grover of the A.D. Grover company (probably best known today for their guitar tuners) and a total of 96 instruments were made. Chris Martin was an eyewitness to a similar fling with banjos in the 1970s, when Martin acquired the Vega company, and he explains the problem: "We could make banjo necks like nobody's business, because they were wood, but when it came to all the metal parts, it befuddled us."

Fortunately for Martin, Hawaiian music and Hawaiian style guitars – played on the lap with a steel bar – were on the rise. In 1915 the Hawaii pavilion at the Pan-Pacific Exhibition in San Francisco featured Hawaiian music, and it quickly became a national fad.

Martin was one of the earliest companies to make guitars exclusively for Hawaiian play – with a raised nut and non-angled, non-compensating bridge. Martin made one 00-21H in 1914 (before the boom), then went into production in 1917.

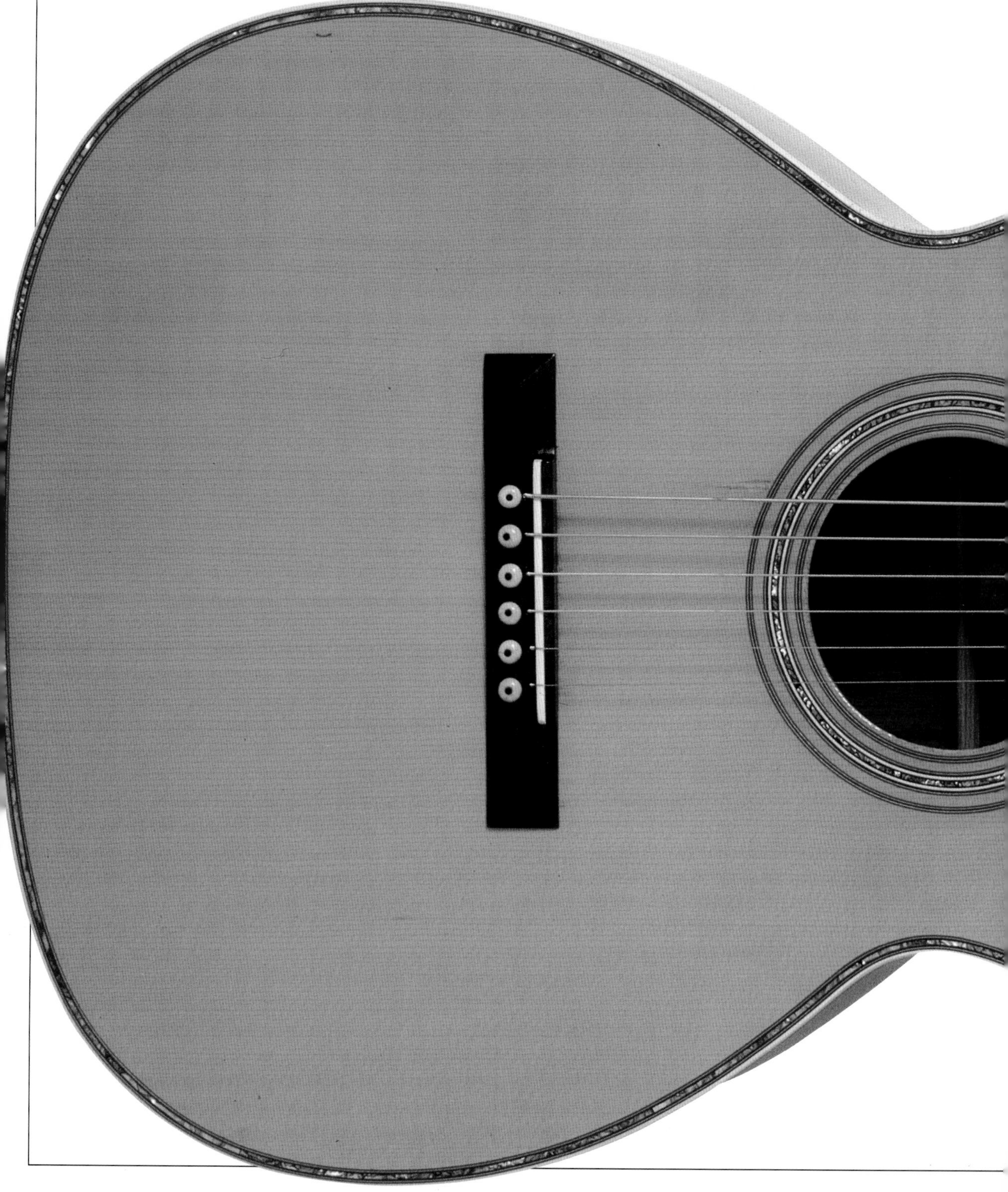

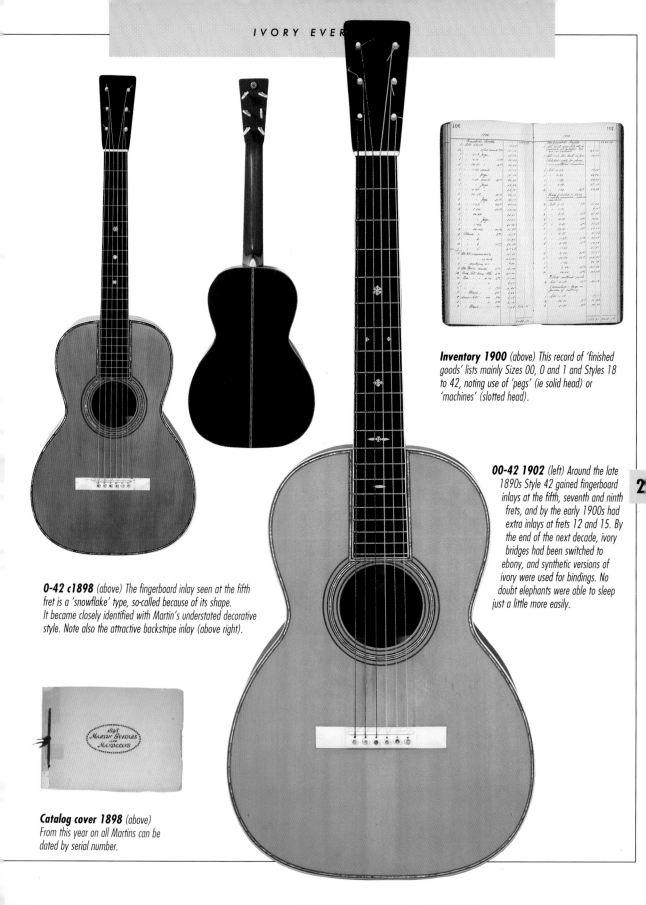

Inventory 1900 (above) This record of 'finished goods' lists mainly Sizes 00, 0 and 1 and Styles 18 to 42, noting use of 'pegs' (ie solid head) or 'machines' (slotted head).

00-42 1902 (left) Around the late 1890s Style 42 gained fingerboard inlays at the fifth, seventh and ninth frets, and by the early 1900s had extra inlays at frets 12 and 15. By the end of the next decade, ivory bridges had been switched to ebony, and synthetic versions of ivory were used for bindings. No doubt elephants were able to sleep just a little more easily.

0-42 c1898 (above) The fingerboard inlay seen at the fifth fret is a 'snowflake' type, so-called because of its shape. It became closely identified with Martin's understated decorative style. Note also the attractive backstripe inlay (above right).

Catalog cover 1898 (above)
From this year on all Martins can be dated by serial number.

2-40 c1886 (left) Ivory is applied to most Style 40 guitars for the top binding strip, outside the distinctive abalone line, but it is also used at this period for the bridge, as on this fine guitar. Ivory comes from the dentine of various animals, and was once taken principally from the especially hard and dense tusks of elephants, which almost became extinct as a result. Such poaching is now illegal.

2-42 c1890 (right) Style 42 was introduced around the 1870s and remained Martin's most ornate Style until the early 1900s. Immediately distinctive is the extra strip of abalone binding on the body around the edge of the fingerboard.

Martin c1860s (above) Martin used ivory for binding, nuts and saddles, as an alternative to wood for bridges, and occasionally for an especially ornate fingerboard (see also pages 14/15 and 19). It is sometimes seen on early 'transitional' Martins made without an obvious Style type, like this attractive example. Note especially the pearl and ivory soundhole decoration, and the exquisite colored wood inlay in the center of the sides (above right), an extra decoration seen on only a handful of Martins of the period.

Pricelist 1888 (above) This notes the use of ivory bridges for Styles 34, 40 and 42.

000-45 1926 (below) Fitting into Martin's line just above the existing Style 42, Style 45 was introduced in the early 1900s as their fanciest yet. The company's craftspeople put abalone and ivory just about everywhere that it was possible, producing a stunningly attractive guitar. Style 45 Martins from virtually any period have become highly sought after.

Back & side (right) Style 45 Martins are instantly identifiable by the superb abalone inlay work on the back and sides.

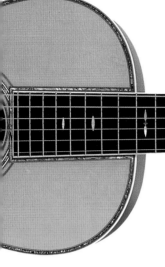

00-45 1914 (below) Typical Style 45 appointments include the lavish 'scroll' inlay work on the guitar's headstock and the delicate 'snowflake'-shaped position markers that are inlaid into the fingerboard.

Catalog 1904 (left) The first publicity for Martin's famous Style 45 pictures a 0-45 and lists models 1-45, 0-45 and 00-45. Martin notes that the Style's "Japan pearl" inlay is "quite narrow and gives a rich effect without being prominent".

000-45 1931 (below) While new left-handed Martins are relatively easy to obtain today, earlier models are very rare. The present owner of this 000-45 believes it to be the only left-handed guitar that Martin made before World War II. More unusual still is that the guitar was originally a seven-string. The mark remaining at the central site of the seventh tuner, which was removed when the guitar was converted to a more manageable six-string, can just be seen at the base of the 'scroll' headstock inlay.

Backstripe (left) Seen here in close-up is the colored wood inlay that makes the backstripe on the back of Style 45. It joins the two back halves.

The new models sported bodies (top, back and sides) of koa, a native Hawaiian wood somewhat similar to mahogany but with lighter color and more figuration. The response was slow that first year – six 0-28Ks, two 1-18Ks and a koa 00-40 – but the line was expanded in 1918 with the 0-18K (which would become the most popular koa model) and 0-21K. (Since all the koa guitars were made for Hawaiian play, they were not designated with an H in the model name.) In the 1920s, the 0-18K was priced at $40, which was $5 more than the regular (mahogany/spruce) 0-18; the 0-28K was $70, the same as the regular (rosewood) 0-28.

LESS GUTS, MORE STEEL

Standard models were also available with Hawaiian setup, including the 00-17H, 00-18H, the 00-40H and – most successful of all – the small, all-mahogany 2-17H. The pearl-trimmed Style 40, which was out of regular production by the 1910s, was revived as the 00-40H and was quite successful from 1928 to '39, outselling any standard Style 42 or 45 model during that time. (A few 00-40Ks were made, but a standard setup 00-40 was not available during the 1920s and 1930s.) The 2-17H was made from 1927 to 1931; the 0-17H was made from 1930 to '39. Occasional koa or Hawaiian examples occur in other styles.

The Hawaiians were an unqualified success. In 1927 models 0-18K and 0-28K together had sales of 650 units and the 2-17H sold 200. These three accounted for over 15 per cent of Martin's guitar production that year.

The popularity of Hawaiian music had a profound effect on the non-Hawaiian Martins. Martin had always made guitars for gut strings, but by the early 1900s some makers, led by Gibson and the Larson Brothers, were designing guitars for steel strings. Hawaiian players preferred the extra volume of steel, and standard guitarists in ensembles needed steel strings to be heard over mandolins and banjos. Martin took a cautious approach, reviving Style 17 in Size 2 only in 1922, fitting it with a heavier-braced mahogany top and steel strings. The price of the 2-17 was right: $25. Martin sold 344 of them in 1922 – more than the company's total annual production in many

years of the previous decade. Sales more than doubled the next year, and the 2-17 peaked in 1926 with an astounding production of 1300 (28 per cent of all guitars made that year).

Steel strings spread quickly: to Style 18 guitars in 1923, Style 28 models in 1925 and across the line by the end of the decade. Chris Martin's explanation: "Banjo and mandolin orchestras were forming and guitar players were jealous. They didn't want to just sit at home and play parlor music, they wanted to go out and gig. So they'd show up at the gig with their gut-string guitar, and it'd be like, 'Go sit in the back.' So there was a demand from the market to put the type of string from the banjo and mandolin on the guitar. Initially in our catalogs, I believe in the 1920s, it said 'gut-string standard, steel-string optional'. And then fairly quickly toward the mid-1920s it began to say 'steel-string standard, gut-string optional'. And then by the 1930s the gut-string guitar and the Martin company started to become two different animals."

Perhaps the most important lesson to be learned from the 2-17 was the appeal of an affordable model. In 1926 the 2-17 listed for $32.50, the 0-18 for $35 and the 0-21, the cheapest rosewood Martin, for $50. Their respective production figures for the year were 1300, 900 and 195. That lesson would come in handy when the Depression hit three years later.

The added tension of steel strings prompted several changes in construction. In the mid-1920s an ebony bar was embedded into the neck (a steel T-bar would replace it in 1934). In 1929 bridges were given a larger surface area to contact with the top. They lost the ornamental pyramids on the ends (Styles 17, 18 and 21 had already lost their pyramids in the mid-1920s) and gained a 'belly'-shaped dip on the edge closest to the endpin.

Hawaiian music helped guitar sales, but the real boon to Martin was ukuleles. Martin had made some ukes as early as 1907, but these were guitar-like, with heavy wood and spruce tops. However, the Hawaiian boom of 1915 was a call to action in Nazareth, and by 1916 Martin was in the ukulele business. Unlike the cheap, novelty ukes that many companies made, Martin ukes were all high-quality, from the plain mahogany Style 0 to the fancy, pearl-trimmed koa Style 5K. In addition to standard or soprano size (6⅜in wide), Martin also made concert (7⅞in) and tenor ukes (8¹⁵⁄₁₆in) and a taro-patch, a double-strung, concert-size uke. An even larger baritone uke (10in) was successfully introduced in the 1960s. Along with Hawaiian guitars, ukuleles carried Martin through the tenor banjo era of the 1920s.

If surviving instruments are any indication, Martin was also apparently the leading maker of the tiple, a small South American folk instrument. With 10 metal strings arranged in four courses (some of them tuned in octaves), the tiple is a sort of cross between a 12-string guitar and a large ukulele. Martin tiples were introduced in 1919 and most were made in Styles 17 (or in the later, similar Style 15), 18 and 28. Production peaked with a total of 681 in 1926, but then leveled off to an annual total of 50–100 that continued into the 1970s.

By 1929, Martin was enjoying increasing guitar sales as banjoists began switching to the more versatile guitar. The leading indicator of this new trend was the tenor guitar. With a tenor banjo neck on a guitar body, the tenor guitar offered the banjo player an easy switchover. Martin offered its first tenor in 1927: the 2-17T. Fifteen were sold. Three 1-18Ts were also sold in 1927, but curiously, thereafter virtually all the Size 1 guitars with a banjo neck were the 'plectrum'-necked 1-18P. (The plectrum banjo was essentially a five-string banjo but without the fifth string. It had a longer scale than a tenor.) A tenor-neck Style 18 was available in Size 0 beginning in 1929 and sales were quite respectable: 34 the first year, 327 in 1930. Although the 0-18T endured through the 1930s and would experience a new surge of popularity in the 1960s, tenor guitars were, for the most part, transitional instruments enabling players to move more gradually from banjo to guitar.

Any optimism for the coming decade was destroyed on October 28, 1929 when the American stock market crashed and the country plunged into a devastating economic depression. Once again, Style 17 was called upon to shore up sales. Martin dropped the binding on the 2-17 so the price could be rolled back to $25. The move worked. The new version, referred to at the time as #25, sold 25 in 1929 and then 750 in 1930, leading all other models. In second place was the tenor version, the 2-17T. Style 17 was also offered in Sizes 0 and 00

beginning in 1930, and was the best-selling Style in those Sizes.

Martin was fortunate during the Depression to have the biggest recording star of the period playing a Martin. Jimmie Rodgers, known as the Singing Brakeman, America's Blue Yodeler and eventually the Father of Country Music, was a longtime Martin man. A picture from the early 1920s shows him with Martin's first steel-string, the 2-17; he played a 00-18 on his first recording session in 1927; as a recording star, his working guitar was a custom-made Martin with pearl trim and his name in block letters on the fingerboard.

PERRY'S PECULIAR REQUEST

As the guitar rose in popularity, better players demanded more room on the neck to show off their talent. One of these was Atlanta multi-instrumentalist Perry Bechtel. As a banjoist, Bechtel was accustomed to having the entire fingerboard at his disposal. He already had a guitar with a 14-fret neck, but it was an archtop (a Gibson L-5). If he wanted a flat-top with 14 frets, he would have to look elsewhere, because Gibson was still a neophyte flat-top maker, having introduced its first small, 13¼in-wide models only in 1926. For a professional-quality flat-top, there was only one place for Perry Bechtel to go: the Martin guitar company.

Chris Martin tells the story as it was handed down to him: "Perry Bechtel came to visit, and he saw the handwriting on the wall. The way I like to describe him, he was the Eddie Van Halen of the banjo and mandolin orchestra era. Perry realized that the banjo and mandolin orchestra thing was playing itself out, and he didn't want to retire. He was a banjo player, but every time he picked up a guitar he couldn't play it because it had a big wide neck, flat fingerboard, 12 frets to the body. So he came up to visit and said, 'Can't you make me a guitar that feels like a banjo?' And my understanding is that my grandfather [C.F. III] and great-grandfather [Frank Henry] thought, 'Gee, he wants a guitar body like this.' [Chris draws a circular body, like a banjo.] No. So they took the 000 and squared off the shoulders, made a 14-fret neck, slimmed it down and radiused the fingerboard. Perry came back, they handed it to him, he may have said, 'Gee, that wasn't what I

31

000-28 1936 (right) Guitars of 000 Size appeared around 1902 and for a time were Martin's largest. Thirties examples like this, with 14 frets clear of the body, are highly prized.

2-44 Olcott-Bickford Artist Model 1930 (below) Martin made a little over 30 guitars in Style 44 from 1913 to 1939, especially for American classical guitarist and teacher Vahdah Olcott-Bickford.

Catalog 1917 (right) A list of guitarists who have "given the Martin their highest praise" includes Vahdah Olcott-Bickford (1885-1980; born Ethel Lucretia Olcott). Also noted is the American virtuoso William Foden (1860-1947) for whom Martin made special guitars in the 1910s.

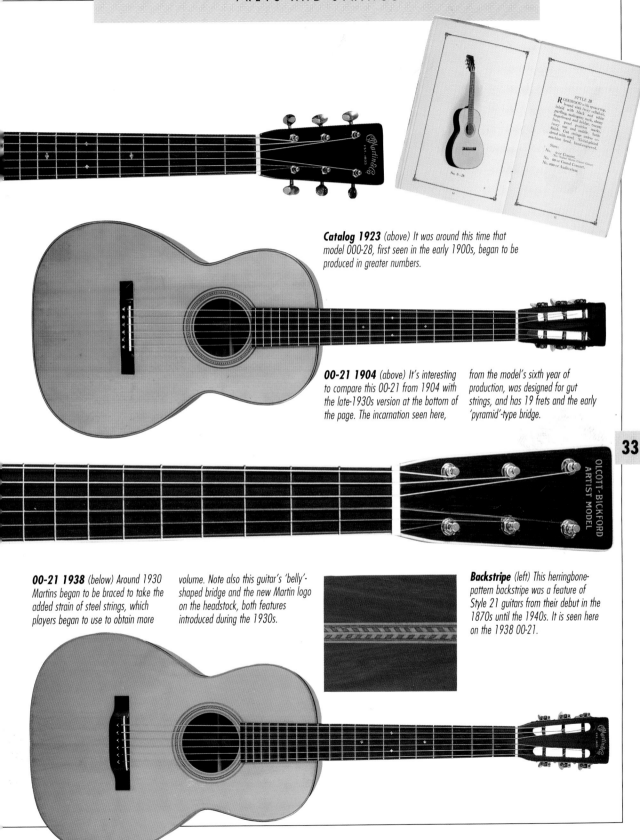

Catalog 1923 (above) It was around this time that model 000-28, first seen in the early 1900s, began to be produced in greater numbers.

00-21 1904 (above) It's interesting to compare this 00-21 from 1904 with the late-1930s version at the bottom of the page. The incarnation seen here, from the model's sixth year of production, was designed for gut strings, and has 19 frets and the early 'pyramid'-type bridge.

00-21 1938 (below) Around 1930 Martins began to be braced to take the added strain of steel strings, which players began to use to obtain more volume. Note also this guitar's 'belly'-shaped bridge and the new Martin logo on the headstock, both features introduced during the 1930s.

Backstripe (left) This herringbone-pattern backstripe was a feature of Style 21 guitars from their debut in the 1870s until the 1940s. It is seen here on the 1938 00-21.

expected to see,' but once he picked it up it worked well enough for him. And he said, 'I'll take one.'" Bechtel's guitar, a 000-28 with a body shortened in length so that it left 14 frets clear, was made in 1929. Martin dubbed it the Orchestra Model. Chris Martin speculates that at the time Martin probably thought that big band players might go for this 'orchestra' model.

ORCHESTRA FADES

The OM was added to the catalog in 1930, available in Styles 18 (initially $60, then dropped to $50 in early 1932, then raised to $55 in late 1933), 28 ($90, $85, then back to $90), 45 ($180, $170 and finally $175) and a special fancy Style 45 Deluxe ($225). The prices were slightly higher – never more than $10 difference – than the comparable 000 models.

In addition to the longer neck, there were several other differences that were probably a result of Bechtel being a plectrum banjo player. The scale (string length) on the OM was 25.4in rather than the 24.9in scale of the 000. (Plectrum banjos, like classic-era five strings, typically had a scale length of 26in or longer.) The peghead was also banjo-style: solid, with straight-through, geared tuners. Except for the occasional Martin with a solid head and ivory friction pegs, Martin guitars had used slotted pegheads with right-angle tuners since 1850. The OMs all came with steel strings, and like earlier steel-stringed, plectrum-played instruments (the mandolin and tenor banjo) the OMs were fitted with a pickguard. It was of celluloid with tortoiseshell coloring, and was glued to the top.

The OMs didn't last long – only until 1933. It wasn't that they were rejected. The 14-fret neck was quickly adopted across most of the line – the 0-17 and 0-18 in 1932, all others by 1934 except, curiously, the rosewood-body 0 and 00 models, which still retain the 12-fret neck. And the pickguard is still standard on all steel-string Martins. The OM was simply merged with the 000 in 1934. These new guitars had the OM's 14-fret neck, reshaped body, solid peghead, pickguard and, for a very short time, the long scale. Except for a change to right-angle tuners, this hybrid guitar was an OM, but Martin opted to maintain tradition and an orderly model nomenclature system, and the new style was called 000. After a few examples had

been made, the 24.9in scale returned (although the 25.4in scale had been established on a new, larger Martin).

The year 1930 brought another small change. Beginning in October, the model name was stamped onto the neck block of every Martin guitar.

Although it was the height of the Depression, it was also the dawning of the guitar era, and Frank Henry Martin proceeded boldly ahead. (Gibson, by contrast, became primarily a wooden toy company from 1931 to 1934.) Most Martin fans think of 1931 as the beginning of the glory years of Martin, the year of Martin's first big-body 'dreadnoughts'. However, in 1931, the dreadnoughts took a back seat to another new style of guitar – one that represents a rare moment of foresight for Martin.

In 1931, for one of few times in history, Martin found itself on the leading edge of an industry trend. This trend was the archtop guitar, a guitar built along violin concepts with a carved top and back. Invented by Orville Gibson in the 1890s and perfected at Gibson by Lloyd Loar in the 1920s, the loud, percussive, f-hole archtop guitar would be the favorite of jazz band players in the 1930s.

In 1931, however, Gibson was still reeling from the devastating effect of the tenor banjo and concentrating on toy production. Epiphone, a prominent New York-based banjo company, did foresee the coming boom and introduced a staggering new line of ten f-hole guitars in 1931. The only other instrument maker to recognize the impending boom was, amazingly, the conservative flat-top maker – Martin.

Martin jumped into the archtop market with uncharacteristic enthusiasm, introducing three models midway through 1931. The bodies were in the new OM style (14-fret 000) but were designated with a C. The tops were carved in the Gibson manner, but the backs were just bent into an arched shape and then secured by braces. Also, like earlier Gibsons, the Martins had a round soundhole. The C-1 was roughly equivalent to a Style 18, with mahogany back and sides; the C-2 had the rosewood body and trim of a Style 28; the C-3 was trimmed with the gold-plated parts and the snowflake fingerboard inlays of a Style 45.

These first archtops were apparently very highly regarded by

Martin, for they sported a new pearl peghead logo: M-A-R-T-I-N inlaid vertically down the peghead. (The initials "C" and "F" framing the "M" would be added by 1934.) The flat-tops got a peghead logo, too, in 1931, but it was simply a silkscreened "C.F. Martin & Co., Est. 1833" (replaced by a decal in 1932).

The archtops were more expensive than their flat-top equivalents: The C-1 was $80 (the 000-18 was $60), the C-2 was $100 (the 000-28 was $90) and the C-3 was $200 (the OM-45 was $180). The C-1, C-2 and C-3 sold 139, 104 and 21, respectively, in their first partial year of production – making 1931 a very good year for Martin archtops.

With such a promising start, Martin moved quickly to expand the line at the low end. The first of these was built in 1932 on a 00-size body of the 12-fret shape. The 14-fret neck would not be available on 00 models until 1933, and at that time the new body shape was adopted on the archtops as well. The top was bent into shape rather than carved on the new models (until 1937, when a carved top was instituted). The first nine 00-size archtops, all made in 1932, had Style 18 appointments and were labeled 00-18S (the letter S signifies a 12-fret neck today, but prior to World War II it was used on any Martin with a special feature). Beginning in 1933 the name was changed to R-18. At $50, the R-18 was a success, with sales of 481 and 486 in the first two years of production, and it remained Martin's leading archtop. In late 1934, an even cheaper model, the mahogany-top R-17 was added at a $40 list, but it never matched the sales of the R-18.

Players showed a preference for f-holes over a round hole, and Martin began to change over late in 1932 on the C-1 and C-2, in early 1933 on the C-3 and later that same year on the R-18.

As America began recovering from the Depression, Martin expanded the line on the high end. The F-7 and F-9, both with a rosewood body, debuted in 1935. The F-7 had hexagonal inlays on six frets, the F-9 on eight. Both had a vertical peghead logo and the fancy Style 45 backstripe of colored wood. The F-9 had gold-plated metal parts. With the F came a new body style, 16in wide with the stretched-out body lines of a 000 – in essence a 0000, the biggest body Martin had ever made, but most noteworthy for its later role in flat-top history.

The F-7 listed for $175, the F-9 for $250. Sales started well, with 91 F-7s and 28 F-9s in the first year, but fell rapidly. The F-series was expanded downward in 1940, with the F-1 and F-2, which had Style 18 and 28 appointments, respectively, and list prices of $85 and $135. They repeated the promising start of the fancier Fs, with initial sales of 54 for the F-1 and 22 for the F-2, and then repeated the immediate drop in sales.

ARCHES COLLAPSE

Martin archtops had several fatal flaws. First, with bodies of rosewood and mahogany, they had a unique tone, to be sure, but they lacked the percussive power of the maple guitars of Gibson, Epiphone and Gretsch. Second, they weren't big enough to compete with the volume their competitors produced. Where other makers had started with 16in guitars, then bumped them to 17in and 18in by 1934, Martin didn't advance to a 16in-wide guitar until 1935. And last, Martins felt awkward. The flat-top body was not modified to accommodate the arched top, and consequently the neck had to be set back at an awkward angle for the strings to clear the top.

In 1942 sales of Martin archtops had fallen to a total of 194 guitars spread over eight models. World War II gave the company reason enough to stop, and production was never resumed. Remnants of archtop design, however, survive in the form of hexagonal inlays, 0000 body style, vertical peghead logo and black-and-white plastic binding layers.

In the meantime, Martin had developed yet another new look for the 1930s, one that would overpower the OMs and archtops. The demand for louder guitars prompted Martin to make a larger flat-top. Curiously, Martin did not take the obvious route, which was simply to blow out the 15in-wide 000 another inch. Instead, Martin took the easiest route, reviving a body shape that had been used only for custom-brand instruments. It featured a thick waist and wide upper bouts – a boxlike shape that would come to be known as the 'square-shouldered' style. Martin had made guitars with these body lines in various sizes for the Oliver Ditson Co. of Boston beginning in 1916.

36

Style 5K ukulele c1924 (left)
When the ukulele fad hit the US during the 1920s, Martin often made more ukes than guitars. This particular uke was made for Daisy Martin by her husband C.F. Martin III, and is now in the Martin museum.

Style 3K ukulele c1930 (right)
Martin have made five main Styles of ukulele, the 5, 3, 2, 1 and 0, and Style 3 and 0 are still made. Hawaiian koa wood was a popular choice for 1920s and 1930s ukes, indicated by the K suffix on the Style.

STYLE 2
Stained mahogany body, top, and neck, ebony nut, rosewood fingerboard, patent pegs. Body bound front and back with ivory-celluloid.
Style 2-K. Similar in design, but body and top of Hawaiian koawood, natural color.

STYLE 3
Stained mahogany body, top, and neck, ivory nut and bridge-saddle, ebony finger-board, seventeen frets, pearl position marks, patent pegs, body ornamented with ivory-celluloid binding and inlay.
Style K-3. Similar in design, but body and top of Hawaiian koawood, natural color.
No. 3 and No. 3-K are designed for professional use.

Style 2

Style 3

Catalog 1925 (above) A Style 2 uke is shown on the left-hand page above a Style 3, with differences in materials, inlay and decoration noted on the right. A footnote delicately points out to readers that "3 and 3K are designed for professional use".

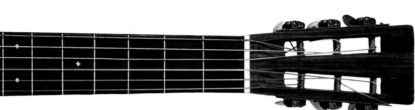

000-21 harp guitar 1902 (above) Only four such guitars were made by Martin, between 1902 and 1911. Modern players might at first glance think that this is just a very early twin-neck, but that ends quickly when one notices that 'the 12-string neck' has no frets, and has widely spaced strings, some of which are not over the fingerboard. They are in fact 'sub-bass' strings intended to add open-string background drones as accompaniment to normal playing on the six-string.

00-18T 1947 (below) Martin tenor guitars first appeared in the late 1920s, and are identified by model numbers with a T suffix. The tenor guitar was designed at a time when the guitar was attracting some banjo players, and offered an easier transition by incorporating a four-string banjo-style neck on a conventional acoustic guitar body. While some banjo players found this set-up comfortable, the instrument was not so pleasing to guitarists, many of whom found the tenor guitar's four short strings constricting.

37

Catalog c1927 (left) The small 5-21T was only some 11 inches across the body, and therefore doubtless of extra interest to banjo players. "For the amateur," Martin says, and with an eye to extra sales: "Useful as a second instrument for the professional."

Catalog 1929 (right) The P (for plectrum) Martins were also aimed at the converting banjoist: 'plectrum' banjos have four strings of longer scale-length. Shown is a 1-17P.

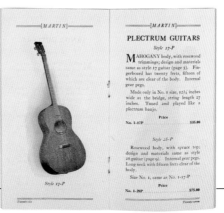

The largest Ditson had been 15⅜in wide, and in 1931 Martin pulled out the paper pattern (it's still in the Martin archives and it bears the penciled date 7/19/16) and made up some of these big guitars in mahogany and in rosewood. Presumably, since these new guitars did not have the body lines of an oversized 000, they received a new designation: D for dreadnought. This was titled after a class of large battleship named for the famous British ship HMS Dreadnought, launched in 1906 as the biggest of its type. Although the dreadnought guitars were essentially Styles 18 and 28, the first examples were stamped D-1 and D-2. In 1932, the model names were changed to D-18 and D-28.

D FOR DREADNOUGHT

The first dreadnoughts had a 12-fret neck and slotted peghead, no doubt because that's what the Ditsons had. Sales were slow – a total of 13 D-18s and 17 D-28s in their first three years. A 14-fret neck and a new, shorter body appeared on the Ds in 1934. They finally seemed secure enough to be added to the price list in 1935. The D-18 listed for $65, the D-28 for $100 – $10 more than their 000 equivalents.

In country and bluegrass, and later folk music and any other musical setting where the guitarist required power and sustain, Martin dreadnoughts were considered to be without equal. Among the first buyers was Luther Ossenbrink, who was better known to listeners of The National Barn Dance on Chicago's WLS radio by his stage name, Arkie the Arkansas Woodchopper. Arkie bought a D-2 (the guitar is now owned by the Country Music Foundation) and probably showed it to his fellow WLS star, "Oklahoma's Singing Cowboy" Gene Autry.

Gene Autry doesn't remember whether he saw Arkie's dreadnought or someone else's, but one thing is for sure, he says: "I've been playing Martin guitars since I could walk, even before I started out in show business. I knew Fred Martin [C.F. III] and his father [Frank Henry], too. And they were always very nice to me, and I wrote to them a number of times and played a lot of those one night stands back in that part of the country. And if I was close enough to the factory in

Nazareth I would take a drive over there and try to see them."

Back in 1926, when he was just a year out of high school and working for the railroad as a telegraph operator, Autry bought a Martin 0-42. A year later, even though he couldn't really afford it, he bought a 00-42. He later had his name inlaid on the fingerboards of these guitars – in block letters on the 0-42 and in script on the 00-42. He also recalls owning a long-neck Martin that was used "more or less like a banjo" – this was probably a plectrum guitar.

THE COWBOY'S 45

Autry remembers buying a D-18 shortly after they were introduced. He is most famous, however, for what was apparently his next Martin – a D-45, the *first* D-45, the most famous guitar ever made by Martin. The guitar has serial number 53177 and it was ordered in 1933 through the Chicago Musical Instrument Co.

Autry was a national star by that time. Those who couldn't tune him in on WLS's 50,000 watt clear channel had heard his huge hit record of 1931, 'That Silver Haired Daddy of Mine.' He ordered a guitar that would be equal to his celebrity – the biggest body and the fanciest Style Martin had (even though Martin didn't offer Style 45 in a D). And he had his name inlaid on the fingerboard in pearl script.

Like the D-18 and D-28 of 1933, Autry's D-45 had a 12-fret neck and slotted peghead. The next D-45, custom-ordered by Milwaukee entertainer Jackie 'Kid' Moore in 1934, also had a 12-fret neck and, like Autry's, its owner's name in script on the fingerboard. Except for one later custom-ordered 12-fret D-45, all the subsequent D-45s had a 14-fret neck.

Autry's D-45 is on display at his Western Heritage Museum in Hollywood, and the guitar shows some playing wear. He recalls that he played his own guitar on many of his records. "I made a lot of records with those guitars," he says of the Martins. At some point, his D-45 was damaged and sent back to the factory for repair, at which time a decal logo was placed on the back of the peghead.

Autry's timing couldn't have been better for Martin. In 1934 he appeared in his first movie, *Tumbling Tumbleweeds*, and he went on to become the most successful of all the singing cowboys. In the movies, however, he did not play the D-45 or any of the other Martins with his name on the fingerboard, even though his character was always named Gene Autry. "I could be photographed with it for exploitation and everything else," he explains, "but in a movie, why, I think that they felt at that time that they might pull a clip out some time when I was using another name. They didn't want to do that."

Autry's D-45 gave Martin some great exposure, but D-45 sales lagged nevertheless. A change in 1939 from the small snowflake fingerboard inlays to larger hexagons, appropriated from the F-series archtops, boosted annual D-45 sales above 10 for the first time. The D-45 debuted on the 1938 price list at $200 and then climbed on up to $250 — not all that expensive compared to Gibson's $400 archtop, the Super 400, but still beyond the reach of the less-affluent rural fans of country and Western singers. Consequently only 91 D-45s were made from 1933 to 1942.

Not surprisingly, the 000-45, priced from $10 to $25 under the D-45, wasn't selling much better. World War II put a halt to all pearl-trimmed Martins — Styles 40 and 42 as well as 45 — as of October 1942. They wouldn't return until 1968.

Amid all the great changes of the 1930s, Martin also made a small modification that, like any change in Martin instruments, should be noted. In 1934, the fretwire was changed from the 'bar' frets — with a rectangular cross-sectional shape — to T-shaped frets.

BACK TO GUTS

Martin made one other foray into new territory during the 1930s. In 1936, two classical models were introduced: the 00-18G and 00-28G. The G stood for gut-string — proof that the changeover to steel strings on standard models was complete and final. The G models had the wood and trim of a standard 00-18 and 00-28, but from there the G-models (or rather their makers) seem to have had a hard time making up their minds what they wanted to be — classicals or Martins. The necks are classical in width, with 12 frets clear of the body; but the bodies are those of a standard 14-fret steel-string Martin. Tops on

some examples are braced in a classical-style fan pattern, but apparently the company that invented the X-brace did not want to abandon it altogether, for some G-models have an X-braced top. The same thing happened with bridges. Some guitars were fitted with a classical-type bridge, where the strings loop through the bridge and are then tied off; others received the standard Martin belly bridge with bridgepins. Any combination of these features was possible on a gut-string Martin of the late '30s. (Eventually, the majority of G-models had fan-pattern bracing and a loop bridge.)

Martin's reintroduction of gut-string guitars seems an odd move in light of the company's changeover to steel strings just a little more than a decade earlier. Maybe the rising popularity of the guitar in general gave to manufacturers a false signal of new interest in classical or semi-classical guitar; nonetheless, Martin was followed into the gut-string market by Epiphone in 1938 and Gibson in 1939.

The 00-18G listed for $50, the 00-28G for $85, and each was priced at $5 more than its non-G equivalent. Curiously, the 00-28G was introduced just as Martin was discontinuing the unpopular 00-28 (last listed in 1937). A few G-versions of Styles 21, 42 and 44 were also made in the first years of G production. G-series guitars sold at a rate of a dozen or two a year through the 1940s.

Most players stayed with steel-string guitars, and by the mid-1930s, in order to get more volume, they had begun using heavier-gauge strings, which took their toll on guitar tops. So Martin made several structural changes to counteract the problem, the first of which was to move the bracing. The braces had crossed to make the X at a point about an inch below the soundhole. That point was moved farther away from the soundhole to provide more support for the bridge — the spot where all the vibration and tension on the top originates. On the smaller guitars (non-dreadnoughts) the move took place by 1935; on the dreadnoughts it occurred in 1939 or '40.

The wooden bars used for the top bracing on Martins had always been 'scalloped' — that is, shaved or trimmed in places to maximize top vibration. According to the notes of factory foreman John Deichmann, this practice was halted in 1944

0-28K 1923 *(this page) Martin were one of the first companies to produce guitars especially for playing in the Hawaiian style, and the 0-28K model launched in 1917 was among the earliest. The main requirements of Hawaiian slide guitars are a special nut (see opposite) to shift the strings high off the fingerboard, and a straight, non-compensated bridge saddle. The K-suffix models were made from koa wood. This is chiefly found in Hawaii and is claimed to produce a more suitable tone than the otherwise similar mahogany. Koa guitars were made in a variety of Styles and Sizes, and the 0-28K was produced between 1917 and 1931, using selected figured koa for the top as well as the back and sides. This superb example has been subsequently converted to 'normal' low-nut use, and has lost its original bridge.*

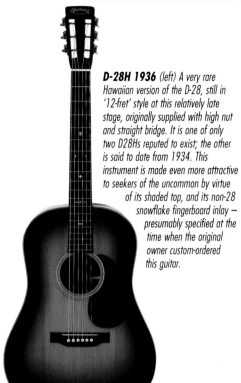

D-28H 1936 (left) A very rare Hawaiian version of the D-28, still in '12-fret' style at this relatively late stage, originally supplied with high nut and straight bridge. It is one of only two D28Hs reputed to exist; the other is said to date from 1934. This instrument is made even more attractive to seekers of the uncommon by virtue of its shaded top, and its non-28 snowflake fingerboard inlay — presumably specified at the time when the original owner custom-ordered this guitar.

Headstock (above) This close-up of the 00-40H shows the raised nut, the consequently high string action, and the special low frets that enabled the Hawaiian-style player to slide away without fear of colliding noisily with the fingerboard.

00-40H 1935 (right) This was the only way to buy a Style 40 Martin in the 1920s and 1930s, the pearl-inlaid Style having been dropped for regular guitars during the 1910s. Martin clearly believed that a fancier Hawaiian instrument would do well, although in retrospect it's not surprising to report that in fact they sold more of the 00-17H, the 00-18H, and especially the Hawaiian version of the small 2-17 (see far right), the 2-17H. In 1928 a 00-40H retailed at $100, while the 2-17H was priced at just $30.

41

2-17 1930 and Catalog 1925 (above) This cheap, plain and spartan guitar (top) was produced from the early 1910s to the late 1930s, and as shown here had a body made entirely from mahogany. In 1922 it had become the first Martin model specifically made to take steel strings (see catalog, center). Martin describes the $25 "amateur size" 2-17 as being handy "for general knock-about use".

with guitar #89926. "I thought we stopped because most of the men went off to fight, and we hired women to build guitars," Chris Martin says. "And I thought that was an extra operation that we didn't want to teach the women how to do. I said this once to my grandfather, and he said, 'That's a crock. The women could do the work just like the men. The reason we stopped was because of heavy gauge strings. We couldn't keep people from using heavy gauge strings. The tops would pull up. We'd end up fixing them, so we said we'll stop scalloping the braces.' I don't think anybody noticed."

World War II, which effectively killed the pearl-trimmed models, also had a severe effect on Style 28 guitars. They emerged from the war in 1946 minus their most famous attribute, the herringbone top trim. Herringbone was a casualty of the war: "Once they ran out of what they had from Germany, they couldn't get any more because we were at war with Germany," Chris Martin explains. "Mike [Longworth] may tell you something different, but it's my understanding that the herringbone trim came from Germany, and the Germans were in no mood to send us herringbone trim. They were in the mood to send us bombs, so that's when we stopped." (Martin historian Mike Longworth has written that although Martin imported wood purfling from Europe for many years, by this time the herringbone vendors were American, and the war had simply made the supply inconsistent in quality as well as availability.) Style 21 guitars retained their herringbone soundhole ring until 1947 and their herringbone backstripe until early 1948.

HERRINGBONE ADRIFT

Style 28 went through several more changes around the time of the war, possibly due to material shortages. The fingerboard inlay changed from small diamonds and squares to dots in 1944. (Style 21 also went to dots.) The backstripe changed from a 'zigzag' pattern to a narrow checkered pattern in early 1947, then to a wider checkered pattern in 1948.

The moving of the X and the removal of the herringbone trim and scalloped braces were all eventually regarded by Martin players as 'mistakes' and were later rectified when a

market appeared for vintage reissues. The HD-28 in 1976 brought back scalloped bracing and herringbone purfling, and various Special Edition models featured the X-brace moved back to within an inch of the soundhole.

Despite all the innovations of the 1930s, Martin emerged from World War II with its leanest model lineup in 100 years. Only four styles were available, none of them fancy, and in limited Sizes – 17 (Sizes 0 and 00), 18 (Sizes 0 through D), 21 (Size 0 with 12-fret neck only for a few years, and Sizes 00 and 000) and 28 (000 and D only). Tenors were also available in 17 and 18, and the classicals were still offered in 18 and 28.

The postwar years also brought a change in Martin leadership. By 1945, Frank Henry Martin had seen two world wars, the rise and fall of the mandolin, the rise and fall of the tenor banjo, and the steady rise of the Martin company. He retired in 1945 and died in 1948.

Frank Henry Martin's oldest of two sons, C.F. Martin III, called Fred or Fritz by friends, succeeded him as president. Unlike Frank Henry, who had been thrown into a position of great responsibility in his early 20s, Fred Martin was 51 years old and a seasoned veteran of the instrument industry. Born in 1894, he came of age in the golden era of mandolin orchestras and played mandolin, guitar and ukulele. He was the only head of Martin who could be called an accomplished musician.

Fred often performed in public with his younger brother of 15 months, Herbert Keller Martin. The two also worked as a team in the family business, with the quiet, sincere Fred working behind the scenes in manufacturing and the more outgoing Herbert handling sales. But Herbert died an untimely death in 1927 when an intestinal obstruction led to peritonitis.

By the 1960s, C.F. III was a revered figure around the Martin factory. "I guess he liked to be called Fred," says employee Dick Boak, "but nobody felt comfortable calling him Fred. He was old enough and he commanded so much respect and everybody loved him so much that everybody was just completely scared to call him that. Everybody said 'Mr. Martin.'

"He loved guitar making. It was his whole heritage, his life, his ancestors, his future, his grandchildren. It was all one thing. Whenever he talked about it, he got choked up."

By 1945, when C.F. III took over as president, the business was totally different from when he had started. The electric guitar had established a foothold and would find its voice with the advent of rock'n'roll in the 1950s. Fortunately for Martin, those were not the only new trends of the early postwar years. Bluegrass music had been introduced by Bill Monroe on the Grand Ole Opry in 1939. By the late 1940s his high-speed fusion of country and blues had become a full-fledged genre of music, thanks in part to the popularity of his former bandmembers Lester Flatt and Earl Scruggs. At the same time, other performers had brought together various forms of roots music – rural, Appalachian, ethnic, blues and protest songs – under the banner of folk music. It would be some years before these styles reached the mainstream of popular music, but by then Martin guitars would be firmly established as the standard-bearers for folk and bluegrass.

Bill Monroe is best known as a mandolin player, but his influence was so profound that whatever guitar his guitarist played was the guitar that every bluegrass guitarist played. And they all played Martins. Martin guitars had won Monroe's approval on their merit. Before he formed The Blue Grass Boys, his partner was his older brother Charlie, who played a Gibson dreadnought. However, in 1939 Monroe bought a D-28. "That was the most powerful herringbone I ever heard," says Monroe's son James. James doesn't remember exactly where and when his dad bought it, but he does remember that Bill played that guitar (not mandolin) during his debut on the Grand Ole Opry in October 1939. Playing 'Muleskinner Blues' on his Martin D-28, Monroe introduced the famous bluegrass 'G-run,' the musical figure that is still the signature riff of bluegrass music.

FROM BLUEGRASS TO BLACKLIST
Lester Flatt was one of many guitarists in The Blue Grass Boys who played a dreadnought. Although he was never known as a lead player, his influence on guitar buyers was still enormous by virtue of his position as the front man for Flatt and Scruggs. In the early 1950s Flatt played a D-18, but his most familiar guitar was his next one: a D-28. He bought it used, and then

had it customized in 1956 by Mike Longworth, then a Chattanooga, Tennessee, high school kid, now Martin's head of customer relations. Longworth inlaid oversized diamonds and squares on the fingerboard, plus a "LESTER" block. He also added an oversized pickguard of leather, which he says was "one of the dumbest ideas I ever had." Soon after, Nashville guitar maker J.W. Gower replaced the leather guard with one of tortoiseshell plastic. By the end of the 1950s, for bluegrass players there was only one guitar: a Martin D-28.

In the Martin line of the postwar years, there was not much else to choose from. There were no pearl-trimmed guitars. Style 28 was the fanciest and it didn't even have herringbone any more. Style 21 was the only other rosewood model. Style 18 was the only choice for mahogany body and spruce top. The mahogany-topped Style 17 completed the line, and it would only last through 1960.

Bluegrass was still a semi-obscure offshoot of country music when folk music began moving toward the mainstream. In 1950, The Weavers recorded an Israeli folk song, 'Tzena, Tzena,' and in the July 1 issue of *Billboard* it reached the No. 2 spot, eventually selling over a million singles. In the next issue of *Billboard*, their version of Leadbelly's 'Goodnight Irene' hit No. 1, where it stayed for the next 13 weeks, eventually selling over two million copies. Their basic instrumentation was banjo and guitar, and that guitar was a Martin 00-28G, a classical strung with silk-and-steel strings.

Weavers guitarist Fred Hellerman bought his 00-28G, his first Martin, in 1950. "They were nice sounding instruments," he says, "so when I had a chance to buy one I did." As a player who fingerpicked and flatpicked, too, he liked the wide classical neck of the G model. Although it was designed for gut strings, he put silk-and-steel on it. The tension pulled the bridge off, so he had it bolted down (the bolt heads were hidden by pearl dots). The tension was still too much for the fan-braced top, and it began to warp. More than 40 years later, the top is still warped, but Hellerman doesn't dare fix it. "I really love this guitar," he says. "You touch it, it sings at you."

The Weavers had hit after hit through 1952, but then in the anti-communist atmosphere fostered by Sen. Joe McCarthy,

OM-28 1930 (right) OM stands for Orchestra Model. It was introduced by Martin in 1929 after banjo player Perry Bechtel came to the company asking for a guitar that was audible in orchestras (in the big-band sense). He also wanted access to more frets, and a narrower neck to which banjo players could adapt. The request resulted in the steel-string OMs, Martin's first guitars with a longer neck giving 14 frets clear of the body, rather than the company's customary 12.

Catalog 1930 (above) OM models were first shown in this catalog's entry, listed as being "designed especially for plectrum playing in orchestra work. Made only for steel strings, in Auditorium size." After 1933 the OM prefix was dropped and the design features were incorporated into the regular 000 Size models.

Headstock (above) For the first year or so of production, OMs were fitted with rear-facing banjo tuners that had large synthetic-ivory pegs. They were soon replaced with standard machines, like those seen for example on the 1932 OM-18 (right).

OM-18 1932 (above) Martin occasionally finished guitars with a sunburst top, although in keeping with the company's generally tasteful image this is referred to as a 'shaded' top. Compare the Style 18's minimal decoration with the famous herringbone trim of the OM-28 (left). A total of 765 OM-18s and 487 OM-28s were made between 1929 and 1933.

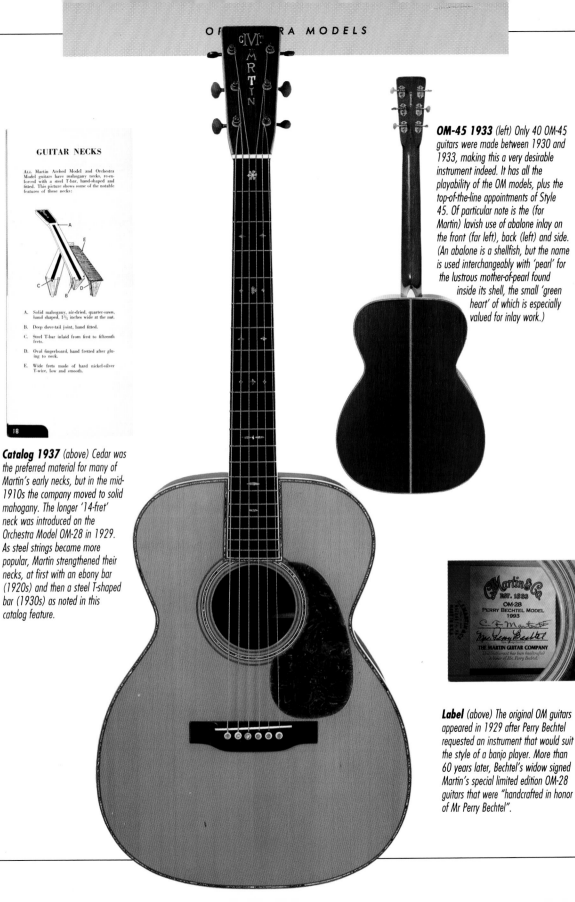

GUITAR NECKS

ALL Martin Arched Model and Orchestra Model guitars have mahogany necks, re-enforced with a steel T-bar, hand-shaped and fitted. This picture shows some of the notable features of these necks:

A. Solid mahogany, air-dried, quarter-sawn, hand shaped, 1¾ inches wide at the nut.

B. Deep dove-tail joint, hand fitted.

C. Steel T-bar inlaid from first to fifteenth frets.

D. Oval fingerboard, hand fretted after gluing to neck.

E. Wide frets made of hard nickel-silver T-wire, low and smooth.

18

Catalog 1937 (above) Cedar was the preferred material for many of Martin's early necks, but in the mid-1910s the company moved to solid mahogany. The longer '14-fret' neck was introduced on the Orchestra Model OM-28 in 1929. As steel strings became more popular, Martin strengthened their necks, at first with an ebony bar (1920s) and then a steel T-shaped bar (1930s) as noted in this catalog feature.

OM-45 1933 (left) Only 40 OM-45 guitars were made between 1930 and 1933, making this a very desirable instrument indeed. It has all the playability of the OM models, plus the top-of-the-line appointments of Style 45. Of particular note is the (for Martin) lavish use of abalone inlay on the front (far left), back (left) and side. (An abalone is a shellfish, but the name is used interchangeably with 'pearl' for the lustrous mother-of-pearl found inside its shell, the small 'green heart' of which is especially valued for inlay work.)

Label (above) The original OM guitars appeared in 1929 after Perry Bechtel requested an instrument that would suit the style of a banjo player. More than 60 years later, Bechtel's widow signed Martin's special limited edition OM-28 guitars that were "handcrafted in honor of Mr Perry Bechtel".

they were effectively blacklisted. McCarthyism kept folk music under wraps, but it could not hold back rock'n'roll. Martin acoustics played a small role in rock's early years. Elvis Presley's most famous guitar of that era was a D-18 that he protected with a leather covering. He put his name on the top with stick-on letters (the S was lost so the guitar today reads E-L-V-I). Also, Eddie Cochran's prominent power-strummed acoustic guitar on his 1958 hit 'Summertime Blues' was a D-28, although he was more closely identified with his stage guitar, a Gretsch electric.

In the meantime, The Weavers maintained their integrity and continued to perform, exerting a huge influence on the conscience as well as the music of the folk movement. Although Fred Hellerman will not take credit for influencing the guitar market, his steel-strung classical was the prototypical 'folk guitar'. Sales of Martin's 00-18G and 00-28G grew steadily through the 1950s, peaking in 1961 with 900 and 177, respectively. That same year, Martin introduced two new 'folk models,' the 0-16NY and 00-21NY, with a sturdier X-braced top and a wide, 12-fret classical-style neck. (NY stood for New York, possibly a reference to the booming folk scene in that city.) The G-series lasted only one more year. The 00-21NY lasted five years, averaging about 175 a year; the 0-16NY soared along at an average production of 500 for 10 years before tapering off.

STRING ALONG

The big break for Martin came in 1958 when The Kingston Trio's modernized version of the Appalachian folk song 'Tom Dooley' hit the charts, and they followed with four albums a year of highly entertaining, politically desensitized folk songs. Their instrumentation was simple: Bob Shane played a D-28; Nick Reynolds played an 0-18T tenor (he also used an 0-17T and a 2-18T); and Dave Guard, the banjoist, occasionally played a D-28 or 00-21.

Shane's biggest influences had been folksingers Josh White and Stan Wilson, both of whom he had seen playing Martins. In 1952, he traded in a Silvertone guitar for a Martin tenor. When he met Nick Reynolds during their freshman year in

college, Reynolds only knew how to play a ukulele, so Shane taught him to play a tenor, and then Shane moved to a six-string, a D-28. He continued playing D-28s until 1987, when he bought a limited edition D-45. He stuck with Martins, he says, because of the sound, the looks and, most importantly, the consistency. "Over the years, I found that if one got broken or lost, you could always get another that sounded exactly the same." Almost 40 years after The Kingston Trio's first hit, Shane, Reynolds and new member (of 19 years) George Grove still play Martins.

Reynolds was the only celebrity of the folk era who played a tenor, and he is responsible for the rise in Martin tenor sales. The 0-18T had languished along at about 60 guitars a year through the 1950s, but in 1959 it jumped over 100 for the first time since 1947, then to a peak of 251 in 1962. It didn't taper off until 1967, when the Trio was no longer having hits.

Like Lester Flatt's influence on bluegrass guitarists, Shane's and Reynolds' influence on the folk crowd was not based on virtuoso guitar playing. Shane and Reynolds were rhythm players – very good rhythm players, but strummers rather than pickers – which meant that almost any amateur guitarist could play along with a Kingston Trio record. Thousands of them did, and they did it on Martins.

Folksinger Tom Paxton sums up the opinion of the 1960s folk crowd: "Martin was the prestige brand of guitar. It was the guitar everyone aspired to own."

Overall sales did not show an immediate jump from the folk boom. Martins became scarce, and rumors started up to explain why. Pres Rishaw, who had joined the sales force in 1962, recounts some of them. "One was, they were made by six little old men in a loft. Another was that we had prayer meetings from 12 to 2. Another one, there was a stable behind the plant because it was Pennsylvania-Dutch, and we all rode to work in a horse and carriage."

Martin couldn't meet the demand – that much was true. Working out of a 100-year-old factory with no room for expansion, the company had long since reached its capacity of about 6,000 guitars per year. In 1964 a new, 62,000-square-foot factory was built on a parcel of land in a new residential

Decoration Style 45
Martins have fine 'green
heart' abalone inlay applied
around the body edge and the
soundhole.

D-28 1941 (above) The D prefix stands for dreadnought, and the name was originally taken from the biggest battleship of World War I, emphasizing at the time the guitar's huge size - it was by far the biggest and loudest in Martin's line. Pre-1947 D-28s feature Martin's discreet herringbone inlay.

D-18 1937 (right) Originally called the D-1, the D-18 was launched in 1931 and, as the base model of the dreadnought line, has been a popular guitar ever since. The restrained level of decoration on Style 18 Martins makes for a rather austere appearance, so the visual distinction as well as the relative rarity of the shaded top would make this late-1930s instrument an especially attractive guitar to collectors as well as players.

D-18 1939 (right) Another exceptional, plain, pre-war dreadnought — in fact this is one of 475 D-18s made in 1939, during which year a D-18 would have set you back $65. By 1953 it had doubled in price. Into the mid-1960s and the D-18 went above $250 for the first time, and by 1973 it had topped $500. In 1981 you would have needed $1033 for a D-18; and as we go to press, 63 years after its introduction, the humble D-18 is listing at a cool $1910.

Catalog 1936 (above) Notice how the name was spelled with an 'a' in this early catalog appearance of Martin's own dreadnought line. It was shown under an Orchestra Model heading, and referred to as a "bass guitar" of "great power and smoothness."

Ditson Dreadnought-style 1924
(above) The big dreadnought-style guitar was first made by Martin in 1916 as a special item for two music stores run by Ditson in Boston and New York. The general design was suggested to Martin by Harry L Hunt, manager of Ditson's New York store.

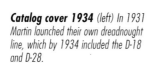

Catalog cover 1934 (left) In 1931 Martin launched their own dreadnought line, which by 1934 included the D-18 and D-28.

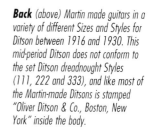

Back (above) Martin made guitars in a variety of different Sizes and Styles for Ditson between 1916 and 1930. This mid-period Ditson does not conform to the set Ditson dreadnought Styles (111, 222 and 333), and like most of the Martin-made Ditsons is stamped "Oliver Ditson & Co., Boston, New York" inside the body.

Shaded top *Martin made just under 100 original D-45s from 1933 to 1942. This 1938 shaded-top example may well be unique.*

Side *(below) Style 45 is unusual in that abalone inlay is also used on the body sides.*

Back *(left) The more expensive Martin Styles feature abalone inlay around the body edge as well as a colored-wood inlaid stripe joining the two halves of rosewood. At the time that the original D-45s were made Martin regularly used Brazilian rosewood. A recent embargo has all but halted its use today.*

D-45 1938 *(above) The D-45 has long been the flagship of the Martin line, having the biggest body size and the most lavish decorative style of any standard model. It was introduced as a custom item in 1933, with a 12th-fret neck/body join; later it moved to this familiar 14-fret style.*

Ledger 1933 *(right) The first Martin D-45 was made for the famous 'singing cowboy' Gene Autry in 1933. An entry (bottom right) records this historic order, made through the Chicago Musical Instrument Co.*

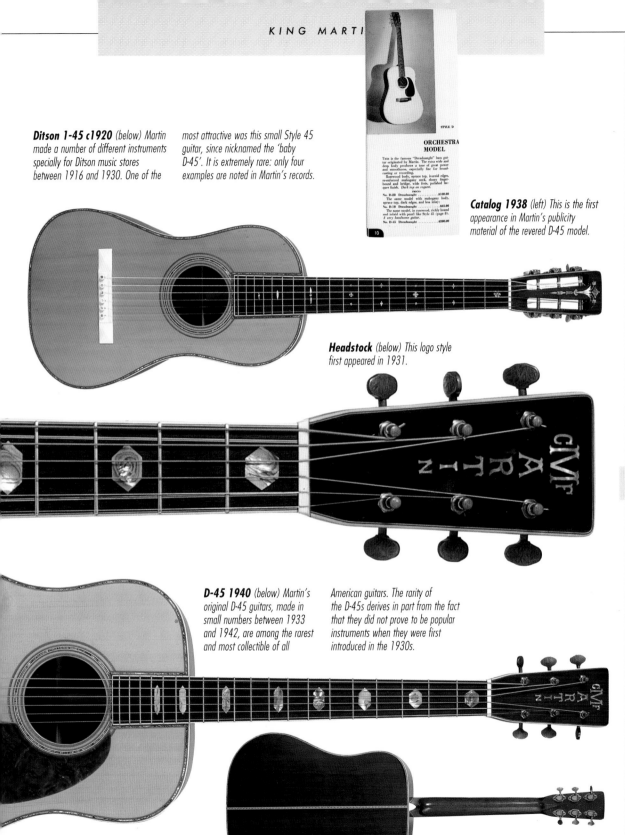

Ditson 1-45 c1920 (below) Martin made a number of different instruments specially for Ditson music stores between 1916 and 1930. One of the most attractive was this small Style 45 guitar, since nicknamed the 'baby D-45'. It is extremely rare: only four examples are noted in Martin's records.

STYLE D

ORCHESTRA MODEL

This is the famous "Dreadnaught" bass guitar originated by Martin. The extra wide and deep body produces a tone of great power and smoothness, especially fine for broadcasting or recording.
Rosewood body, spruce top, ivoroid edges, re-enforced mahogany neck, ebony fingerboard and bridge, wide frets, polished lacquer finish. Dark top on request.

PRICES

No. D-28 Dreadnaught $100.00
   The same model with mahogany body, spruce top, dark edges, and less inlay:
No. D-18 Dreadnaught $65.00
   The same model, in rosewood, richly bound and inlaid with pearl like Style 45 (page 4).
A very handsome guitar.
No. D-45 Dreadnaught $200.00

10

Catalog 1938 (left) This is the first appearance in Martin's publicity material of the revered D-45 model.

Headstock (below) This logo style first appeared in 1931.

51

D-45 1940 (below) Martin's original D-45 guitars, made in small numbers between 1933 and 1942, are among the rarest and most collectible of all American guitars. The rarity of the D-45s derives in part from the fact that they did not prove to be popular instruments when they were first introduced in the 1930s.

development on the outskirts of Nazareth (land that co-incidentally had been owned in earlier times by the Martin family). Production jumped in 1965 to over 10,000 for the first time in history and then went on to an all-time record in 1971 of 22,637.

TWELVES, ELECTRICS, BELLBOTTOMS...

The new plant was 'christened' by folksingers Tom Paxton and Judy Collins, who performed on the loading dock. Paxton had been imprinted with the Martin brand as an aspiring folksinger in the 1950s. He remembers first reading about a Martin in Burl Ives' autobiography *Wayfaring Stranger*, in which Ives said he always played a Martin (despite his Gretsch endorsement in the early 1950s). As a high school kid in Oklahoma, Paxton recalls, "A couple of my pals and I had an ersatz Kingston Trio group, and were very aware of Martin. We lusted after Martins. They [the Trio] were on the cover of *Life* jumping into a swimming pool with their guitars, and we were the first to say aha, they're not the Martins, they're some cheap Silvertones or something."

Paxton finally got his first Martin the day he got out of the Army in 1960. It was a used D-28 with a hole in the back that had been repaired by legendary archtop guitar maker John D'Angelico. That was the guitar he played at the new Martin factory in 1964.

Paxton and Collins were each given a special guitar for their appearance. In the move to the new facility, two old Style 45 tops had been discovered. They had the abalone soundhole ring already inlaid but not the border trim. Martin had no more abalone, so the tops were trimmed out with the last of the herringbone purfling left over from the old-style D-28s.

The folk boom and the discovery of Huddie Ledbetter (Leadbelly, who died in 1949) and his 12-string guitar forced Martin to produce a new model. At first Martin protested. A 1964 ad in *Sing Out!*, the folk song magazine, explained that despite the demand, Martin would not make a 12-string because the string tension was just too great on the top. But the company finally gave in and put a model on the market by the end of the year. The D12-20 had a 12-fret neck with slotted peghead, but in virtually all other respects it appeared to be similar to a D-18 (except for a Style 28 backstripe).

A rosewood 12-string followed in 1965 and, curiously, Style 35 was chosen. Both models were quite successful, with the D12-20 selling over 1,600 in 1969 and again in 1970 and the more expensive D12-35 peaking at 928 in 1970. That success prompted more 12-strings: Style 45 in 1969, Style 28 (with 14-fret neck) and Style 41 in 1971, and Style 18 (with 14-fret neck) in 1973. By the end of the 1970s, the 12-string craze had died down, and by the 1990s, the D12-28 was the only folk-era 12-string still produced in significant numbers (more than 10 a year). Two recent models with the enlarged-000 bodies are the J12-40 (rosewood) and the J12-65 (maple).

Even in the middle of the folk boom, the electric guitar market looked appealing. Leo Fender, the pioneer of electric solidbody guitars, had tried out a pickup in the late 1940s by screwing it onto a Martin 000-18. Ten years later, in 1959, Martin did essentially the same thing, putting a single-coil DeArmond pickup on the 00-18E and D-18E and two pickups on the D-28E. The 00-18E retained the X-bracing, but the dreadnoughts had lateral top braces (following Gibson's example with its small CF-100E and dreadnought J-160E). DeArmond pickups had been used on Gretsch guitars in the mid-1950s, but by the time they appeared on the Martins, they were *passé*. Martin's electrified flat-tops didn't sound very good, no matter if they were played as electric, acoustic or amplified-acoustic guitars. The D-18E lasted only a year; the other two models were last made in 1964.

It would have been a good time to kiss the electric market goodbye, but Martin plowed on ahead with newly designed thin-bodied archtops in 1961. A single-cutaway was available with one pickup (still a DeArmond) or two, designated F-50 and F-55, respectively, and the double-cutaway F-65 had two pickups. These lasted four years before being replaced by the single-cutaway GT-70 and double-cutaway GT-75 (both with two pickups) in 1965. The GTs were last listed in 1968.

Through their 10 years of production, Martin electrics were competitively priced – the 00-18E debuted at $190, the F-series ranged from $225 to $310, the GTs from $340 to $395 (and $425 for a 12-string GT-75). The D-28E, being made of rosewood, was the costliest, listing by 1965 for $490. And the electrics were by no means a commercial disaster. The 00-18E and D-18E both topped 300 in their first year of production. Each of the Fs had three years of 100-plus sales. The GT-75 peaked at a very respectable sales figure of 576 in 1966. Martin had stayed with less successful models in years past, and with a new plant (finished in 1964), the time seems to have been right for expanding the line. But demand for acoustics was growing so fast that the electrics were abandoned.

The folk boom kicked off the most successful and ultimately the most tumultuous period in Martin's history. At the center of it was Frank Herbert Martin, son of C.F. III. Unlike his forebears, Frank had not grown up believing it was his destiny to take over the family business. Born in 1933, he was a star athlete in high school years. He had a passion for car racing, and in 1956 he and his brother-in-law talked C.F. III into funding an import dealership in Saylorsburg, a small town about 20 miles north of Nazareth. By 1962 a failed business, a serious automobile accident and the responsibility of fatherhood (Christian Frederick Martin IV had been born in 1955) convinced Frank to join Martin as sales manager.

Frank was the antithesis of his father. Frank was an outgoing man who liked to socialize and have a drink – sometimes too many drinks – with the guys. C.F. III was a quiet man who was known to have made only one joke in his life. At a trade show, the story goes, he was having dinner with Gibson president Ted McCarty, and when the waiter took drink orders, McCarty ordered a Gibson. C.F. III countered with a "Martin-i."

Although Frank, as the son of the boss, was clearly in line to become the boss, his father remained the chairman, the chief executive officer. Dick Boak, who was hired by Frank in 1986, observes: "Certainly in any family, especially when you have six generations of a family, it's pretty common to have a generation that doesn't quite fit in with the program, and I guess Frank has to be historically seen as that person. Frank had his problems; Frank had attributes. He was extremely committed to the employees. He had no trouble making a decision. His

decisions were spontaneous and very, very clear in his own mind, so those things are good things." Frank was responsible for Martin's image as a progressive company, Boak says. "There were people with bellbottom trousers and there's no ties, and Frank with longer hair, beard and moustache. It was refreshing. And to be tied to the company that was somehow tied to Tom Paxton and David Bromberg and Joan Baez and Judy Collins and Bob Dylan, there was a pretty unique feeling that I would attribute to Frank."

One of Frank Martin's first moves after joining the company in 1962 was to form Martin Sales. The move would lead directly or indirectly to the hiring of Pres Rishaw, Bob Johnson and Mike Longworth – three employees who would make an impact on the Martin guitar line far beyond what they were originally hired to do. Martin Sales was a separate company, located on the Nazareth town square in a building that also housed a grocery store. Bob Johnson was a representative from IBM who rented Martin its first computer, then came to work for Martin. From socializing with Johnson, Frank hired Johnson's friend Pres Rishaw as the first full-time employee of Martin Sales.

AN AWFUL LACK OF ROSEWOOD FROM BRAZIL

Martin hadn't had an active sales staff in years. "Mr. Martin would go to the Chicago show [the National Association of Music Merchants, or NAMM, trade show] every year and take the orders, and that was it," Rishaw says. "They hadn't had anybody on the road since the Depression. Frank hired me full-time and a month or two later I hired a guy named Dave Magagna, who later became president of Guild. And jees, in a year's time we had production sold out for about four years." Martin Sales also represented Pan and Crucianelli accordions, Guild guitars and Vega banjos until 1968, when Sales was integrated into the guitar company.

Rishaw left in 1963 but returned in 1967, again as a result of socializing with Frank. "My wife and I owned a little restaurant in Allentown, and the guys – Frank, Bob, Tigger [computer consultant Hugh Bloom] – would come in and have a drink or lunch, whatever," he says. A talk with

53

C-3 1931 (right) Despite Martin's almost total identification in many players' minds as the foremost producer of flat-top acoustic guitars, the company was among the first American guitar makers to recognize and act upon the trend toward archtop guitars in the early 1930s. This first-year example of the C series archtops demonstrates Martin's early combination of a round-soundhole 000-size body with an arched top and back. The C-3, with its bound ebony fingerboard (the inlays here are not entirely original), was the top model of a line that also included the C-1 and C-2, all with shaded tops. The vertical 'C.F. MARTIN' headstock logo first appeared in 1931, on these models. A year later Martin introduced the similar 00-size R series archtop guitars.

Catalog 1935 (above) Martin's largest archtops were the F series models, launched in 1935. This listing shows the top-of-the-line F-9, described as "the guitar de luxe for the modern player".

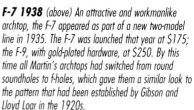

F-7 1938 (above) An attractive and workmanlike archtop, the F-7 appeared as part of a new two-model line in 1935. The F-7 was launched that year at $175; the F-9, with gold-plated hardware, at $250. By this time all Martin's archtops had switched from round soundholes to f-holes, which gave them a similar look to the pattern that had been established by Gibson and Lloyd Loar in the 1920s.

Back & side (left) Note the beautiful figured maple. As on Martin's other archtop guitars, this instrument has a carved top, while the arched back is formed by internal bracing rather than carving.

F-5 1940 (left) This rare guitar is one of only two trial F-5 models made at the Martin factory during 1940. One can assume that the company at first intended this spruce-top, maple-back-and-sides guitar to sit in the middle of their F series – two humbler models, the F-1 and F-2, were added to the bottom of the line in the same year. But the F-5 never went into production. Certainly maple was an unusual material for Martin to use: they had traditionally employed rosewood for guitar backs and sides. But maple was the premier wood used for backs and sides by Gibson for its respected archtop guitars, so perhaps Martin decided to back off from such direct competition with Gibson?

55

F-1S 12-string 1941 (above) This instrument is the only example of a 12-string F-series guitar that Martin made, and according to the company's records is one of only six documented pre-war Martin 12-string guitars.

56

Frank about rising prices and their effect on Martin's general sales position in the market led to an invitation to him to rejoin the company. Rishaw accepted and stayed until 1983.

The year 1965 was a time to look forward with optimism, but one problem loomed ahead. Brazilian rosewood was getting hard to find in pieces big enough to make the two-piece back of a Martin dreadnought. A most unlikely source – Bob Johnson, the computer man – came up with a solution. Johnson knew a few chords on guitar but had not grown up in guitar manufacturing. And it's a good thing. If he had been steeped in the Martin tradition, he probably never would have suggested making a dreadnought with a three-piece back, utilizing smaller pieces of rosewood.

Johnson recalls that C.F. Martin III dug out some old reference to Martins with three-piece backs. (Historian Mike Longworth is not aware of any such instruments, and C.F.'s point of reference may have been the old bowlback mandolins, some of which had as many as 42 separate ribs forming the back.) The bracing of a three-piece guitar back would have to be different from a two-piece, and after some experimentation, 000-type braces were adopted on the back (00-type on the top). Not only did the three-piece back work, it gave the new guitar a distinct sound – not as booming as the two-piece back but retaining the deep resonance of rosewood. With a bound fingerboard and peghead, it was fancier than Style 28, and though it did not have the abalone soundhole ring found on earlier 30-series models, it was designated Style 35.

The D-35 debuted in 1965 at $425, which was $50 more than the D-28. It was an unqualified success, pulling almost even with the D-28 by 1970 and for several years in the mid-1970s outselling the D-28. (At times the price difference was as little as $20.) The D-35S (12-fret neck) also equaled the D-28S in popularity.

The father of the D-35, Bob Johnson, eventually became Martin's vice president of operations, a position that put him in charge of manufacturing. His tenure at Martin ended in 1977 after a factory strike.

The rosewood problem was not altogether solved by the D-35. In 1969 Brazil put an embargo on rosewood logs,

and guitar-quality wood was no longer available in quantity. That year Martin switched to Indian rosewood.

After the D-35, the next suggestion for a new model came from Pres Rishaw. "When I came back and started on the road again, a lot of people were asking me about this guitar called the D-45," Rishaw recalls. "So I sort of dug into that. I was between trips sitting in the office. I said to Hugh Bloom, 'Jees, I'm bored sitting around. There's just so many phone calls I can make,' and Tigger says, 'Well, why don't you get yourself a project and jump on it and keep yourself busy?'"

Rishaw went to work finding materials suitable for a new D-45. There were a few 'acme' tops – highest grade spruce – still around, and he found pearl-cutters in New York who could supply the abalone inlays. In the meantime in Chattanooga, Tennessee, a repairman named Mike Longworth was filling the demand for D-45s by "D-45-izing D-28s" (as Rishaw describes it). In other words, taking a D-28 and inlaying pearl borders, new fingerboard inlays and pearl "C.F. Martin" peghead logo so that the finished product looked like a D-45. Frank Martin knew of Longworth and suggested that he supervise the pearl work on Martin's new D-45. Longworth accepted the offer and moved to Nazareth.

The D-45 debuted in 1968 at the astronomical price of $1,200 – almost three times the price of a D-35, almost twice the cost of Gibson's most expensive flat-top, the J-200. But Rishaw had correctly read the market. Annual sales would range from a low of 40 in 1978 to a high of 291 in 1979, and for many guitarists the D-45 would always represent Martin's greatest achievement.

FORTY-SOMETHING

Mike Longworth's inlaying expertise was crucial to the revival of the D-45, but his contributions to Martin had just begun. He saw a place for another new model. "We had the D-35 with the three-piece back, and we had the D-45," he explains. "And, of course, being a historical type person I knew that we had made Styles 40 and 42 in the past. So I just inlaid the top of a guitar and suggested to the company that we offer something in the middle, and I had suggested we call it a D-40. The Style 40 didn't have a pearl headstock; the Style 40 from the Hawaiian days just had a decal. And they wanted to put pearl on it, so they called it a D-41. And that was the origin of the guitar."

Longworth downplays his role, saying that most new models at Martin are the result of a team effort. "Sure, I came up with the idea, but it can't be totally mine because they changed it by putting pearl in the headstock," he says. "Like everything here it ends up being a cooperative effort."

In Longworth's pre-Martin years, when he was making D-28s into D-45s, he had always been careful to leave the D-28 model stamp intact so that future owners would not be deceived, and in building the prototype D-41 fingerboard he built in a safety feature against anyone who might try to upgrade it to a D-45. "I moved all the inlays [from a D-45]," he says. "What I did was take the No. 1 inlay and start it at the third fret, so everything was in the wrong fret, or we say a different fret, and it had six instead of eight [inlays]. And I did that on purpose so that nobody would be able to add the other two." In other words, the third-fret inlay of the D-41 is the same size as the first-fret inlay of the D-45. Adding a D-45 inlay to the D-41 at the first fret would not work, since it would be same size as the inlay at the third fret (it should be larger).

Introduced in 1969 at a price of $800, midway between the D-35 and D-45, the D-41 did exactly what a well-conceived model for that niche would be expected to do. It offered the less-affluent buyer a chance to own a pearly Martin without having to spend the money for a D-45. Sales of the D-41 for its first seven years stayed at a level that was between two to four times that of the D-45.

In 1968, in a repeat of the 1930s, the excitement of a guitar boom prompted Martin once again to introduce a fan-braced classical guitar. The mahogany body N-10 and rosewood N-20 looked more like traditional classicals than had their G-series predecessors, with such features as a wood-marquetry rosette and a 25.4in scale. In 1970, they were further distinguished by a fancier peghead shape and an even longer scale length of 26⅜in. But after a promising start of 265 N-10s and 262 N-20s in 1969, sales fell steadily downward.

By the end of the 1960s, the folk boom had died down, but folk elements had worked their way into rock music. The emergence of Crosby, Stills and Nash brought acoustic and electric camps together. Their 1969 hit 'Suite: Judy Blue Eyes' prominently featured Stephen Stills' acoustic guitar. Not much of the guitar was visible on their album cover, but the unbound peghead and the white body binding made it easy for a Martin aficionado to identify it as a D-28. It signaled a second wave of acoustic guitar buying that was bigger than that of the early 1960s.

By this time there were some formidable new movers in the guitar market, and cheap imports had already killed off long-established American makers such as Kay and Harmony. In 1970 Martin covered its bets with its own import brand, Sigma (the Greek letter sigma, when turned on its side, is the letter M).

Frank Martin expanded the company considerably in 1970 by buying Vega Banjo Works of Boston, Fibes Drum Company (makers of fiberglass drums) and Darco String Co. (owned by D'Addario family members, who left in 1973 to form a new string company under their own name). Martin had for years marketed Martin strings, and with the acquisition of Darco's equipment began to make Martin strings in-house for the first time. In 1973 Martin bought the Levin guitar company of Sweden.

In hindsight, the problems that these acquisitions would bring are easy to see. Chris Martin points to a sales chart, to the steep upward climb of the late 1960s: "All this is happening and we're generating revenue from this, but we're not pumping it back into guitar building."

Although C.F. Martin III was the CEO, he let Frank have his head because C.F. III had never seen anything but a flat-line sales chart for guitars. Chris Martin illustrated the wild pattern of the company's growth with the story of Fibes drums: "My grandfather was in the hospital. My dad comes in: 'We think we'd like to buy this drum company.' And my grandfather says, 'Well I think we should analyze this situation, take a look at the pros and cons.' My dad says, 'I'm sorry, I already bought it today.' My dad was gullible. When someone would say, 'I need you to decide today because if you don't buy it, Gibson's going

Martin ad 1962 (left) These wide-necked NY 'folk models' were another reaction to the 1960s folk boom.

D-35 1968 (below) The innovative feature of this model, introduced in 1965, was its new back (see right). Still in production, the D-35 has proved a successful addition to the dreadnoughts.

D12-45 1969 (below) Other than a few rare early guitars (see, for example, page 55), Martin did not start to make 12-strings until the 1960s folk boom defined the market. The luxurious Style 45 appeared in 12-string form late in the decade: this first-year example was one of three made in 1969.

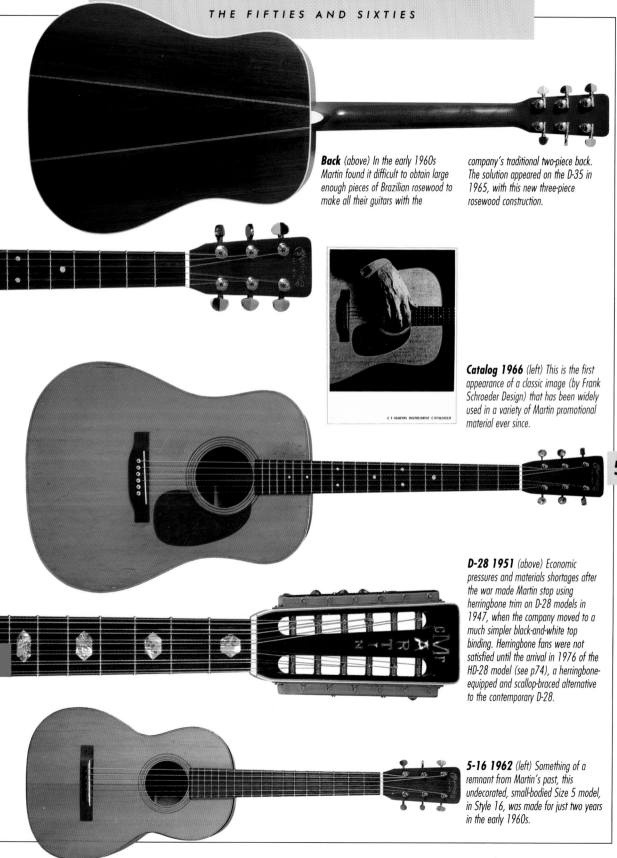

Back (above) In the early 1960s Martin found it difficult to obtain large enough pieces of Brazilian rosewood to make all their guitars with the company's traditional two-piece back. The solution appeared on the D-35 in 1965, with this new three-piece rosewood construction.

Catalog 1966 (left) This is the first appearance of a classic image (by Frank Schroeder Design) that has been widely used in a variety of Martin promotional material ever since.

D-28 1951 (above) Economic pressures and materials shortages after the war made Martin stop using herringbone trim on D-28 models in 1947, when the company moved to a much simpler black-and-white top binding. Herringbone fans were not satisfied until the arrival in 1976 of the HD-28 model (see p74), a herringbone-equipped and scallop-braced alternative to the contemporary D-28.

5-16 1962 (left) Something of a remnant from Martin's past, this undecorated, small-bodied Size 5 model, in Style 16, was made for just two years in the early 1960s.

59

to buy it,' he believed them, whether it was true or not." Frank's father did not question his purchases, and the banks encouraged him. "The banks loved us," Chris recalls. "Business was good. We'd call them up and say we need some money, they'd say, 'How much? We'll send a truck over today.' So they were in bed with us."

Salesman Pres Rishaw credits Frank Martin for much of the company's success in the 1970s. "Frank has apparently some detractors, but I hope somebody gives Frank credit for the genius that he was," Rishaw says. "He was a brilliant fellow, really brilliant. His basic philosophy was, surround yourself with people you trust and let them go do their job."

New Martin, Old Martin

On the strength of one dealer in Australia, Frank sent Rishaw on a trip to generate more overseas business. The response from foreign dealers was phenomenal. "One time I wanted to go to Hong Kong and then from Hong Kong to Singapore, Singapore to Australia and New Zealand," Rishaw recalls. "Frank said, 'You have to sell $50,000 in guitars on this trip just to afford the ticket.' Hell, I sold it in Hong Kong, my first stop, in about 30 minutes."

Stateside, Rishaw and Mike Longworth began traveling to bluegrass festivals to give Martin a higher profile among those players. Rishaw also initiated a relationship with Opryland theme park in Nashville when it opened in 1972. Martin started by sponsoring one of the live shows, which was held in the Martin Guitar Music Theater. When Martin questioned the return on an investment of $15,000-20,000 per year, Rishaw talked the park into naming Martin guitars the official acoustic guitars of Opryland. Each year at contract time, Rishaw gained another point. Fibes became the official drums, Darco the official strings.

In the meantime, interest in older Martins was on the rise, fueled in part by the preference of players such as Stephen Stills and Neil Young for vintage guitars. Sales of used guitars didn't directly benefit Martin, of course. Martin historian Mike Longworth (whose official title is Consumer Relations Manager) observes, "The biggest competitor of new Martins is

old Martins." Longworth made this remark in a conversation at a vintage guitar show in Nashville in 1988, but Martin was well aware of it in the 1960s, when the company began designing new guitars that met the old ones head-on with such vintage features as herringbone purfling, abalone trim, 12-fret bodies, scalloped bracing and the X-brace close to the soundhole.

The 12-fret dreadnought had already returned, although not yet under the Martin brand. The E.U. Wurlitzer company of Boston had ordered a D-28 with a 12-fret neck in 1954 and then continued to order one or two a year. These were labeled D-28S, S being the designation for any special feature. In 1962 a W was added to the Wurlitzer special-orders: D-28SW. Finally in 1967 the 12-fret D joined the Martin line, available in Styles 18, 28 and 35. All three were well-received, with each selling over 100 a year (as many as 250 in some years) for the next seven years.

One new Martin of the 1970s grew out of some customized Martins from the 1960s that had been originally built in the 1930s and 1940s. The story starts with the 16in-wide rosewood-body archtops, the F-7 and F-9. A total of 248 were made between 1935 and 1942, and for more than 20 years they were the answer to a trivia question: What is Martin's largest body size on a production model? With a body of rosewood, these archtops sounded more like flat-tops, but it took a fortuitous accident before the obvious idea hit.

About 1965, a man walked into Mark Silber's New York guitar shop with literally a wreck of an F-7 or F-9. "He'd been playing it in the car and had a wreck and the top got crashed," recalls Silber. "He had put a piece of plywood on it. He wanted to trade for any old guitar. I think I traded him a Guild that was worth 100 dollars."

Silber put the carcass away in the back of his shop. He considered making a new arched top for it, but he'd never had any interest in archtops. Eventually the idea came to him to put a flat top on it, and he bought a spruce dreadnought top from Martin. (The untrimmed top was large enough to fit the 16in body.) The finished guitar sounded great, and Silber wrote Martin suggesting that they make a production model, but with the back and the sides constructed from maple.

Silber recalls his guitar being a hit with the Greenwich Village folk crowd, which included an up-and-coming player named David Bromberg. In the meantime Matt Umanov, who had worked for Silber, opened his own store in the Village. He recalls: "A few years later, Bromberg found an F-7 and asked me to do a similar job for him. It was my feeling that a long-scale neck belonged on that, because the F-7 and F-9 had 24.9in scale lengths [shorter than dreadnought scale]." Umanov got a neck blank from Martin and inlaid the fingerboard with some Style 45 pearl he had bought from a New York pearlcutter. Bromberg has toured with the guitar for the last 25 years. "He thinks it's the greatest guitar in the world," Umanov says.

Like Silber, Umanov suggested that Martin put a 0000-body flat-top into production, but with no response. He continued to convert archtops, always using a long-scale neck. In the 1970s, Bromberg "really started hammering on them," Umanov says. "I think probably as a result of David getting on someone's case down there, it got into production – with of course Indian rosewood and that yellow dye on top."

Chris Martin explains the delay: "A lot of research – probably a lot more research than was necessary – went into the development of the M, because basically Mark Silber, Matt Umanov and Dave Bromberg created the M, but we had to justify it by researching the hell out of it."

C FOR CUTAWAY

Martin debuted the new size – called M – in 1977. The model was in the upper middle area of ornamentation, with a rosewood body, bound fingerboard and peghead, and a pearl soundhole ring. The pearl ring was typical of the traditional styles in the 30-series, so the new model was designated M-38. One of its early champions was folksinger Tom Paxton, who still uses one as his main guitar.

The M-38 listed for $1200, in between a D-35 and a D-41. It sold 275 units in its first year – not a threat to the D-28 or D-35, but outdistancing the D-41 that year. That was good enough for Martin to try the new body on a familiar style. Style 35 seems an odd choice – the three-piece back was still a rather radical new design – but the D-35 was selling well, so the M-35 was introduced in 1978. The model name was changed to M-36 after 26 guitars were made. It sold as well as the M-38.

The next obvious style for the M would be Style 28, but when it finally came, in 1981, it brought a new look to Martin, for it was only offered as a cutaway – the MC-28. A new dreadnought cutaway, the DC-28 also debuted.

Matt Umanov says he had been hammering away at Martin since the 1960s to make a cutaway. In the 1970s, he loaned Martin several examples from other manufacturers: a Gibson CF-100, a Gurian (both with a pointed cutaway) and a rounded-cutaway guitar. Martin's response, according to Umanov: "They scratched their head for another six or seven years."

Somebody at Martin had in fact built a cutaway in the 1960s. Mike Longworth recalls seeing it when he arrived in 1968. "The guitar actually had been made and then not sold and was hanging around the final inspection area," he says. "The guys get together and play music during lunch hour. They had a couple of Martin guitars sometimes without even any finish on them, and they had that cutaway. As far as I know it never did have any finish on it – kind of a rough test."

The MC-28 was more of a departure from Martin tradition than just a simple cutaway. It had an oval soundhole and a 22-fret fingerboard rather than the standard 20 frets. Umanov relates the story as told to him by people at Martin: "They said, 'Well, we're making a cutaway. You know that big heavy brace under the soundhole that ends up being under the last fret of the fingerboard? On the Gurian that brace stopped at the cutaway, and on the Gibson it also stopped at the cutaway. We didn't like that. We wanted it to go all the way across.' The only choice was to bring it down below the cutaway. 'We can't mess with the X-brace, so we better squash down the soundhole.' Then the fingerboard was too short. 'Oh, gee, I guess we better lengthen the fingerboard.' They told me that's why the fingerboard is longer."

Martin finally offered the M body in two traditional styles, 18 and 21, in 1985, and also added maple versions, the M-64

61

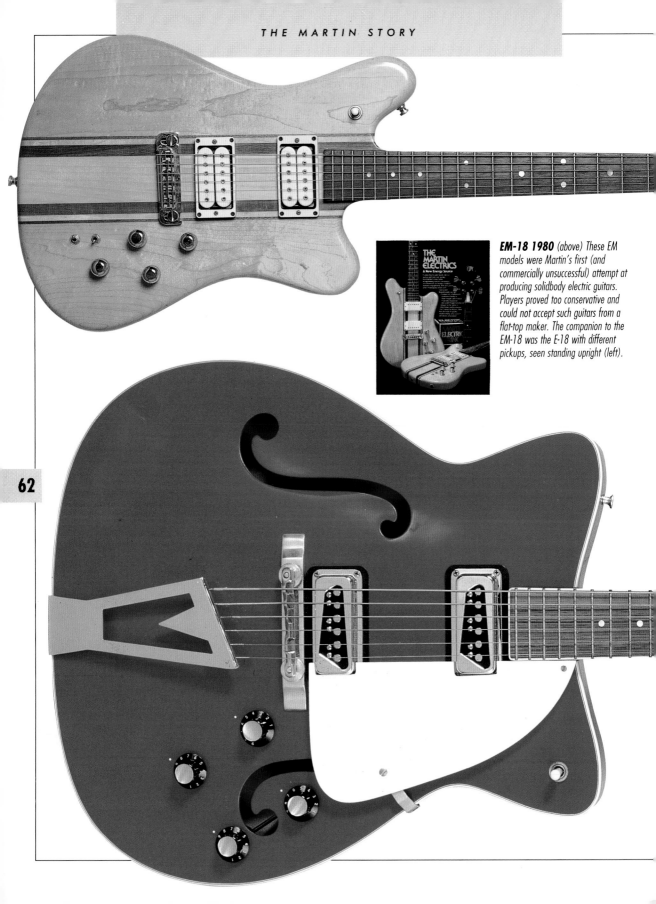

EM-18 1980 *(above) These EM models were Martin's first (and commercially unsuccessful) attempt at producing solidbody electric guitars. Players proved too conservative and could not accept such guitars from a flat-top maker. The companion to the EM-18 was the E-18 with different pickups, seen standing upright (left).*

F-55 1962 (left) Demand among players for thin-bodied archtop guitars in the early 1960s led Martin to offer three electric F series models from 1961 to 1965: the single-pickup F-50, this F-55, and the twin-cutaway F-65.

00-18E 1964 (right) A rather more bizarre electric episode was Martin's attempt to amplify several of their flat-top guitars. A DeArmond pickup is mounted over the soundhole, linked to body-mounted controls. (The tuners on this example are not original.)

Catalog 1959 (above) This launch-year brochure shows one of Martin's two dreadnought-sized E series electric flat-tops. The guitars were dropped some five years later, and have seldom proved to be attractive to acoustic or electric players.

Catalog 1962 (above) The electric F series also included the double-cutaway F-65 model. The Bigsby vibrato was an optional extra.

F-65 Double-cutaway, double pickup with mixing switch, allows full use of all frets in all positions, steel T-bar in neck, adjustable plexiglass bridge (pictured with Bigsby unit—available on all models at extra cost) shaded honey maple top, solid back and sides. Hard case $445, Soft case $245.

63

GT-75 1967 (above) Produced between 1965 and 1968, the GT series was a later attempt by Martin at electric archtop models, but it still proved difficult to entice players away from Gibson and other established makers of such guitars. The GTs were issued in burgundy or black finishes; this unusual red example was probably a factory sample. The series also included a single-cutaway GT-70 model.

Catalog 1960 (left) Included here are all three of Martin's E series electric flat-tops: the 00-18E (which sold that year for $199.50), the D-18E (retailing at $289.50), and the gold-hardware D-28E (which was listed on the 1960 pricelist at $410).

and MC-68. But M sales were still slow. The M-36 and M-38 had topped 300 in only one year, 1979, and had fallen down to 40 or 50 a year. Although the M remained in production, Chris Martin had a better idea: a deep-bodied M that would debut in 1985 as the J-size.

In the meantime, several prewar features were revived on the D-28, specifically the herringbone trim, scalloped bracing and 'zigzag' backstripe. Introduced in 1976 as the HD-28, it was an immediate success, with 500 sold the first year and 1,486 in 1977. By the 1990s it would become Martin's best-selling model. In 1978 a herringbone D-35 was introduced, but it was not nearly as well received as the HD-28.

Guitar production, which had fallen off from the early 1970s peak, slowed to a trickle in 1977 when Martin's workforce went on strike. The local cement workers union (Nazareth is the birthplace of Portland cement) had seen its ranks depleted and sought to grow with the addition of Martin workers. Management was not responsive to the worker's complaints and the workers struck. "I was in college," Chris Martin recalls. "I would come home and somebody would let the air out of my tires. My dad got beat up. Some thugs came to his house one night and beat him up." Managers, supervisors and office staff were put on the line, and they got out six guitars a day. The string division and the Sigma imports generated enough revenue to keep the doors open.

Solid. Electric. Martin?

The unionization attempt failed and the strikers came back, but the guitar market was falling fast in the face of new developments in keyboard instruments and an economic recession. Despite the hard times, Martin decided to give the electric guitar one more try. The new model of 1979 had a fresh peghead shape that suggested the scroll of the old Stauffer-style Martins of the 1830s. The double-cutaway body was made of three pieces of maple with attractive laminate strips of rosewood or walnut. The E-18 ($660) had two humbucking DiMarzio pickups; the EM-18 ($700) had two exposed-coil pickups with coil-tap capability. A companion bass, the EB-18 ($650), was also offered.

The next year, another model was added, with a contoured mahogany body (no laminate strips). The E-28 ($1,200) had special Seymour Duncan pickups, active electronics and a phase-shifter. There was also a bass, the EB-28 ($1,200).

Martin stuck with the solidbodies through 1983. The EM-18 was the best seller, averaging over 250 a year, with the EB-18 bass coming in second at over 150 a year. Dick Boak, who was hired by Martin in 1976 as a draftsman and was put in charge of the E-18 project (and was fired over his objections to the final product but eventually returned to Martin), believes the solidbodies might have succeeded had Martin continued to refine them. But Martin abandoned the solidbody market.

Now Martin's acquisitions became liabilities (except for Darco strings). "The Vega thing never worked out because we could never get the volume up to a level that was efficient," Chris Martin says. "And all those metal parts drove us nuts. We didn't know from hooks and flanges. Fibes... We went out into the marketplace with what we thought was the best drum in the world, and the people in the drum business for 50 years beat us up and down the block." Levin, Chris says, turned out to be "a pig in a poke" whose "socialist workforce" was "uninspired." In 1979, Martin bankrupted Levin and sold Vega and Fibes, although debts from these ventures would continue to plague the company.

The guitar business continued on its downhill slide. Around 1979, Chris recalls a NAMM show in Atlanta where they went the entire first day without writing a single order. When they got back to Nazareth after the disastrous show they began downsizing, putting workers on partial workweeks and laying off many of the middle- and upper-level management people who had been hired in the boom time.

Times got worse. As recently as 1977, Martin had shipped over 10,000 guitars (less than half of the 1971 record year, but still not bad). In 1982, total production was only 3,153 instruments, the lowest since World War II. "We needed leadership then," Chris Martin says, "even if it was just to walk around and say, 'It'll be okay, we'll figure this out.' It was the time he [Frank] should've said, 'All right, when the going gets tough...' The tough don't go drink." Frank Martin happened to be having a drink with Pres Rishaw at the very moment his father and the board of directors voted to ask for his resignation. On May 5, 1982, Frank Martin 'retired' at the age of 49. He moved to Florida, officially to "pursue other interests," and he died on Thanksgiving Day, 1993.

On June 15, 1986, with the Martin company still struggling in a downsliding guitar market, C.F. Martin III, the heart and soul of the company, passed away. Christian Frederick Martin IV, the only descendant of the founder working for Martin, would seem to have inherited control of the company. But it was not that simple.

When Frank Martin resigned in 1982, longtime vice president Hugh "Tigger" Bloom became president. Chris Martin had been in the business for four years. His destiny suddenly looked uncertain. At that point, he says, "I take a deep breath, because my grandfather's still alive. But my grandfather did realize that he needed to do something symbolic for me." In 1985, C.F. III went into a board meeting, announced that Chris was going to be vice president of marketing and practically ordered all in favor to say: "Aye."

Chris had worked in the sales department and done various office jobs to get a feel for them. He admits the best experience would have been on the road, but "I just wasn't sure what was going on, with Tigger in charge and my grandfather being that old." He was afraid if he were out of sight, he would be out of the minds of the board of directors.

C.F. THE FOURTH

Chris was 28 years old when his grandfather died. He remembers: "One of the directors said, 'Well, we could make Tigger the CEO,' and I said, 'I think the chairman should remain the CEO and I think I'm ready.' And they looked at me and they said, 'Okay, maybe you are.' So they made me the chairman. And I was scared to death."

C.F. III had envisioned Chris as a successor, and Chris recalls his grandmother being "hell-bent" on raising him to take over the company. Dick Boak, who was a fellow Rotary Club member with C.F. III, says, "I know that C.F. spent a lot of energy, a lot of time trying to breed Chris with the type of

integrity that he saw as crucial to the position and the longevity of the company."

Chris' father, however, had very little relationship with him. Chris' parents had divorced when he was three, and he grew up with his mother in New Jersey and Ohio, spending only summer vacations in Nazareth with his grandparents. His mother remarried and at one point had Chris change his last name to her new husband's name. His childhood experiences in the business were limited to helping a bandsaw operator by pushing wood scraps into the trash can, and to packing strings.

Like most Martins, Chris was not much of a musician. When he was 11, his mother lined him up with a guitar teacher, but when the teacher found out his pupil was the heir to the Martin company, he decided this was his chance to create a virtuoso. All Chris wanted was to learn some chords so he could play along at campfires at summer camp. Formal training was no fun, and consequently Chris today feels more comfortable on a piano than a guitar.

After high school, Chris decided he should learn how to build a guitar as a summer project. For the record, it was a D-28S with a thin neck. He tells the true story: "I went out in the shop and said I want to build this guitar. Now everyone out there was so proud of what they did, and they realized I had no clue basically on how to work with wood. They would give me some reject D-18 parts to work on and they would show me how the job was done on my guitar. Like, 'Let me demonstrate how the neck should be carved, Chris. Give me your neck.' So they really built the guitar. I was right there and I got to do some stuff that they knew I really couldn't screw up too bad."

Chris entered the University of California at Los Angeles, and his name landed him a job at Westwood Music. He started in sales. "They would say, 'This is Mr. Martin,' but young Mr. Martin didn't know what he was talking about," he explains. Then he was moved to the repair department, where he discovered he was probably never going to be a woodworker.

College life in California was not right for Chris, so he returned to Nazareth and went back to the factory to really learn how guitars are made. "They put me on the line, starting with some simple tasks," he says. "I'd do something

M38
GRAND AUDITORIUM

The M-38 is a flat-top version of the Martin "F" style carved-top guitar manufactured between 1935 and 1942. An important characteristic of the M style Grand Auditorium body is the acoustic properties that make it ideal for sound system and recording studio use.

The sides and traditional two-piece back are made of solid rosewood. A light stain adds character to the solid spruce top which is supported by bracing scalloped in the pre-war style. The soundhole rosette is hand inlaid with abalone pearl and the body finish is polished lacquer.

Body bindings are white with black and white inlay around the top, sides and back. An unusual feature is a connecting link of binding and inlay adjacent to the heel of the neck. (See detail, page 29.)

The slim mahogany neck joins the body at the 14th fret and features chrome plated, enclosed gear tuning machines. The headstock and fingerboard are bound in white with black and white trim. Unique to this model is the combination of an ebony fingerboard and rosewood bridge.

A very special guitar.

Catalog 1977 (above) The M-38 was introduced in 1977, the first of Martin's new M series. The Ms had a thinner, jumbo-size body, derived from flat-top conversions that some players had been concocting from Martin's old archtop guitars.

M-36 1993 Offering the unusual teaming of a rosewood bridge with an ebony fingerboard, the M-36 (left) was launched in 1978. This member of the Martin M series is designed to produce a bassier tone, which is probably helped by its distinctive three-piece rosewood back (right), recalling that of the earlier D-35 model (see page 59). The M Size is less deep than a D, and slightly larger in outline.

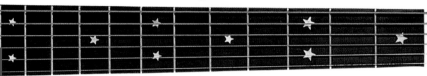

Catalogs The Rolls Royce status of the D series is underlined in a 1972 brochure (far right). Sigma was Martin's own imported guitar brand (right), launched in 1970.

D-76 1976 (above) The D-76 limited edition guitar was built to celebrate the 200th anniversary of the Declaration of Independence, the statement made in 1776 that based the United States on the right "to life, liberty, and the pursuit of happiness". Martin gave the D-76 special star-shaped fingerboard inlays and an eagle on the headstock, and built 1,976 guitars, plus 98 D-76E models for employees, and this single prototype (serial-numbered 000000).

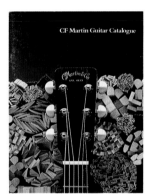

Catalog 1977 (left) While the traditional craft aspects of working with wood were emphasized on the cover of this brochure, in the Martin factory more modern industrial practices were being felt, and in 1977, at a time of declining sales for guitars, Martin's workforce went on strike. The unionization attempt failed.

67

Martin ad 1962 (left) This was the year in which Martin's old G-suffix classical models came to the end of a long run, replaced by the C series, as exemplified by the 000-28C that this well balanced young woman is so taken with. Also in the series were the 00-16C, 00-18C and the later 00-28C.

N-20 1972 (above) Martin had made guitars designed for classical players, with wide fingerboards, slotted headstocks and loop bridges, since the 1930s, but had never fared particularly well in this specialist market. The N-10 and N-20 classicals, with characteristic wide-waisted classical body shapes, were launched in the 1960s. They were produced throughout the 1970s, with the better-appointed N-20 surviving into the 1990s.

for a week and then I'd move." Again he realized he was not a born woodworker, and he began working toward finishing his degree. He graduated from Boston University in 1978 with a business degree and immediately joined the Martin company.

Despite the show of self-confidence that gained him the chairmanship, he wasn't comfortable as CEO. "I realized I was not a born leader," he says. "I was the shy kid in high school. I couldn't speak in public. And now all of a sudden I'm the chairman of the board." A public speaking course helped him communicate better, but he still wasn't getting through to the veteran workers. He credits the Outward Bound program for the team experience that he could relate to his managers.

Before he could instill a positive attitude of teamwork, however, he had to make sure he had a company to run. The settlement of his grandfather's estate required a stock evaluation, which required the company to furnish a business projection. Chris proudly presented the auditors with a flat projection of 7,000 guitars a year for the next five years. The accounting firm came back with a recommendation that C.F. Martin & Co. be liquidated.

SURVIVING THE EIGHTIES

"It was a godsend," Chris says. "It was the kick in the pants that we needed to say no, we're in charge of this thing, we can make it happen. I got into strategic planning, and one of the elements of that is to define your business. So I sat down with a group of people and said, 'We're in the acoustic flat-top steel-stringed guitar business. Let's admit it. Let's just do the one thing we're known for.'"

Martin's "Vision Statement" starts with the goal of "continuous improvement in the quality of performance within all departments of our company that will lead to improved customer satisfaction, reputation, competitiveness, market share and profitability."

Chris says, "We communicated that to the employees. They didn't need to be reminded. They needed to know that management was getting back to what we should have been doing all along. Coincidentally, about 1985 the guitar business

started to pick up. Just a little, but it was a ray of hope. Then '86 a little more and '87 and '88 and '89. And now it's crazy."

With his background in sales and marketing, Chris was aware of a demand for Martins that Martin didn't make. "Being a member of the Guild of American Luthiers, I would go to these conventions and I was insanely jealous of these luthiers who were making copies of [older] Martin models," he says. Martin certainly had the ability to make those models – a Custom Shop had been inaugurated formally in 1979 – but the orders weren't coming in. Then a Custom Shop ad showed an OM model with black binding and snowflake inlay. It was just one example of what the shop could do, but orders began coming in for that guitar. The conclusion, according to Chris, was that customers wanted to have decisions made for them.

SMALL ISN'T BEAUTIFUL

As a result, the Guitar of the Month program began in October 1984. The original idea of a new, custom-featured guitar every month was trimmed back to only four or five limited-run models a year. They have ranged from the 00-18V or D-18V, with vintage-style features (including an old V-shaped neck) to an ultra-fancy J-45M Deluxe. They are fitted with special paper labels, signed by C.F. Martin IV (and, until his death, C.F. Martin III).

Even before he became CEO, Chris Martin was intent on making his mark in Martin history with an innovative model. In 1980 an idea came to him on a trip to Japan. "You go to these bluegrass clubs in Tokyo and these guys, five-foot-three, 100 pounds, get up there and climb over their dreadnought," he says. When he got back home, he designed a ⅞-size dreadnought – perfect, or so he thought, for kids, women or Japanese men. Six months later he brought the first 7-28s to Japan. "They thought it was a toy," he says. "So that was a dud."

On a more positive note, Chris thought the M size, introduced in 1977, was a viable idea, even though its reception had been lukewarm. "The idea of a balanced-sounding guitar, harkening back to the tight waist like the 000 – there's validity there," he says. "I was certainly aware of what Gibson had done with their jumbos [the large-bodied, tight-waisted J-200-style flat-tops]. I looked at our line and said, 'We don't have a jumbo.' So very simply, I went out into the shop one day and I said, 'Take an M, make the sides as deep as a dreadnought, throw it together.' The damn thing worked! It was like Prototype Number One worked.

"At that point it was built like a D-28 with scalloped bracing. And I gave it to one of my colleagues, John Marshall. John didn't know what it was, and he started to smile when he played, and I thought, there's something here. And then I gave it to someone else, and they started to smile. There's something here. And then Dick DeWalt got involved, the sales manager, and he was astute enough to realize, let's not just clone it and make it look like a D-28. He went in and talked to Stan Jay [founder of Mandolin Brothers, one of the leading vintage dealers], and he said, 'This guitar is probably going to be a front guitar. The person who's in front's going to play it. Why don't you jazz it up a little, put the hexagons in the fingerboard, put the gold tuning machines on.'"

They did just that and put the new J (for Jumbo) in the exalted range of the 40-series guitars. The J-40M (the M suffix was dropped in 1990) led an entire line of deep-bodied Ms that debuted in 1985, including the plainer J-21M, the fancy maple J-65M, and two 12-strings, the J12-40M and the J12-65M.

The J size seemed perfect, but tradition-minded (read dreadnought-minded) Martin players still had to be convinced. Chris asked Diane Ponzio, who performs on the lecture/clinic presentations Chris gives at stores, to swap her D-35 for a J-40. Once she tried it, she liked it. Audiences liked it, too, but Chris says it's still a hard-sell to dealers. "I still go into stores that do not have a J-40, after six or seven years. They go, 'No, give me a 28, give me an 18.' Try a J-40! It's big! It's loud! It will satisfy your customer's demands."

J FOR JUMBO

"That's my guitar," says Chris Martin. "That's the guitar that some day people are going to say, 'What did Chris do for the company? Chris put together the J-40.'"

The J-40 started off with sales of 259 in its first year and went upward, settling in the 1990s at an average of a little over 300 a year. A black version, the J-40BK – the only color finish other than shaded (sunburst) Martin has ever offered – was added in 1988, and it added another 50 or so a year to J-40 sales totals. A cutaway version, the JC-40, was introduced in 1987 and added about 100 guitars a year to the J-40 sales figures. By comparison, Martin's most popular models, the HD-28 and D-28, have averaged about 1,200 and 1,100 a year, respectively, in the 1990s.

Chris again tried to buck Martin tradition with the introduction of maple-bodied guitars in 1985. The five new models offered something for everyone: J, M and D bodies, plus a cutaway M and a 12-string J. They also ushered in a new series of style numbers, the 60-series. The J-65 was the most successful, but its peak sales figure was only 91 in 1988. Chris Martin sums up the results: "We thought we'd get into the maple guitar business. Have not had a lot of luck. Not a lot of luck."

One magic ingredient for new models has been the limited run. "We've done limited editions out of quilted maple, quilted mahogany, figured walnut," Chris says, "and if we keep the numbers low, boy there's a lot of interest. I'm afraid if we came out and said we're gonna make a thousand walnut guitars it'd be a hard sell, but when you do 10 of them and they're numbered [consecutively], poof, they're gone."

FUN WITH THE OVER-45S

Another Chris Martin contribution is what he calls "the ultra-fancy, above-45 guitars." After going to vintage shows, he decided that there was room above Style D-45 for something fancier. He tested the market with a super fancy J-45 (officially Custom J-45M Deluxe), which was a 1986 Guitar of the Month. Seventeen were sold, which Chris says was 16 more than anyone expected. The next year was the 50th anniversary of the first production D-45s, and Chris had a run of 50 made of Brazilian rosewood, priced at $7500. The sales staff had so little confidence that no guitars were to be made unless orders were taken for them. Chris recalls: "Three days later they were all gone, and everybody was like, 'Gee, maybe that upper end was more lucrative than we thought.'"

OM-45 Custom 1983 (right) Through its custom service, Martin offers made-to-order guitars to players who want their own particular combination of features. High on the list of requested details is extra inlay, as on this ornately finished custom OM-45 model, made in the early 1980s.

MC-28 1982 (above) Martin finally issued a flat-top with a cutaway when this model was added to the line in 1981. This particular MC-28 has an internal factory-mounted pickup, the controls for which are on the upper body side. Martin have offered various pickup options since the mid-1970s.

Catalog 1986 (right) Mid 1980s economics caused Martin to import the laminated-body Shenandoah models in kit form from Japan and assemble them into finished instruments at their Pennsylvania factory. For a time this allowed the company to market a low-priced Martin-branded guitar.

C.F. MARTIN SHENANDOAH SERIES

Martin guitars and Quality: two terms which have been closely related for over 150 years. This association continues with Martin Shenandoah Series guitars.

The development of Martin Shenandoah guitars resulted from years of thorough planning and research. Regardless of style, Martin Shenandoah instruments are designed with a "vintage style" easy play V-shaped neck, a solid spruce top for tonal quality, and an attractive tortoise style pickguard. In addition each guitar is equipped with a high-output acoustic pickup that allows the player the choice of acoustic or acoustic-electric play.

Although this is our least expensive line of Martin instruments, every guitar is subject to Martin's rigid standard of quality. Experienced Martin craftsmen assemble, finish and inspect each Martin Shenandoah to insure the industry's highest quality standards. We back our "statement of quality" with a limited lifetime warranty on all Martin Shenandoah guitars.

Play a Martin Shenandoah and discover the Martin difference.

D-2832 SHENANDOAH DREADNOUGHT

Modeled after Martin's world renowned D-28, the D-2832 features rosewood veneer back and sides and a select solid spruce top. Hand sprayed to a high gloss lacquer finish, the D-2832 has decorative white body binding, genuine pearl fingerboard position markers and chrome enclosed tuning machines.

The twelve string counterpart D12-2832 (not shown) is designed with a modified top bracing pattern and a specially reinforced neck.

The Martin Dreadnought tone is evident whether you play the guitar as an acoustic or an acoustic-electric. If value for your dollar is important, you'll appreciate the affordable quality of the D-2832 and the D12-2832.

D-3532 SHENANDOAH DREADNOUGHT

The rich Dreadnought sound of the D-3532 is projected from a select solid spruce top. A three-piece back of rosewood veneer is responsible for the deeper bass response of the D-3532.

A high output acoustic pickup amplifies the natural sound of the D-3532 without coloring or distorting the tone. The only way to appreciate the full potential of this guitar is to play it.

JUMBO SIZE INSTRUMENTS

Jumbo size instruments are the most recent additions to the line of handcrafted Martin guitars. Combining an "M" or Grand Auditorium body profile and a "D" or Dreadnought body depth creates an instrument with a big, powerful sound that remains balanced from bass to treble.

As Rick Turner stated when reviewing the Jumbo M in the May 1986 GUITAR PLAYER Product Profile column, "Steel string players, the guitar I tested is one of the two or three finest new instruments I've ever played. It is acoustic, and very powerful instrument, beautifully made in the best C. F. Martin tradition. If there are still people around who think the historic Pennsylvania company 'doesn't make them like they used to', then these entire should get to the nearest Martin dealer with that pick in hand. The Jumbo M is the next definitive guitar from Martin."

Jumbo M guitars are constructed using the world's finest selection of solid rosewood and maple for the body woods and highest grade, vertical grain spruce for the sound board. The six-string Jumbo guitars are designed with antisloped bracing to add to the robust tone of these instruments and a "low profile" neck design for that special "flat artist" feel. Whether you're accustomed to playing an electric guitar or an acoustic guitar, this new neck design adds to your playing comfort. Every Martin Jumbo M instrument is superior in tone, playability and craftsmanship to any other guitar in its price range.

> The Martin Jumbo guitar is destined to become the Dreadnought of the '90s.
> C. F. Martin IV

Catalog 1986 (above) The J series, a version of the earlier M series with a full-depth body, first appeared in the Martin line during 1985.

J-40M JUMBO M

Rapidly becoming one of Martin's most popular guitars, the J-40M is in demand for its outstanding tone and appearance. As a Martin "40 Series" instrument, the J-40M is handcrafted using the world's very finest spruce, rosewood, mahogany and ebony. Eight abalone pearl hexagon fingerboard inlays and gold enclosed tuning machines give the J-40M that Martin "40 Series" look. Inlays are ½ the size of the D-45—a new and different style that is consistent with the 40's tradition.

To add extra "punch" to the tonal power of the J-40M, each spruce top-brace is masterfully scalloped by hand to just the right thickness. The solid, one-piece mahogany neck is hand shaped in a "low profile" contour that provides players with a smooth, comfortable feel over the entire length of the neck.

Why choose a guitar for tone, playability or beauty when you can have all three in one instrument?

J12-40M JUMBO TWELVE STRING

This twelve-string version shares many of the features of its six-string counterpart. Body woods, bindings and inlays are identical. A special neck design and innovative bracing pattern accommodate the additional tension of six extra strings. As Martin's only "40 Series" twelve-string, the J12-40M has hexagon abalone of pearl fretboard inlays and its twelve gold tuning machines with ebony buttons.

J-21M JUMBO M

Rich, dark binding sets off the quartersawn rosewood back and sides of the J-21M (not shown). A select spruce top is fitted with a rosewood belly bridge while the fingerboard is also of rosewood specially selected for its durability.

Handcrafted in the finest Martin tradition, the J-21M has a rich, warm tone that is amplified by scalloped top-bracing. The "low profile" neck design is comfortable for acoustic or electric guitar players.

Without sacrificing tone or quality, Martin has made the J-21M its most affordably priced Jumbo M size guitar.

JC-40 1994 (above) The new J series body design was first produced with a cutaway on the JC-40 model, which made its debut in 1987. The J models are some ¾ in deeper than the M series, the same depth as a dreadnought. At first Martin used a rather unwieldly model numbering system for the J series guitars by adding an M after the Style number (for example, J-40M). Now the J (or JC for cutaway versions) stands alone.

71

J12-65M 1985 (above) This 12-string version of the full-depth J-65 shares with its six-string cousin a figured maple back-and-sides (not shown), rather than the customary rosewood. Both guitars first appeared as part of the Martin line in 1985. The design of the soundhole ring recalls the D-28 model.

D-42LE 1988 (right) The 1980s saw Martin launch an impressive marketing scheme with LE (Limited Edition) and 'Guitar of the Month' instruments, made in relatively small quantities and usually with signed and numbered labels.

Perhaps the most ambitious fancy limited-run model came about after Chris' visit in 1993 to Gene Autry's Western Heritage Museum in Hollywood, where Autry's original D-45 is displayed. The result was not one but two Gene Autry models — one with Autry's name in script on the fingerboard, the other with snowflake inlay and a small Autry signature at the 12th fret. Each model will be made in a limited run of 100.

ONLY SIXTEEN

Martin stepped into the modern age of neck construction in 1985 with two major changes. The first was an adjustable truss rod. The device had been patented by Gibson in 1921 and most manufacturers had adopted it in some form or another as soon as Gibson's patent ran out, but Martin had used the non-adjustable T-bar since 1934 (and an ebony rod during World War II when metal was in short supply). In early 1985 Martin began phasing in a U-bar with a rod that was adjustable at the neck block. A non-adjustable square bar was also available as an option, and those examples are designated by the letter Q after the model name. Next came the "low profile" or thin neck, which Chris Martin admits was popularized by Taylor guitars. By 1987 it was standard on the popular large-bodied guitars (Ds, Ms and Js) and was optional on any other model with a 14-fret neck and adjustable rod.

Martin experimented more in 1986 with special runs of Style 16 guitars. These did not strictly adhere to the specs of the 0-16NY. Instead, they were designed as trade show specials. The first was the D-16M, a mahogany dreadnought. Its plain ornamentation and semi-gloss finish allowed for a list price of $1070, which was $225 less than the next cheapest dreadnought, the D-18. Then came limited runs with ash and walnut bodies, followed by a cutaway, the 000C-16. Through various permutations, Style 16 guitars have been quite successful and have gained a reputation as a true bargain in a solid wood guitar.

In 1988, Martin made a decidedly untraditional change in a traditional style, eliminating the familiar Style 18 soundhole ring design, the grouping of nine black and white rings bordered on either side by a single black ring. The new ring configuration, adopted on Styles 18, 21, 16 and any other non-cutaway guitar (except those with a pearl soundhole ring), was the standard D-28 grouping of nine rings between two groups of five black and white rings. The move up to a fancier ring was, ironically, made for purely economic reasons. The company had to put aside guitar tops to cure, and these tops would have soundhole rings already inlaid. With limited inventory space, the tops had to be allocated among the various Styles. When orders for guitars came in, if the orders didn't match up with the allocation, Martin might end up with, say, a surplus of Style 18 tops and a shortage of Style 28 tops. If the number of different ring types was reduced to two — Style 28 or pearl — then the chances of surpluses and shortages would be reduced, too. So that's what Martin did.

The Stinger line, budget-priced Korean-made solidbodies that are set up in Nazareth and distributed by Martin, appeared in 1985. Stingers, Sigmas and the strings and accessory products together make up an important part of Martin's overall business.

Martin has also worked on developing pickups for acoustic flat-top guitars. The Martin Thinline was originally a Barcus Berry product and is now a Fishman. Retrofitting onboard controls has not been as successful, because players have been reluctant to cut a hole in the side of a solid wood guitar. The latest design is the MEQ-932, with a four-band EQ control and both a mic (cannon) jack and a standard guitar cord jack.

The Backpacker, a small travel guitar developed by New Jersey luthier/musician Bob McNally, has put Martin's factory in Mexico into the instrument business. The factory was bought for Darco string production in 1991, and pickup production was also moved there, but Chris' goal was to make a wood product (and eventually a guitar model) in the new facility. He had no great expectations for the Backpacker — projected production was about eight a day. Martin showed it at NAMM in January 1994 and took orders for 5,000. Then on March 4, the Backpacker literally took off when astronaut Pierre Thuot took his Backpacker along on a Space Shuttle mission.

The newest Martin model is the D-1. Chris Martin credits his employees with the push that led to it. It started back with the Shenandoahs – guitars with laminated back and sides that Martin began importing in 1985. The Shenandoahs arrived from Japan in kit form – an unfinished body and neck – and were assembled and finished in Nazareth. (The Shenandoahs bore regular Martin model numbers but with 32 added, thus a D-2832 was the Shenandoah version of the D-28.)

The Shenandoah bodies were made to take a polyester finish, but Martin was putting on a thinner lacquer finish, which required a finer degree of sanding and filling. Consequently, it was taking more time to finish a Shenandoah than it was to finish a Martin. At the same time, a complaint from a competitor regarding the labeling forced Martin to identify the guitars as being assembled in the USA from components made in Japan. "We weren't proud of the Shenandoah," Chris says. "It was the only thing we could do in the price range at that time. Sales were declining, the yen was going crazy, so parts were getting more and more expensive, and the impetus to the D-1 was the employees saying, 'Damn it, let us build this thing from scratch here.'"

THE RESPONSIBLE USE OF WOOD

The D-1, with laminated mahogany sides (but solid back) became a test model of sorts, allowing Martin to introduce some innovative designs that the company had been afraid to try, including a new bracing pattern and new neck joint. "I'd have to say that this guitar is the first that is made of laminated materials that was designed to optimize those materials," says Dick Boak, director of the Association of Stringed Instrument Artisans and Martin's director of advertising. The greater rigidity of the laminated sides was viewed as a positive feature by Martin engineer Mike Drezner, who experimented with various bracing patterns to find the one that worked best. The new pattern includes a bridgeplate (the plate that supports the underside of the top in the bridge area) mounted at an angle. The D-1 necks are 'carved' by machine, and they have a new rounded neck joint rather than the traditional Martin dovetail. The neck fastens with a bolt. The finish is a semi-gloss, which does not require the considerable labor cost of polishing a glossy finish.

"It's designing the dreadnought to be built in 1990 instead of 1890," Chris says, adding that this is not at odds with the Martin tradition. "My feeling about mechanization is that my family has utilized mechanization since 1833. It's just that the state of the art has changed."

After a mahogany guitar, the next would have to be rosewood, and that would be the D-1R. Because of the difficulty in matching a solid back with veneered sides, however, the D-1R has a laminated back as well as sides.

The introduction of laminated woods represents more than a cost-saving move. It's a harbinger of a materials problem that all guitar makers are facing. Consequently, new materials rather than new body shapes will be the focus of future designs, Chris Martin believes. "All of us in the guitar business have done too good a job convincing people that rosewood and mahogany and ebony and spruce are the only or the best woods for guitars. Hopefully we'll always make a few guitars out of rosewood and ebony but it's not going to be in the volume that it is today. It's just not."

Dick Boak adds that the future efforts of C.F. Martin & Co. will be "toward development of new technologies and towards efficient manufacturing and use of alternative materials in respect to veneers. It's his [Chris Martin's] feeling that veneers are probably, unfortunately, the wave of the future because of the rain forest situation, and certainly it represents a more responsible use of the wood."

Boak, like all Martin guitar lovers, has mixed feelings about the inevitable future. "I love the sound of solid wood guitars, and I hope that we can make them as long as there is a demand for them," he says. "And if a tree is going to come down, if you were to ask the tree what it wanted to be before it came down, certainly the answer in many cases would be a Martin guitar. I can't imagine being anything quite that nice."

As of 1994, Martin is in the enviable position of having production sold out at least a year in advance. Having learned from the boom and bust of earlier years, Chris Martin is taking cautious steps forward, slowly expanding the plant, slowly adopting new technologies and materials, keeping C.F. Martin & Co. focused on the product that it has always made the best: acoustic flat-top guitars.

73

HD-28P 1990 (left) After making guitars for 157 years, Martin finally produced their 500,000th instrument in 1990. The building of half a million guitars could not go unmarked, and so the instrument concerned, an HD-28P (which translates as a herringbone-trim D-28 with low-profile neck), was signed on the top by Martin's entire workforce, and now resides in a glass case in the company museum. No hierarchy is evident — apparently people signed the guitar as and when they turned up. Sharp-eyed readers may care to check the position of company boss Chris Martin IV's signature. (Clue: it's somewhere between autographs 65 and 67 in the first column).

Catalogs 1993 (above) Proving that Style 45 is still seen as Martin's flagship, the recent covers of both the general fretted instrument catalog (above) and the Martin brochure (top) picture guitars of this luxurious top-of-the-line Style.

74

J-40BK 1994 (above) This black version of the J-40 was introduced by Martin in 1988. It's the first color option that the company has offered, other than the 'shaded-top' (or sunburst) finish that provided an earlier contrast to the familiar natural spruce look.

D-45 Deluxe Limited Edition 1993 (left)
This magnificent tribute to the skill of the inlay artist features an overflowing 'tree of life' decoration on the fingerboard. It is number 50 of a limited run of 50 guitars, and is owned by the current head of the company, Chris Martin IV.

Gene Autry (above) The most famous 'singing cowboy', Autry owned the first Martin D-45, custom built for him in 1933, and is pictured here with the special edition 1990s version.

CHD-28 1994 (above) As it became obvious that traditional guitar-making woods would not always be available, Martin began to experiment with timbers unfamiliar to the company. This new optional version of the HD-28, using cedar in place of the conventional spruce top, is one such example.

D-45 Gene Autry 1994 (above)
This is the production prototype for a limited edition guitar that aims to recapture the very first Martin D-45 built over 60 years ago for Autry, complete with his name inlaid into the fingerboard, just as on the original.

The reference section that takes up the rest of this book consists of three main parts: Model Identification (starting here and continuing to page 81); Reference Listings (pages 82 to 104); and Dating Martins (104-105).

The MODEL IDENTIFICATION section that starts here is designed to help you work out an instrument's model name. Martin guitars have a two-part model name, separated by a hyphen. The first part is the body *Size*, the second part the decorative *Style* (for example 000-28, where 000 is the Size and 28 the Style). Once a model name is determined, then the individual entry in the Reference Listings section can provide specific details of each variation.

The REFERENCE LISTINGS (starting on page 82) give further information on individual models once a guitar has been identified. All the variations of the model are described (the 000-28, for example, has 18 different variations, including Hawaiian, gut-string, plectrum, koa and electric). Some of these variations are indicated by additional suffixes, mostly letters (for example a 000-28H is a Hawaiian version), and these can be interpreted in the Suffix chart on page 81. Also shown in the Reference Listings are general specs, production years and, in most cases, a production total for each variation.

The DATING MARTINS section (pages 104-105) helps to determine the year of manufacture of an instrument through a general chronology of changes made by Martin, and a list of serial numbers to pinpoint the exact date of Martins made from 1898.

76

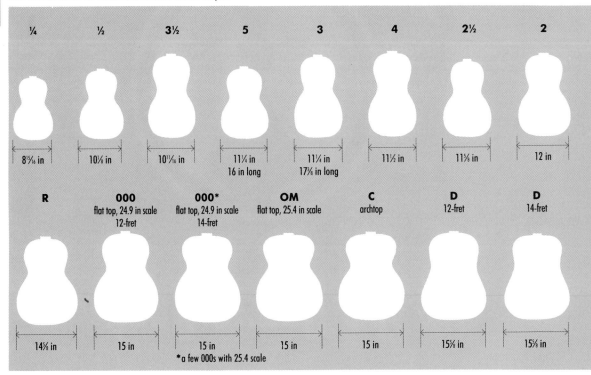

If you're trying to identify an acoustic or electric archtop, or a solidbody electric, see the charts on page 81. If it's a flat-top Martin you want to identify, first find out whether it was made before or after 1898. Do this by looking for a serial number stamped on the neck block inside the body. Look right inside the soundhole, toward the neck.

IF THE GUITAR HAS NO SERIAL NUMBER it was made before 1898. Go to page 82.

IF THE GUITAR HAS A SERIAL NUMBER it was made from 1898 onwards. Sometimes you can tell the model name too: Martins made since September 1930 have the model name stamped on the neck-block with the serial number. Keep reading...

IF YOU NOW KNOW THE GUITAR'S MODEL NAME go straight to the Reference Listings of Martins made from 1898, which start on page 84.

IF YOU STILL DON'T KNOW THE MODEL NAME, either because it isn't stamped on the neck-block or because you don't have access to the guitar in question, then see the body outlines and measurements below and read the related info on page 78. This will help you to work out the guitar's body Size. Then go on to page 79 and 80 where you can determine the decorative Style. Combine the two – Size and Style – and you have the model name.

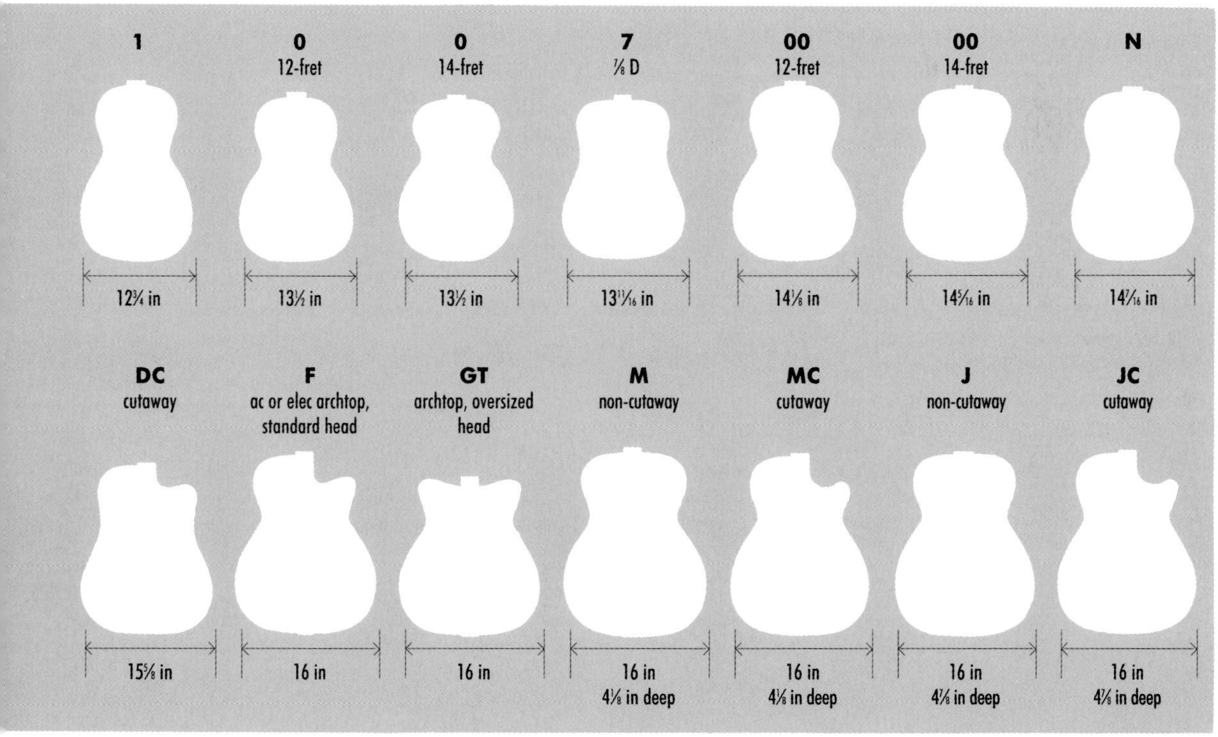
1
12¾ in
0
12-fret
13½ in
0
14-fret
13½ in
7
⅞ D
13 11/16 in
00
12-fret
14⅛ in
00
14-fret
14 5/16 in
N
14 7/16 in
DC
cutaway
15⅝ in
F
ac or elec archtop, standard head
16 in
GT
archtop, oversized head
16 in
M
non-cutaway
16 in
4⅛ in deep
MC
cutaway
16 in
4⅛ in deep
J
non-cutaway
16 in
4⅞ in deep
JC
cutaway
16 in
4⅞ in deep

BODY SIZES

Almost all Martin body Sizes are delineated by body width, and this is most easily measured across the widest part of the back of the body. The body outlines of all Martin's Sizes are illustrated in the drawings shown across the bottom of the previous two pages (76 and 77). The outlines include the width measurement information, and also list the characteristics that differentiate any body Sizes that have similar widths.

If you don't have the guitar to measure, then try to match up the instrument's body shape with the outlines. Of course, some of the body outlines are more similar than others, but it should be possible for you to tell apart the more distinctive of the body Sizes.

You should bear in mind that not all body Sizes were available in all years, and the Chronology Of Sizes chart (below) is designed to be of use in eliminating certain Sizes that appear to be similar but that were only available at particular periods. Clues to help you pinpoint more exactly the year in which a particular Martin guitar was made can be found in the Dating Martins section, which includes the all-important serial number list. Martin is one of the few guitar makers with strictly sequential serial numbers that allow accurate dating.

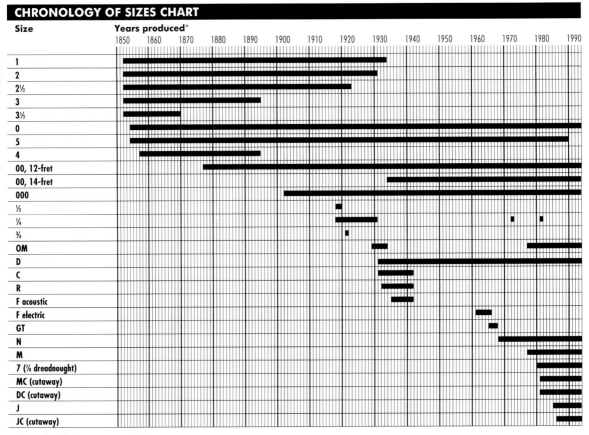

CHRONOLOGY OF SIZES CHART

*Occasional special-order appearances not included.

DECORATIVE STYLES

Style identification keys are divided into three periods. First try to place the guitar into one of these three general periods according to the following characteristics. Note that these eras may overlap by a few years.

FIRST PERIOD

▌ No serial number.
▌ None with dark top (no mahogany, koa or sunburst finish).
▌ No 000 size or larger.
▌ Most with no fingerboard inlay.
These characteristics indicate a Martin made between **1833** and **1898**. See pages 82-83.

SECOND PERIOD

▌ Serial number on guitar.
▌ No pickguard (except for a few 1929-31).
▌ No peghead decal.
▌ No D size.
These characteristics indicate a Martin made between **1898** and **1931**. See key below.

THIRD PERIOD

▌ Serial number on guitar.
▌ Pickguard on most.
▌ Peghead decal (or "C.F. Martin" head inlay).
These characteristics indicate a Martin made **since 1932**. See key on following page.

1898-1931 STYLE KEY

No pearl, no decorative top edge trim	Unbound fingerboard	1 to 4 soundhole rings	**17**
		1-9-1 soundhole ring grouping	**18**
	Bound fingerboard	**44**	
Herringbone trim	Herringbone soundhole ring	**21**	
	Herringbone around top edge	**28**	
Pearl soundhole ring but no pearl edge trim	Wood bridge	Diagonal wood purfling	**27**
		Herringbone purfling	**30**
	Ivory bridge	**34**	
Pearl top edge border	No pearl on top around fingerboard	**40**	
	Pearl on top around fingerboard	Unbound peghead	**42**
		Bound peghead	**45**

1932 – current STYLE KEY FOR FLAT-TOPS

No top binding
- All single-dot fret markers → **15**
- Two dots at 7th fret → **17** | **#25 (2-17)** | **0-55 (00-17)**

1- or 3-ply binding with dark outer layer
- Bridge pins angled → **1 newstyle**
- Bridge pins on line perpendicular to strings → **16**

Multiple binding with dark outer layer
- Mahogany back and sides
  - Natural spruce or koa top
    - Non-12-string → **18** | **D-1 oldstyle**
    - 12-string → **D12-20**
  - Dark-stained spruce top → **19**
- Rosewood back and sides
  - No herringbone edge trim → **21**
  - Herringbone edge trim → **HD-28CTB** | **HD-28GM** | **HD-28PSE**
- Maple back and sides
  - Unbound fingerboard
    - Maple peghead face → **D-60**
    - Rosewood peghead face
      - D size → **D-62**
      - M size → **M-64**
  - Tortoiseshell fingerboard binding
    - Snowflake inlay → **D-62LE**
    - Dot inlay → **65**
- Koa back and sides → **25K**

Maple (light wood) outer binding → **D-18MB**

White body binding, no pearl edge trim
- Wood-marquetry soundhole rings (no herringbone)
  - Mahogany body → **N-10**
  - Rosewood body → **N-20**
- Non-pearl soundhole rings
  - Unbound fingerboard
    - 2-piece rosewood back
      - Star-inlays → **D-76**
      - Other inlay → **D-2 oldstyle** | **28** | **Cust. 15**
    - 3-piece rosewood back → **CM-0089**
    - Koa back → **28K**
    - Mahogany back → **HD-28M**
  - Bound fingerboard
    - 3-piece rosewood back → **35** | **36**
    - 2-piece rosewood back → **J-40**
    - 2-piece mahogany back → **D-93**
    - 2-piece maple back → **68**
- Pearl soundhole ring
  - Bound peghead → **38**
  - Unbound peghead → **37**

White body binding, pearl edge trim
- Unbound peghead
  - Top: no pearl round fingerboard → **40 (non-J)**
  - Top: pearl round fingerboard → **42**
- Bound peghead
  - Top: no pearl round fingerboard → **41**
  - Top: pearl round fingerboard → **45**

80

MODEL NAME CHART FOR ACOUSTIC ARCHTOPS

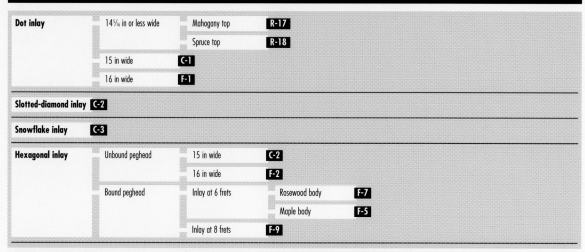

Dot inlay	14⁵⁄₁₆ in or less wide	Mahogany top	**R-17**
		Spruce top	**R-18**
	15 in wide	**C-1**	
	16 in wide	**F-1**	

Slotted-diamond inlay **C-2**

Snowflake inlay **C-3**

Hexagonal inlay	Unbound peghead	15 in wide	**C-2**
		16 in wide	**F-2**
	Bound peghead	Inlay at 6 frets	Rosewood body **F-7**
			Maple body **F-5**
		Inlay at 8 frets	**F-9**

MODEL NAME CHART FOR ELECTRIC ARCHTOPS

Single cutaway	1 pickup	**F-50**
	2 pickups	Standard rectangular peghead **F-55**
		Large, flared-top peghead **GT-70**
Double cutaway	Sunburst finish	**F-65**
	Burgundy or black finish	**GT-75**

MODEL NAME CHART FOR ELECTRIC SOLIDBODIES

Maple body with dark laminates	Selector switch and 1 mini-switch	**E-18**
	Selector switch and 2 mini-switches	**EM-18**
Mahogany body, shaded (sunburst) finish	**E-18**	

KEY TO STYLE SUFFIXES

A	ash back and sides	**GM**	Grand Marquis special edition	**MBLE**	M-style suffix on J models – Brazilian rosewood
AC	ash back and sides, classical	**GOM**	guitar of the month (limited edition)		back & sides, limited edition
B	Brazilian rosewood back & sides	**H**	Hawaiian set-up, herringbone soundhole ring	**MC**	M-style suffix on J cutaway models
BK	black finish		(1990s) or huda wood (D-18H 1966 only)		(1985–1990)
BLE	Brazilian rosewood back & sides, limited edition	**K**	koa wood (back & sides; or top, back & sides)	**MP**	Morado rosewood back & sides, low-profile
BSE	Brazilian rosewood back & sides, signature	**KLE**	koa top, back & sides, limited edition		neck
	edition	**K2**	koa wood (top, back & sides)	**N**	standard-profile neck (i.e. not low-profile)
C	classical or cutaway	**L**	left-handed version		and/or non-scalloped braces
C16	cutaway	**LE**	limited edition	**NY**	'New York': wide fingerboard, 12-fret, slotted
C LSH	cutaway, large soundhole, herringbone trim	**LSH**	large soundhole, herringbone trim		head
C.T.B.	CFM inlay, tortoise binding	**M**	M-style suffix on J models 1985-1990 or	**P**	'plectrum' four-string neck (1920s/1930s),
E	electric flat-top (1950s/1960s) or employees-		mahogany back and sides		or low-profile neck (1987–89)
	only model (1970s)	**MB**	maple binding	**PSE**	low-profile neck, signature edition
G	gut-string (today =nylon)	**MBK**	M-style suffix on black J-40 1985-1990	**Q**	old-style non-adjustable square truss-rod

R	rosewood back or adjustable truss-rod (1985-86)
S	'special' = anything unusual or 14- or 12-fret neck (whichever is non-standard)
SE	signature edition
SF	satin finish
SW	'Special Wurlitzer' made for E.U. Wurlitzer company
T	tenor four-string
TE	tenor electric
T8	tenor eight-string
V	'vintage' features and/or V-profile neck
W	walnut back & sides
2R	double herringbone soundhole ring

REFERENCE LISTINGS

This section is divided into two parts. First on these two pages are the pre-1898 Martins. Then starting on page 84 is the main listing of flat-top, archtop, electric archtop and electric solidbody Martins made from 1898.

KEY TO DECORATIVE STYLES PRE-1898

4 rosewood soundhole rings	Checkered-pattern soundhole ring	**17**	
	Rope-pattern soundhole ring	No edge purfling	**17** **18**
		Diagonal-pattern edge trim	**24**
	Herringbone soundhole ring	**20** **21** **22** **23**	
	Zipper-pattern (1 horizontal between 2 diagonal) soundhole ring	**26**	
	Herringbone around top edge	**28**	
Pearl soundhole ring, no pearl edge trim	Wood bridge	Diagonal colored wood edge trim	**27**
		Herringbone edge trim	**28** **30**
		Wide herringbone edge	**33**
	Ivory bridge	**34**	
Pearl top edge border	No pearl on top around fingerboard	**40**	
	Pearl on top around fingerboard	**42**	

■ **MARTIN GUITARS MADE BEFORE 1898** – Work out the decorative style from the key, and then look for more information under the relevant heading opposite.

The pre-1898 guitars are listed by Styles only, as there is little information regarding the availability of various Sizes. You may be able to ascertain the Size of a specific guitar by using the charts on pages 76/77.

Note that specs may vary from the following descriptions. Models are noted in Martin sales books beginning in 1856, but model specs are not listed. Sizes and Styles were typically written on a label affixed to the case rather than the guitar, so identifications can't be absolutely positive, since cases can be switched.

GENERAL CHARACTERISTICS

Most pre-1898 guitars with:
■ Brazilian rosewood back and sides, spruce top.
■ Ebony bridgepins with pearl dots.
■ 12-fret neck, slotted peghead, ebony fingerboard with no inlay.

In addition to the features listed, pre-1898 models may have some of the following characteristics:
■ Line of wood around center of body
■ Inner body lining of spruce veneer
■ "Ice cream cone" neck heel
■ Clock key neck adjustment
■ Solid peghead with friction tuners
■ Scrolled peghead with six-on-a-side tuners (1833-1840s)

Style 17 *1856–97*
Plainest standard style.
▌2 or 4 rosewood soundhole rings (early with checkered purfling in center of rings, green-and-white rope-pattern ring in center by 1870s, no rope pattern by 1897).
▌5-ply top binding with rosewood outer layer, unbound back.
▌White backstripe.
▌Brass tuner plates, ivory tuner buttons.
No documented distinction between Styles 17 and 18.

Style 18 *1857 onward*
No top edge purfling, rope-pattern soundhole ring.
▌Rope-pattern colored-wood soundhole ring.
▌5-ply top binding with rosewood outer layer, unbound back.
▌Brass tuner plates, ivory tuner buttons.
No documented distinction between Styles 17 and 18.

Style 20 *1850s*
▌Herringbone soundhole ring of red, white and green wood.
▌5-ply top binding and 3-ply back with rosewood outer layer.
▌Herringbone backstripe of red, white and green wood.
Very obscure style. Little distinction between Styles 20 and 21.

Style 21 *1860s onward*
Herringbone soundhole ring and backstripe (fancier than Style 20).
▌Colored-wood herringbone soundhole ring between 4 rosewood rings (between 2 groups of 5 rings from 1869).
▌5-ply top binding with rosewood outer layer, 3-ply back binding with ivory outer layer.
▌Colored-wood herringbone backstripe
▌Diamond-pattern figures on endpiece, engraved tuner plates, ivory buttons.
Little distinction between Styles 20 and 21.

Styles 22, 23 *1850s*
▌Herringbone soundhole ring between 2 groups of 5 rings.
▌4-ply top binding with ivory outer layer (possibly with colored-wood purfling), ivory-bound back.

▌No other specs available.
Very obscure styles.

Style 24 *1850s–1880s*
Green and white Z-pattern soundhole ring.
▌Soundhole ring of green and white wood in Z-pattern (line of long diagonals between 2 short diagonal lines) between two groups of 5 rings.
▌Rosewood top binding, top purfling of green and brown wood in diagonal pattern (some with additional checkered-pattern lines), thin line of side binding, 2-ply back binding with rosewood outer layer.
▌Backstripe of red, green, brown and white wood in long arrow-pattern.
▌Engraved brass tuner plates, ivory tuner buttons, diamond-pattern figures on endpiece.
Obscure style.

Style 26 *1850s–80s*
Black and white rope pattern around top.
▌Soundhole rings in 5-9-5 grouping.
▌Ivory-bound top, black and white rope-pattern top purfling, 1- or 3-ply back binding with ivory outer layer.
▌Zigzag backstripe.
Obscure style.

Style 27 *1857 onward*
Pearl ring, greenish colored wood purfling.
▌Soundhole rings of 4 groups of 5 rings with pearl ring in center.
▌Ivory-bound top, top purfling of green and brown wood in long diagonal pattern, 3-ply back binding with ivory outer layer.
▌Zigzag backstripe.
▌Ivory-bound fingerboard and peghead.

Style 28 *1860s onward*
Herringbone trim around top.
▌Pearl soundhole ring through 1870, later with black and white rings in 5-9-5 ring grouping (2 ivory rings in center).
▌Herringbone top purfling, ivory-bound top, 3-ply back binding with ivory outer layer.
▌Zipper-pattern (horizontal pieces between to diagonal lines) backstripe.

Style 30 *1860s–onward*
Pearl ring, herringbone trim, wood bridge.
▌Soundhole rings of 4 groups of 5 rings with pearl ring in center.
▌Herringbone purfling around top border, ivory binding on top, back and fingerboard.
▌Fingerboard inlay by 1898 of slotted diamonds at frets 5 and 9, Maltese cross at fret 7, German silver tuner plates, pearl tuner buttons.

Style 33 *late 1800s*
▌Pearl soundhole ring, wide herringbone purfling around top border.
Very obscure style.

Style 34 *1870–onward*
Ivory bridge but no pearl around top edges.
▌Pearl soundhole ring, top purfling of red, green and white herringbone.
▌Ivory-bound top, 3-ply back binding with ivory outer layer, ivory-bound fingerboard.
▌Fingerboard inlay by 1898 of slotted diamonds at frets 5 and 9, Maltese cross at fret 7, ivory bridge, German silver tuners; pearl tuner buttons.

Style 40 *1860s onward*
▌Pearl top borders but not around fingerboard.
▌Pearl soundhole ring.
▌Pearl trim around top edge, ivory-bound fingerboard.
▌Zipper-pattern (line of horizontal inlays between 2 diagonal lines) backstripe.
▌Ivory bridge, German silver tuners, pearl tuner buttons.

Style 42 *1870 onward*
Pearl top border goes around fingerboard.
▌Pearl soundhole ring.
▌Pearl trim around top edge, pearl trim on top around fingerboard, ivory-bound fingerboard.
▌Zipper-pattern (line of horizontal inlays between to diagonal lines) backstripe
▌Inlays at frets 5, 7 and 9 by 1898; listed in 1870 with "screw neck" (clock key), ivory bridge, German silver tuners; pearl tuner buttons.

83

MARTIN FLAT-TOP MODELS, 1898-CURRENT

Models are grouped in order of body Size, in alphabetical/numerical order: D, J, M, N, OM, ¼, ½, ¾, 0, 00, 000, 1, 2, 2½, 3, 5, 7. Within Size groups, models are listed in ascending Styles.

Odd prefixes
CHD models are listed under . . . D
CM . . . . M
CMJ . . . . J
Custom 15 . . . . D

DC models are listed under . . . . D
D3 . . . . D
HD . . . . D
HJ . . . . J
HOM . . . . OM
JC . . . . J
LHD . . . . D
MC . . . . M
M2C . . . . M
OMC . . . . OM
SD . . . . D

SOM models are listed under . . OM
#25 2

Unless otherwise noted, all guitars have:
■ Spruce top.
■ Dot fingerboard inlays.

Note also that shaded (sunburst) finish tops occur occasionally from around 1928 onward.

84

Entries in this flat-top section are laid out as follows:

Model name *Years of production*
Quick identifying feature(s).
■ Body materials, finish.
■ Body trim: soundhole ring, binding, purfling, pickguard, bridgepins, backstripe.
■ Fingerboard material and inlay, neck style, peghead trim.
Production total (when available; through 1993).
Other comments.
Related models, in alphabetical order.

SIZE D

D-1, 1st version *1931*
Prototype of D-18.
■ Mahogany back and sides.
■ Soundhole rings in 1-9-1 grouping, rosewood body binding.
■ 12-fret neck, slotted peghead, unbound ebony fingerboard.
Production: 2.
DC-1, 1934, carved-top prototype, black binding, production: 2.

D-1, 2nd version *1992–current*
Mahogany body, non-gloss finish, U-shaped neck heel.
■ Solid mahogany back, 3-ply laminated mahogany sides, satin non-gloss finish, modified X-bracing.
■ Soundhole ring in 5-9-5 grouping, tortoise-bound top and back, tortoise pickguard, slanted bridgeplate, slanted bridgepin holes, white bridgepins with black dots, thin black backstripe.
■ Unbound rosewood fingerboard, U-shaped (non-dovetail) neck joint,

mahogany heel cap, chrome enclosed tuners.
D-1R, 1994–current, solid rosewood back, 3-ply laminated rosewood sides.

D-2 *1931–34*
Prototype of D-28.
■ Brazilian rosewood back and sides.
■ Soundhole rings in 5-9-5 grouping, ivoroid binding, herringbone top purfling, zigzag backstripe.
■ Unbound ebony fingerboard, slotted-diamond inlay, 12-fret neck, slotted peghead.
Production: 7.

Custom 15 *1980–current*
HD-28 (see later entry) with added features
■ Tortoise pickguard.
■ Unbound ebony fingerboard, slotted-diamond inlay, V-neck, chrome tuners.
Production: 741.
Named after the 15th custom-ordered guitar of 1980.

D-16 *1986–current*
Minimal trim, offered as annual NAMM show special, woods and other specs change from year to year.
■ Mahogany back and sides, scalloped braces, gloss finish (1989–90 version).
■ Soundhole ring varies, tortoise-bound top (black, 1994), unbound back, black bridge pins.
■ Unbound rosewood fingerboard, small dot inlay, chrome Grover tuners.
D-16A, limited runs from 1987, ash back and sides, production: 1987: 7; 1988: 751; 1990: 60.

D-16H, 1991–current, limited runs, mahogany back and sides, satin finish, herringbone soundhole ring, zigzag backstripe, larger dot inlay (1992), abalone dot inlay (1993), black bridgepins (black with white dots, 1993), chrome Gotoh tuners.
D-16K, 1986 limited run, koa back and sides, black binding, white bridgepins with black dots, gloss finish, production: 390.
D-16M (D-16 from 1991), 1986–current, mahogany back and sides, satin (non-gloss) finish, tortoise top binding, production: 1986: 88; 1987: 590; 1989: 660; 1990: 782.
D-16W, limited runs from 1987, walnut back and sides, black binding on top and back, production: 1987: 100, 1990: 38.

D-18 *1932–current*
Mahogany body, dark outer binding.
■ Mahogany back and sides.
■ Soundhole rings in 1-9-1 grouping (5-9-5 from 1988), 5-ply top binding and 1-ply back with rosewood outer layer (tortoise by 1936, black from 1966), tortoise pickguard by 1934 (black from 1966) black bridgepins, black backstripe.
■ Unbound ebony fingerboard (rosewood 1947), early (first 29 guitars) with 12-fret neck, 14-fret neck from 1934.
Production 65,070.
D12-18, 1973–current, 12-string, 14-fret neck, solid peghead, production: 1,739.
D-18E, 1958–59, 2 DeArmond pickups, lateral top bracing, production: 302.

D-18H, 1934–36, Hawaiian, flat fingerboard, high nut, flush frets, non-slanted bridge, production: 3.

D-18H Huda (type of wood, species unknown), 1966, production: 2.

D-18LE, 1986–87, quilted or flamed mahogany back and sides, scalloped braces, tortoise binding, black bridgepins with white dots, herringbone backstripe, ebony fingerboard and bridge, V-neck, gold tuners with ebony buttons, production: 32.

D-18M, specs unavailable, 1961, production: 1.

D-18MB, 1990 Guitar of the Month, X brace 1in from soundhole, maple binding, white bridgepins with red dots, top signed by shop foremen.

D-18P, standard version of D-18 from 1987, P dropped 1989, production included in D-18 total.

D-18Q, 1986–93, square non-adjustable truss rod, production (included in D-18 total): 180.

D-18S, 1967–93, 12-fret neck, slotted peghead, production: 1,637.

D-18T, 1962, tenor, production: 1.

D-18V, 1983–84, tortoise binding, tortoise pickguard, ebony fingerboard, V-neck, production: 151; then Sept. 1985 Guitar of the Month, production: 56.

D-18 Vintage, see Vintage D-18.

D3-18, 1991 Guitar of the Month, 3-piece back, X-brace within 1in of soundhole, aging toner on top, slotted-diamonds inlaid on bridge ends, black bridgepins with white dots, tortoise-bound ebony fingerboard with black-white purfling, slotted-diamond fingerboard inlay, chrome tuners with embossed M on buttons.

HD-18LE, Oct. 1987 Guitar of the Month, scalloped braces, tortoise binding with herringbone top trim, black bridgepins with white dots, ebony tuner buttons, production: 51.

Special D-18, 1989 Guitar of the Month, scalloped braces, rosewood binding, tortoise pickguard, black bridgepins with pearl dots, slotted-diamond fingerboard inlay, low-profile neck.

Vintage D-18, 1992 Guitar of the Month, scalloped braces, aging toner on top, soundhole rings in 1-9-1 grouping, tortoise binding, tortoise pickguard,

black bridgepins with white dots, ebony bridge with saddle slot right through bridge, ebony fingerboard, V-neck with lower profile than original V-neck, brand stamp on back of peghead.

D-19 *1976–88*
Deluxe mahogany dreadnought, dark-stained top, optional mahogany top (1980-88).
▌ Mahogany back and sides.
▌ Soundhole rings in 5-9-5 soundhole ring grouping, 5-ply top binding with black outer layer, 3-ply back binding.
▌ Unbound rosewood fingerboard.
Production: 30.

D12-20 *1964–91*
Mahogany 12-string.
▌ Mahogany back and sides.
▌ Soundhole rings in 1-9-1 grouping (5-9-5 from 1988), 5-ply top binding and 1-ply back with tortoise outer layer (black from 1966), tortoise pickguard (black from 1966), chainlink backstripe.
▌ Unbound rosewood fingerboard, 12-fret neck, slotted peghead, white plastic tuner buttons.
Production: 10,350.
SD6-20, 1969, 6-string version of D12-20 (12-fret neck, top braced for 12-string), production: 1.

D-21 *1955–69*
Rosewood body, dark outer binding.
▌ Brazilian rosewood back and sides.
▌ Soundhole rings in 1-9-1 grouping, 5-ply top binding and 1-ply back with tortoise outer layer (black from 1966), tortoise pickguard (black from 1966).
▌ Unbound rosewood fingerboard, chrome tuners.
Production: 2,933.
D-21LE, Nov. 1985 Guitar of the Month, Indian rosewood back and sides, herringbone soundhole ring, tortoise binding, tortoise pickguard, V-neck, production: 75.
D-21 Special Edition, 1985, Indian rosewood back and sides, black pickguard, bound fingerboard, production: 75.
D-21V, 1984, Brazilian rosewood back and sides, tortoise binding, tortoise pickguard, V-neck, ebony fingerboard, production: 1.

D-25K *1980-89*
Koa body, no pearl around soundhole.
▌ Koa back and sides.
▌ Soundhole rings in 5-9-5 grouping, 5-ply top binding with black outer layer, tortoise pickguard.
▌ Unbound fingerboard, dot inlay.
Production: 925.
D-25K2, 1980–89, koa top, black pickguard, production: 512.

D-28 *1931–current*
Rosewood body, unbound peghead.
▌ Brazilian rosewood back and sides (Indian 1969).
▌ Soundhole rings in 5-9-5 grouping, ivoroid-bound top (non-grained white from 1966), herringbone top purfling (6-ply with white outer layer from 1947), tortoise pickguard by 1934 (black from 1966), white bridgepins with black dots, 3-ply back binding with ivoroid outer layer (non-grained white from 1966), zigzag-pattern backstripe (narrow chainlink from early 1947, wide chainlink from 1948)
▌ 14-fret neck (earliest with 12-fret), unbound ebony fingerboard, slotted-diamond inlays (dots from 1946).
Production: 12-fret neck: 41; 14-fret neck, herringbone trim: 2,054; non-herringbone: 78,548.
CHD-28, 1991–current, cedar top, scalloped braces, herringbone trim, zigzag backstripe.
Custom 15, see listing opposite under Custom 15.
D12-28, 1970–current, 12-string, 14-fret neck, production: 4,704.
D-28 (1935 Special), 1993 Guitar of the Month, 1935 features, Indian rosewood back and sides, scalloped braces, X-brace within 1in of soundhole, ivoroid binding, tortoise pickguard, zigzag backstripe, saddle slot right through bridge, V-neck, wider string spacing, square tapered peghead with Brazilian rosewood veneer.
D-28 Cocobolo, 1987, cocobolo is Central American wood related to rosewood, production: 2.
D-28 Custom, Nov. 1984 Guitar of the Month, scalloped braces, ebony fingerboard, snowflake inlay, torch peghead inlay, stamped logo on back of peghead, production: 43.

85

D-28E, 1959–64, 2 DeArmond pickups, lateral top bracing, production: 238.

D-28G, 1937, 1961, gut string, production: 2.

D-28H, 1934, 1936, Hawaiian, flat fingerboard, high nut, flush frets, non-angled saddle, production: 2.

D-28LSH, 1991 Guitar of the Month, large soundhole, 2 pearl soundhole rings, ivoroid binding, herringbone top purfling, snowflake inlays on bridge ends, zipper-pattern backstripe, snowflake fingerboard inlay, gold tuners with ebony buttons inlaid with snowflakes, production: 200.

D-28P, 1988–89, low-profile neck (standard on D-28 from 1990), production: 1,322.

D-28Q, non-adjustable square bar in neck, production (included in D-28 total): 417.

D-28S, 1954–93, 12-fret neck, production: 1,789.

D-28SW, 1962–68, 12-fret neck, made for Wurlitzer, production: 30.

D-28T, 1964, tenor, production: 1.

D-28V, 1983–85, Brazilian rosewood, scalloped braces, X-brace *not* within 1in of soundhole, ivoroid binding, herringbone top purfling, tortoise pickguard, slotted-diamond inlay, white-black-white backstripe, production: 268

DC-28, 1981–current, cutaway, oval hole, scalloped braces, soundhole rings in 5-9-5 grouping, production: 300.

DC-28P, 1988, cutaway, low-profile neck, P designation dropped, production: 1.

HD-28, 1976–current, scalloped braces, herringbone top purfling, black pickguard, zigzag backstripe, production: 17,328.

HD-282R, 1992–current, large soundhole with double herringbone ring, zigzag backstripe.

HD-28BLE, Dec. 1987, prototype of HD-28BSE, without signatures, production: 1; then 1990 Guitar of the Month, herringbone soundhole ring, tortoise pickguard, white bridgepins with red dots, low-profile neck, chrome tuners, production: 100.

HD-28BSE, Dec. 1987, signature edition (underneath top signed by Martins and foremen), Brazilian rosewood back and sides, aging toner on top, ivoroid binding, tortoise pickguard, V-neck, slotted-diamond inlay, ebony tuner buttons, production: 92.

HD-28C LSH, 1993 Guitar of the Month, cutaway, scalloped braces, sunburst top, large soundhole, herringbone top purfling, tortoise pickguard, white bridgepins with red dots, rosewood peghead overlay, built-in pickup.

HD-28 Cocobolo, 1987, cocobolo is Central American wood related to rosewood, herringbone trim, production: 2.

HD-28 C.T.B., 1992 Guitar of the Month, aging toner on top, slotted peghead, tortoise binding, tortoise pickguard, white bridgepins with red dots, herringbone backstripe, slotted diamonds at frets 3, 5, 7, 9, CFM script at 12, torch-pattern inlay on peghead, brand stamp on back of peghead, gold tuners with embossed M on buttons, production: 104.

HD-28GM, 'Grand Marquis', 1989 Guitar of the Month, scalloped braces, tortoise binding, herringbone top purfling, herringbone soundhole ring and backstripe, tortoise pickguard, snowflake inlaid at ends of bridge, black bridgepins with abalone dots, snowflake inlay, vertical pearl *CF Martin* inlay on peghead, *Grand Marquis* decal on back of peghead, gold tuners with embossed M on buttons.

HD-28GM LSH, 'Grand Marquis', 1994 Guitar of the Month, aging toner on top or shaded top finish, 2 herringbone soundhole rings, large soundhole, herringbone top purfling, unbound ebony fingerboard with snowflake inlay, *Grand Marquis* in pearl script inlaid at fret 12, vertical *CF Martin* pearl logo on peghead, gold tuners with embossed M on buttons.

HD-28LE, Dec. 1985 Guitar of the Month, scalloped bracing, X brace 1in from soundhole, aging toner on top, herringbone top purfling, tortoise pickguard under the finish, white bridgepins with red dots, V-neck, slotted-diamond inlay, square peghead, production: 87.

HD-28M, 1988 Guitar of the Month, mahogany back and sides, scalloped braces, aging toner on top, herringbone top purfling, tortoise pickguard, white bridgepins with tortoise dots, gold tuners with pearl buttons.

HD-28MP, 1990, Morado (Bolivian) rosewood back and sides, scalloped braces, herringbone top purfling, white bridgepins with black dots, zigzag backstripe, low-profile neck.

HD-28N, 1989–current, scalloped braces, herringbone top purfling, white bridgepins with black dots, black pickguard, standard neck.

HD-28P, 1987–89, scalloped braces, herringbone top purfling, black pickguard, white bridgepins with black dots, zigzag backstripe, low-profile neck (standard on HD-28 from 1987, P designation dropped 1989), production (included in HD-28 total): 1,959.

HD-28PSE, 1988 Guitar of the Month, signature edition, signed on underside of top by C.F. Martin IV and foremen, scalloped braces, aging toner on top, tortoise binding, herringbone top purfling, tortoise pickguard, white bridgepins with tortoise dots, low-profile neck, snowflake inlay, squared-off peghead, ebony tuner buttons.

HD-28SE, Sept. 1986 Guitar of the Month, signature edition (underneath top signed by Martins and foremen), ivoroid binding, herringbone top purfling, tortoise pickguard, diamonds-and-squares inlay, V-neck, ebony tuner buttons, production: 138.

HD-28V, 1984, Brazilian rosewood back and sides, scalloped braces, X-brace within 1in of soundhole, ivoroid binding, herringbone top purfling, tortoise pickguard, production: 1.

LHD-28, 1991–92, larch (similar to spruce) top, scalloped braces, herringbone top purfling.

D-35 *1965–current*
3-piece back.

▌ Brazilian rosewood back and sides (Indian from 1969), 3-piece back.

▌ Soundhole rings in 5-9-5 grouping, 6-ply top binding and 3-ply back with white outer layer, 2 black lines on side binding, tortoise pickguard (black form 1966), white bridgepins with black dots, white-black-white backstripes.

▌ Bound ebony fingerboard.
Production: 59,731

86

CHD-35, 1992–current, cedar top, scalloped braces, herringbone top purfling, zigzag backstripes, locking tuners.

D12-35, 1965–93, 12-string, 12-fret neck, slotted peghead, production: 6,480.

D-35P, 1986–90, low-profile neck, standard on D-35 from 1987 (labeled until 1990), production (included in D-35 total): 1,485.

D-35Q, 1986–93, non-adjustable truss rod, production (included in D-35 total): 289.

D-35S, 1966–93, 12-fret neck, slotted peghead, production: 1,831.

D-35SW, 1966–68, 12-fret neck, slotted peghead, made for Wurlitzer, production: 3.

D-35V, 1984, Brazilian rosewood, aging toner on top, tortoise pickguard under the finish, mitered fingerboard binding, production: 50.

HD-35, 1978–current, herringbone top purfling, zigzag backstripes, production: 2,835.

HD-35P: 1987–89, low-profile neck, standard on HD-35 from 1987, P dropped 1989, production (included in HD-35 total): 166.

LHD-35, 1992, larch (similar to spruce) top, scalloped braces, herringbone top purfling.

SD8-35, 1969, 8-string, production:1.

SD-35S9, 1968, 9-string, D12-35 body, made for Fats Johnson of the New Christy Minstrels, production: 1.

D-37K *1980–current*
Koa body, pearl soundhole ring.
▌ Koa back and sides, non-scalloped braces.
▌ Pearl soundhole ring, 6-ply top binding and 3-ply back with white outer layer, tortoise pickguard.
▌ Unbound ebony fingerboard, diamond-and-triangles inlay at frets 5 and 9, Maltese cross at fret 7, unbound peghead.
Production: 348.

D-37K2, 1980–current, koa top, black pickguard, production: 256.

HD-37K2, 1982, herringbone top purfling, production: 1.

D-40BLE *1990 Guitar of the Month*
Pearl top border but not on top around fingerboard.
▌ Brazilian rosewood back and sides, X-brace 1in from soundhole.
▌ Pearl soundhole ring, pearl top border, white top binding, 3-ply back binding with white outer layer, 1 black line on side binding, tortoise pickguard, 2 6-point snowflakes inlaid in bridge, white bridgepins with pearl dots.
▌ White-bound ebony fingerboard, snowflake inlay beginning at fret 1, white-bound peghead with pearl borders, engraved gold tuners.
Signed by C.F. Martin IV and Mike Longworth.
Production: 50.

D-41 *1969–current*
Pearl trim on top border, hexagonal inlay.
▌ Rosewood back and sides, scalloped braces
▌ Pearl soundhole ring, pearl top border, tortoise pickguard, white bridgepins with pearl dots, zipper-pattern (row of horizontal inlays between 2 diagonal lines) backstripe.
▌ Bound ebony fingerboard, hexagon inlay, low-profile neck from 1988, no inlay at first fret (first fret inlay, 7/8 of D-45-size from 1987), bound peghead, vertical *CF Martin* logo, gold enclosed tuners.
Production: 6,669.

D12-41, 1988–current, 12-string, 14-fret neck, solid peghead, production: 8.

D-41BLE, 1989 Guitar of the Month, Brazilian rosewood back and sides, scalloped braces, X-brace within 1in of soundhole, aging toner on top, tortoise pickguard, low-profile neck, gold tuners with large ebony buttons, production: 31 (to commemorate 31 Brazilian rosewood D-41s in 1969).

D-41N, 1989–current, standard neck.

D-41Q, 1986–93, retains non-adjustable truss rod, production (included in D-41 total): 7.

D-41S, 1970–93, black pickguard, 12-fret neck, slotted peghead, production: 17.

D-42S *1934*
Pearl trim on top around fingerboard, no pearl on sides.
▌ Brazilian rosewood back and sides.
▌ Abalone soundhole ring, abalone borders on top around fingerboard and edge, ivoroid-bound top and back, tortoise pickguard, zipper-pattern (rows of horizontal inlays between 2 diagonal lines) backstripe.
▌ Ivoroid-bound ebony fingerboard, snowflake inlay beginning at fret 5. Production: 1.
Special features (S designation) not documented.

D-42LE, 1988 Guitar of the Month, signed on underside of top by C.F. Martin IV and foremen, scalloped braces, white binding, tortoise pickguard, small hexagonal inlay, low-profile neck, gold tuners with large ebony buttons, production: 75.

D-42V, 1985, Brazilian rosewood, scalloped braces, ivoroid binding, V-neck, hexagonal inlay, production: 12.

D-45 *1933–42, 1968–current*
Pearl trim around side borders.
▌ Brazilian rosewood back and sides (Indian, 1969).
▌ Pearl soundhole ring, pearl borders on top around fingerboard and edge, pearl side borders, ivoroid binding on top and back (white from 1968) tortoise pickguard (black 1966), white bridgepins with pearl dots, zipper-pattern (rows of horizontal inlays between 2 diagonal lines) backstripe.
▌ Ivoroid-bound fingerboard and peghead (white from 1968), snowflake inlay beginning at fret 1 (hexagonal 1939), vertical *CF Martin* pearl logo, gold enclosed tuners.
Production: 1933–42: 91; 1968–93: 3,378.

D12-45, 1969–current, 12 string, 12-fret neck, slotted peghead, production: 87.

D-45 Deluxe, 1993 Guitar of the Month, Brazilian rosewood back and sides, 'bear-claw' figured spruce top, aging toner on top, ivoroid binding, fossilized ivory bridgepins with pearl dots, inlay on bridge and pickguard, highly figured pearl fingerboard inlays, pearl borders around fingerboard and peghead, gold tuners with large gold buttons embossed with M, production: 50.

D-45KLE, 1991 Guitar of the Month, koa back, sides and top, X-brace within 1in of soundhole, pearl border around peghead, gold tuners with embossed M on buttons, custom-built Mark Leaf case, production: 50.

D-45LE, Sept. 1987 Guitar of the Month, Brazilian rosewood back and sides, tortoise pickguard, hexagon outline at bridge ends, hexagon outline fingerboard inlays, gold tuners with ebony buttons, production: 50.

D-45N, 1989–current, standard neck.

D-45P, 1987, low-profile neck, production: 1.

D-45Q, 1986–93, retains non-adjustable truss rod, production (included in D-45 total): 32.

D-45S, 1969–93, 12-fret neck, slotted peghead, production: 23.

D-45S Deluxe, 1992 Guitar of the Month, scalloped braces, ivoroid binding, tortoise pickguard, snowflakes inlaid at bridge ends, 12-fret neck, pearl border around fingerboard, solid peghead, pearl borders on top and side of peghead, gold tuners with ebony buttons inlaid with pearl M.

D-45V, 1983–85, Brazilian rosewood, scalloped braces, aging toner on top, ivoroid binding, tortoise pickguard under the finish, snowflake inlay, production: 62.

D-45 Gene Autry, 1994 Guitar of the Month, like Gene Autry's original 1933, scalloped braces, X-brace within 1in of soundhole, 12-fret neck, offered with *Gene Autry* in pearl script inlaid on fingerboard or with snowflake inlay and *Gene Autry* engraved into 15th fret inlay, torch inlay on peghead, decal logo on back of peghead.

SD12-45, 1971, 1973, 12-string, 14-fret neck, production: 2.

D-60 1989–current
Birdseye maple.
■ Birdseye maple back and sides, scalloped braces, aging toner on top.
■ Tortoise binding, tortoise pickguard, white bridgepins with tortoise dots.
■ Ebony fingerboard, gold tuners with ebony buttons.

D-62 1987–current
Flamed maple body.
■ Flamed maple back and sides, scalloped braces, X-brace 1in from soundhole, aging toner on top.
■ Soundhole rings in 1-9-1 grouping (5-9-5 from 1988), tortoise-bound top and back, tortoise pickguard, white bridgepins with red dots.
■ Unbound ebony fingerboard, chrome tuners with pearl buttons.
Production: 121.

D-62LE, Oct. 1986 Guitar of the Month, label signed by C.F. Martin IV, white bridgepins with tortoise dots, snowflake inlay, production: 48.

D-76 1975–76
Stars on fingerboard, eagle on peghead.
■ Indian rosewood back and sides, 3-piece rosewood back.
■ Herringbone soundhole ring, 6-ply top binding and 3-ply back with white outer layer, black pickguard, white bridgepins with black dots, herringbone backstripes.
■ Unbound ebony fingerboard, star inlays, pearl eagle on peghead, brass plate on neck block.
Production: 1975: 200; 1976: 1,976

D-76E, for employees, label signed by C.F. Martin III (1976), production: 98.

D-93 1993 Guitar of the Month
Mahogany body, bound peghead.
■ Mahogany back and sides, aging toner on top, X-brace 1in from soundhole.
■ Herringbone soundhole ring and backstripe, diamond inlay at bridge ends, white binding, tortoise pickguard, white bridgepins with red dots.
■ Bound ebony fingerboard, slotted-diamond inlay, *CFM* inlay at fret 3, bound peghead, Brazilian rosewood head veneer, gold tuners with ebony buttons.
160-year commemorative guitar.

SIZE J

All J-size models have scalloped braces. J models have M suffix until 1990, e.g. J-18 was J-18M until 1990.

J-18M (J-18 from 1990) 1987–current
Mahogany body.
■ Mahogany back and sides, aging toner on top, satin (non-gloss) finish.
■ Soundhole rings in 1-9-1 grouping (5-9-5 from 1988), 5-ply top binding and 1-ply back with tortoise outer layer, tortoise pickguard, black bridgepins with white dots.
■ Rosewood fingerboard, chrome tuners with ebony buttons.
Production: 312.

J-21M (J-21 from 1990) 1985–current
Rosewood body, black binding.
■ Indian rosewood back and sides.
■ 5-ply top binding and 1-ply back with black outer layer, tortoise pickguard, black bridgepins with white dots, chainlink backstripe.
■ Rosewood fingerboard, chrome tuners.
Production: 226.

J-21MC, 1986 Guitar of the Month, cutaway, 9-ply soundhole ring, chrome tuners with ebony buttons, production: 57.

HJ-28 1992 Guitar of the Month
Rosewood body, herringbone top purfling.
■ Rosewood back and sides, aging toner on top.
■ Soundhole rings in 5-9-5 grouping, ivoroid outer binding, herringbone top purfling, tortoise pickguard, white bridge pins with red dots, 3-ply back binding with ivoroid outer layer.
■ Unbound ebony fingerboard, slotted-diamond inlay, chrome tuners with embossed M on buttons.

HJ-28M, 1994 Guitar of the Month, mahogany back and sides, herringbone top purfling, white bridgepins with tortoise dots, herringbone backstripe, striped Madagascar ebony fingerboard and bridge, chrome tuners with large ebony buttons inlaid with pearl M.

J-40M (J-40 from 1990) 1985–current
Rosewood body, hexagonal inlays.
■ Indian rosewood back and sides.
■ Soundhole rings in 5-9-5 grouping, 8-ply top binding and 4-ply back with white outer layer, black pickguard, white bridgepins with pearl dots, chainlink backstripe.
■ Triple-bound ebony fingerboard,

small hexagonal inlays, unbound peghead, gold tuners.
Production: 2,886.

J12-40M (J12-40 from 1990),
1985–current, 12-string, non-scalloped braces, 14-fret neck, solid peghead, gold tuners with ebony buttons, production: 419.

J-40MBK (J-40BK from 1990), 1988–current, black finish, gold tuners with large buttons, production: 325.

J-40MBLE, Nov. 1987 Guitar of the Month, Brazilian rosewood back and sides, aging toner on top, tortoise pickguard, gold tuners with large pearl buttons, production: 17.

J-40MC (JC-40 from 1990), 1987–current, cutaway, oval hole, 9-ply soundhole ring, production: 635.

Custom J-45M Deluxe Oct.–Dec. 1986 Guitar of the Month
Rosewood body, hexagonal inlays, tortoise binding.
■ Indian rosewood back and sides.
■ Pearl soundhole ring, pearl borders around top, pearl on top around fingerboard, pearl side borders, tortoise binding, tortoise pickguard, black bridgepins with pearl dots, zipper-pattern (row of horizontal inlays between 2 diagonal lines) backstripe.
■ Bound ebony fingerboard, hexagonal inlay, gold tuners with small ebony buttons.
Production: 17.

J-65M (J-65 from 1990) 1985–current
Maple body.
■ Flamed maple back and sides.
■ Soundhole rings in 5-9-5 grouping, 6-ply top binding and 3-ply back with tortoise outer layer, tortoise pickguard, white bridgepins with tortoise dots, zipper-pattern (horizontal row between 2 diagonal lines) backstripe.
■ Tortoise-bound ebony fingerboard, gold tuners with large pearl buttons.
Production: 391.

CMJ-65 (Custom J-65), 1993–current, modeled after special guitar used by C.F. Martin IV at clinics, cherry sunburst finish, white binding, black pickguard, white bridgepins with pearl dots, hexagonal inlay, MEQ-932 active electronics.

J12-65M (J12-65 from 1991),
1985–current, 12-string, 14-fret neck, solid peghead, production: 148.

SIZE M

All M-size guitars have low-profile neck and scalloped braces, unless noted.

M-18 1984-88
Mahogany body, black outer binding.
■ Mahogany back and sides.
■ Soundhole rings in 1-9-1 grouping (5-9-5 in 1988), 5-ply top binding and 1-ply back with black outer layer, black pickguard, black bridgepins, black backstripe.
■ Unbound rosewood fingerboard.
Production: 106.

M-21 Custom Dec. 1984 Guitar of the Month
Rosewood body, black binding.
■ Indian rosewood back and sides, aging toner on top.
■ Soundhole rings in 5-9-5 grouping, 5-ply top binding and 1-ply back with tortoise outer layer, tortoise pickguard, black bridgepins with white dots.
■ Unbound rosewood fingerboard, slotted-diamond inlay.
Production: 16

MC-28 1981–current
Rosewood cutaway, oval soundhole.
■ Rosewood back and sides.
■ 9-ply soundhole ring, 6-ply top binding and 3-ply back with white outer layer, black pickguard, chainlink backstripe.
■ Ebony fingerboard, chrome tuners.
Production: 938.
M2C-28, 1988 Guitar of the Month, double cutaway, pearl soundhole ring, zipper-pattern backstripe, optional pickguard, white bridgepins with pearl dots, gold self-locking tuners with ebony buttons, Thinline pickup optional.
MC-28N, 1990–current, standard neck.

M-35 1978
Early version of M-36 (same specs).
Production: 26.

M-36 1978–current
3-piece back, bound fingerboard.

■ Indian rosewood back and sides, 3-piece back, aging toner on top.
■ Soundhole rings in 5-9-5 grouping, 6-ply top binding and 3-ply back with white outer layer, tortoise pickguard, rosewood bridge, white bridgepins with black dots, zipper-pattern (horizontal row between 2 diagonal lines) backstripes (also with white-black-white backstripes).
■ White-bound ebony fingerboard, low-profile neck, unbound peghead.
Production: 1,690.

MC-37K 1981–82, 1988–current
Koa cutaway.
■ Koa back and sides, cutaway, oval soundhole,
■ Pearl soundhole ring, white outer binding layer, tortoise pickguard.
■ Unbound ebony fingerboard, slotted-diamond inlay at frets 5 and 9.
Production: 1981–82: 18, 1988-93: 35

M-38 1977–current
Pearl soundhole ring.
■ Rosewood back and sides, aging toner on top.
■ Pearl soundhole ring, 7-ply top binding and 3-ply back with white outer layer, tortoise pickguard, white bridgepins with pearl dots, zipper-pattern (horizontal row between 2 diagonal lines) backstripe.
■ Ebony fingerboard, white-black-white binding on fingerboard and peghead, diamond volute on back of peghead.
Production: 1,814.
M-38N, 1990–current, standard neck.

M-64 1985–current
Maple non-cutaway.
■ Flamed maple back and sides.
■ Soundhole rings in 5-9-5 grouping, 6-ply top binding and 3-ply back with tortoise outer layer, tortoise pickguard, white bridgepins with tortoise dots, zipper-pattern (horizontal row between 2 diagonal lines) backstripes.
■ Unbound ebony fingerboard, chrome tuners.
Production: 110.

MC-68 1985–current
Maple cutaway.

■ Maple back and sides, oval soundhole.
■ 9-ply soundhole ring, 6-ply top binding and 3-ply back with white outer layer, 2 black lines on side binding, tortoise pickguard, white bridgepins with pearl dots, chainlink backstripe.
■ White-bound ebony fingerboard, white-bound peghead with vertical CF Martin inlay, gold tuners, diamond neck volute.
Production: 174.

CM-0089 *1979*
3-piece back, unbound fingerboard.
■ Rosewood back and sides, 3-piece back.
■ Soundhole rings in 5-9-5 grouping, 6-ply top binding and 3-ply back with white outer layer, tortoise pickguard, white bridgepins with black dots, white-black-white backstripes.
■ Unbound ebony fingerboard, unbound peghead.
Production: 25.
Made for Fantasy Records' promotion of David Bromberg album.

90

SIZE N

N-10 *1968-93*
Mahogany body classic.
■ Mahogany back and sides, fan bracing.
■ Wood-marquetry soundhole ring, 5-ply top binding and 3-ply back binding of wood with black outer layer, no pickguard, loop bridge with rounded ends.
■ Unbound rosewood fingerboard, 12-fret neck, 25.4in scale (26.44in from 1970), slotted peghead (protrusion at top from 1970), pearloid tuner buttons.
Production: short scale: 280; long scale: 555.

N-20 *1968–current*
Rosewood body classic.
■ Rosewood back and sides, fan bracing.
■ 5-ply top binding and 3-ply back binding of wood with black outer layer, black side stripe, wood marquetry soundhole ring, no pickguard, loop bridge with rounded ends, white-black-white backstripe.

■ Unbound ebony fingerboard, 12-fret neck, 25.4in scale (26.44in from 1970), slotted peghead (protrusion at top from 1970), pearloid tuner buttons.
Production: short scale: 277; long scale: 824.
N-20B, 1985–86, Brazilian rosewood, production 2.

SIZE OM

OM-18 *1930–33*
Dark outer binding.
■ Mahogany back and sides.
■ Soundhole rings in 1-9-1 grouping, 5-ply top binding and 1-ply back binding with rosewood outer layer (black from 1932), small tortoise pickguard (larger current-size from 1931), belly bridge, black bridgepins, black backstripe.
■ Unbound ebony fingerboard, 14-fret neck, 25.4in scale, solid peghead, banjo tuners (right-angle from 1931).
Production: 765.
OM-18P, 1930–31, plectrum neck, production: 95.
OM-18T, 1931, tenor neck, production: 1.

OM-21 *1992–current*
Rosewood body, dark outer binding
■ Indian rosewood back and sides, scalloped braces.
■ Herringbone soundhole ring, 5-ply top binding and 2-ply back binding with tortoise outer layer, tortoise pickguard, black bridgepins with white dots, herringbone backstripe.
■ Unbound rosewood fingerboard, 14-fret neck, 25.4in scale, chrome tuners.
OM-21 Special, 1991 Guitar of the Month, aging toner on top, herringbone soundhole ring, tortoise pickguard, herringbone backstripe, striped rosewood bridge and fingerboard, slotted-diamond fingerboard inlay, tortoise-bound peghead with black-white purfling, gold tuners with pearloid buttons.

OM-28 *1929–33, 1990–current*
■ Brazilian rosewood back and sides (Indian from 1990).
■ Soundhole rings in 5-9-5 grouping, ivoroid binding on top and back (white from 1990), herringbone purfling, small

tortoise pickguard (larger current size from 1931, black from 1990), pyramid-end bridge (belly from 1930), zigzag backstripe.
■ Unbound ebony fingerboard, slotted diamond inlays, 14-fret neck, 25.4in scale, solid peghead, banjo tuners (right-angle from 1931).
Production 1929–33: 487; 1990–93: 179.
OM-28LE, Oct. 1985 Guitar of the Month, aging toner on top, ivoroid binding, tortoise pickguard, V-neck, production: 41.
OM-28P, 1931–32, plectrum neck, production: 5.
OM-28T, 1930, tenor neck, production: 1.
OM-28V, 1984, Brazilian rosewood, ivoroid binding, tortoise pickguard, V-neck, production: 1.
OM-28 Perry Bechtel, 1993 Guitar of the Month, label signed by Mrs. Ina Bechtel (Perry Bechtel's widow), aging toner on top, herringbone top trim, ivoroid binding, tortoise pickguard, zigzag backstripe, pyramid bridge, V-neck, slotted-diamond inlay, chrome tuners with embossed M on buttons, brand stamp on back of peghead.
OMC-28, 1990 Guitar of the Month, cutaway, X brace within 1in of soundhole, tortoise pickguard, white bridgepins with red dots, low-profile neck, gold tuners with small pearl buttons.
SOM 28, 1969, reissue of original model, production: 6.

HOM-35 *1989 Guitar of the Month*
3-piece back, herringbone trim.
■ Brazilian rosewood back and sides, 3-piece back, aging toner on top.
■ Soundhole rings in 5-9-5 grouping, ivoroid binding on top and back, herringbone top purfling, tortoise pickguard, white bridgepins with red dots, zigzag backstripe.
■ Ivoroid-bound ebony fingerboard, 14-fret low-profile neck, slotted-diamond inlay, 25.4in scale, gold tuners.
Production: 60.

OM-40LE *1994 Guitar of the Month*
Double pearl borders.
■ Indian rosewood back and sides.

■ Double-narrow pearl soundhole ring, double-narrow pearl border around top, white bridgepins with pearl dots, zipper-pattern backstripe.
■ Unbound ebony fingerboard with snowflake inlay, vertical *CF Martin* pearl logo on unbound peghead, gold tuners with large ebony buttons inlaid with 4-point pearl snowflakes.

OM-42 *1930*
Pearl top borders, pearl around fingerboard on top.
■ Brazilian rosewood back and sides.
■ Pearl soundhole ring, pearl top borders, pearl border around fingerboard on top, ivoroid-bound top and back, small tortoise pickguard, zipper-pattern (line of horizontal inlays between 2 diagonal lines) backstripe.
■ Ivoroid-bound ebony fingerboard, snowflake inlay beginning at fret 5, 14-fret neck, 25.4in scale, solid peghead with ivoroid binding, vertical *CF Martin* logo, banjo tuners with gold-plated metal.
Production: 2.

OM-45 *1930–32, 1977–current*
Pearl borders around top, pearl side borders.
■ Brazilian rosewood back and sides (Indian from 1977)
■ Pearl soundhole ring, pearl top borders, pearl border around fingerboard on top, pearl around sides, ivoroid-bound top and back (white from 1977), small tortoise pickguard (larger current size from 1931, tortoise from 1970), white bridgepins with pearl dots, zipper-pattern (line of horizontal inlays between 2 diagonal lines) backstripe.
■ Ivoroid-bound ebony fingerboard (white from 1977), snowflake inlay at 8 frets beginning at fret 1 (hexagonal from 1977), standard neck (low-profile neck from c.1988), ivoroid-bound peghead (white-black-white from 1977) with 'torch' pearl inlay (vertical *CF Martin* from 1977), banjo tuners with gold plated metal (right-angle from 1931).
Production: 1930–32: 40; 1978–93: 128.
SOM-45, 1977, first examples of OM-45, production: 56.

OM-45 Deluxe *1930*
Pearl inlay in pickguard.
■ Brazilian rosewood back and sides.
■ Pearl soundhole ring, pearl around top borders of fingerboard and edge, pearl side borders, ivoroid-bound top and back, pearl design inlaid into small tortoise pickguard, snowflake inlays on ends of bridge, zipper-pattern (line of horizontal inlays between 2 diagonal lines) backstripe.
■ Ivoroid-bound ebony fingerboard, snowflake inlay at 8 frets beginning at fret 1, ivoroid-bound peghead with 'torch' pearl inlay, banjo tuners with gold-plated metal.
Production: 14.

SIZE ¼

¼-18 *1918–31*
Mahogany body, dark outer binding.
■ Mahogany back and sides.
■ Soundhole rings in 1-9-1 grouping ('white' rings are not actually inlaid but are the natural color of the top wood), 5-ply top binding with rosewood outer layer, rosewood-bound back, black backstripe.
■ Unbound ebony fingerboard.
Production: 22.

¼-28 *1972, 1981*
White binding, unbound fingerboard.
■ Indian rosewood back and sides.
■ Soundhole rings in 5-9-5 grouping, 6-ply top binding with white outer layer, black pickguard, 3-ply back binding with white outer layer, chainlink backstripe.
■ Unbound ebony fingerboard.
Production: 14.

¼ 12-string *1918*
Specs unavailable.
Production: 6.

SIZE ½

½-18 *1918–19*
Mahogany body, dark outer binding.
■ Mahogany back and sides.
■ Soundhole rings in 1-9-1 grouping ('white' rings are not actually inlaid but are the natural color of the top wood), 5-ply top binding with rosewood outer layer, rosewood-bound back, black backstripe.
■ Unbound ebony fingerboard.
Production: 18.

½-21 *1919*
Rosewood body, dark outer binding.
■ Rosewood back and sides.
■ Herringbone soundhole ring between 2 groups of 5 rings, 5-ply top binding with rosewood outer layer, 2-ply back binding with rosewood outer layer, herringbone backstripe.
■ Unbound ebony fingerboard, slotted-diamond inlays.
Production: 1.

SIZE ¾

¾-18 *1921*
Mahogany body, dark outer binding.
■ Mahogany back and sides.
■ Soundhole rings in 1-9-1 grouping ('white' rings are not actually inlaid but are the natural color of the top wood), 5-ply top binding with rosewood outer layer, rosewood-bound back, black backstripe.
■ Unbound ebony fingerboard.
Production: 4.

¾-21 *1921*
Rosewood body, dark outer binding.
■ Rosewood back and sides.
■ Herringbone soundhole ring between 2 groupings of 5 rings, 5-ply top binding with rosewood outer layer, 2-ply back binding with rosewood outer layer, herringbone backstripe.
■ Unbound ebony fingerboard, slotted-diamond inlays.
Production: 1.

SIZE 0

All rosewood-body Size 0 models have 12-fret neck and slotted peghead throughout production.
All mahogany-body Size 0 models have 12-fret neck and slotted peghead until 1934, 14-fret neck and solid peghead thereafter (except where noted).

91

0-15 *1935, 1940–61*
All-mahogany, no double-dot fingerboard inlays.
■ Mahogany back, sides and top, non-gloss finish.
■ Soundhole ring of thin white-black-white lines, unbound top and back, rectangular (non-belly) bridge, black bridgepins.
■ Unbound rosewood fingerboard, single-dot inlays.
Production: 1935: 2; 1940–61: 10,703.
Style 15 is almost identical to Style 17, with gloss or non-gloss finishes very hard to differentiate. All Style 15 models have a model stamp on the neck block.
0-15H, 1939, Hawaiian, flat fingerboard, flush frets, high nut, non-slanted saddle production: 12.
0-15T, 1960–63, tenor neck, production: 476.

0-16 *1961*
■ Mahogany back and sides, satin (low-gloss) finish.
■ Soundhole rings in 1-9-1 grouping, 3-ply top binding with black outer layer, tortoise pickguard, rectangular (non-belly) bridge, black bridgepins.
■ Unbound rosewood fingerboard.
Production: 6
0-16NY, 1961–current, unbound extra-wide rosewood fingerboard, no inlay, 12-fret neck, slotted peghead, production: 6,138.

0-17, 1st version *1906–17*
Only Size 0 model with mahogany back and sides during first run.
■ Mahogany back and sides, spruce top.
■ 3 black soundhole rings, 3-ply top binding with rosewood outer layer, rosewood-bound back.
■ Unbound ebony fingerboard.
Production: 420.

0-17, 2nd version *1929–48, 1966–68*
All-mahogany body, double-dots at 7th fret.
■ Mahogany top, back and sides.
■ Soundhole ring of 3 thin white-black-white lines, 3-ply top binding with rosewood outer layer (unbound from 1930), tortoise pickguard optional from

1932 (standard from 1934, black from 1966), rectangular (non-belly) bridge, rosewood-bound back (unbound from 1930), thin black backstripe.
■ Rosewood fingerboard, double-dot inlays at 7th fret, 14-fret neck from 1932.
Production: 1929–48: 10,003; 1966–68: 7.
Style 17 is almost identical to Style 15, except that Style 17 has a glossier finish (in the years when both styles were produced) and fingerboard inlays with two dots at the 5th fret.
0-17H, 1930–39, Hawaiian, flat fingerboard, high nut, flush frets, non-slanted saddle, production: 369.
0-17T, 1932–60, tenor neck, production: 2,238.

0-18 *1898–current*
Dark outer binding.
■ Rosewood back and sides (mahogany from 1917).
■ Soundhole rings in 1-9-1 grouping (colored-wood rope-pattern until 1902, 'white' lines in 1-9-1 not actually inlaid until mid 1930s, 5-9-5 grouping from 1988), 5-ply top binding and 1-ply back binding with rosewood outer layer, (black from 1932, tortoise from 1936, then black from 1966), tortoise pickguard from 1932 (black from 1966), rectangular (non-belly) bridge, black backstripe.
■ Unbound ebony fingerboard (rosewood, some examples from 1935, all from 1940), no dot inlay until 1902.
Production: 23,472.
0-18H, 1920, Hawaiian, flat fingerboard, high nut, flush frets, non-slanted saddle, production: 1.
0-18K, 1918–35, koa top, back and sides, production: 3,132.
0-18S, 1932, 14-fret neck (12-fret was standard at the time), production: 3.
0-18T, 1929–current, tenor neck, production: 3,797.
0-18T Carl Fisher, 1930, special order for New York dealer, production: 31.
0-18TE, 1959, 1962, electric, tenor neck, single pickup, production: 2.
0-18T8, 1969–70, 8-string tenor neck, production: 5.
0-18TD, 1977, specs unavailable, production: 1.

0-21 *1898–48*
Rosewood body, dark outer binding.
■ Rosewood back and sides.
■ Herringbone soundhole ring between 2 groups of 5 rings (non-herringbone 1-9-1 ring grouping from 1947), 5-ply top binding and 2-ply back binding with rosewood outer layer (black from 1932, tortoise from 1936), herringbone backstripe.
■ Unbound ebony fingerboard (rosewood from 1941), slotted diamond inlays (dots from 1944), 12-fret neck throughout production (except for 3 with 14-fret in 1930).
Production: 2,051.
0-21H, 1918, Hawaiian, flat fingerboard, flush frets, non-slanted saddle, production: 1.
0-21K, 1919–29, koa top, back and sides, production: 66.
0-21P, 1929, plectrum neck, production: 1.
0-21T, 1929–35, tenor neck, production: 5.

0-28 *1898–1931, 1937, 1969*
Herringbone top borders through 1937, white binding and unbound fingerboard in 1969.
■ Brazilian rosewood back and sides.
■ Soundhole rings in 5-9-5 grouping, ivory-bound top (ivoroid from 1918, non-grained white from 1966), herringbone purfling (6-ply with white outer layer from 1947), zigzag backstripe (chainlink from 1947).
■ Unbound ebony fingerboard, slotted diamond inlays (no inlays before 1901, dots from 1944).
Production: 1898–1931: 1,347; 1937: 6; 1969: 1.
0-28E, 1963, electric, dot inlay, production: 1.
0-28H, 1928, Hawaiian, flat fingerboard, high nut, flush frets, non-slanted saddle, production: 2.
0-28K, 1917–35, koa top, back and sides, production: 641.
0-28NY, 1968–69, production: 2.
0-28P, 1930, plectrum neck, production: 1.
0-28T, 1930–64, tenor neck, production: 1930–31: 71; 1941: 1; 1961: 1; 1964: 1.

0-30 *1899–1921*
Pearl soundhole ring, wood bridge.
▪ Brazilian rosewood back and sides.
▪ Pearl soundhole ring, ivory-bound top and back (ivoroid from 1918), herringbone top purfling.
▪ Ivory-bound fingerboard and peghead (ivoroid from 1918).
Production: 162.

0-34 *1898–99, 1907*
Pearl soundhole ring, ivory bridge.
▪ Brazilian rosewood back and sides.
▪ Pearl soundhole ring, ivory-bound top and back, herringbone top purfling, ivory bridge.
▪ Ivory-bound ebony fingerboard, slotted-diamond inlay at frets 5 and 9, Maltese cross inlay at fret 7, ivory-bound peghead.
Production: 1898–99: 18; 1907: 1.

0-40 *1912–13*
Pearl top borders, no pearl around fingerboard on top.
▪ Brazilian rosewood back and sides.
▪ Pearl soundhole ring, pearl top borders, ivoroid-bound top and back, ivory bridge.
▪ Unbound ebony fingerboard, snowflake inlay pattern at 5 frets beginning at fret 5.
Production: 6.

0-42 *1898–42*
Pearl top borders, pearl around fingerboard on top.
▪ Brazilian rosewood back and sides.
▪ Pearl soundhole ring, pearl top borders, pearl border around fingerboard on top, ivory-bound top and back (ivoroid from 1918), tortoise pickguard from 1932, ivory bridge (ebony from 1918), zipper-pattern (line of horizontal inlays between 2 diagonal lines) backstripe.
▪ Ivory-bound ebony fingerboard (ivoroid from 1918), snowflake inlay at 3 frets beginning at fret 5 (at 5 frets from 1901), 12-fret neck throughout production, ivory-bound peghead (ivoroid from 1918).
Production: 389.

0-44 *1913–31*
▪ Brazilian rosewood back and sides.

▪ Soundhole rings in 5-9-5 grouping, 6-ply top binding (white alternating with brown and/or black) with ivory outer layer (ivoroid from 1918), 3-ply back binding with ivory outer layer (ivoroid from 1918), backstripe of black and white lines with wide white line in center.
▪ Ivory-bound ebony fingerboard (ivoroid from 1918), ivory-bound peghead (ivoroid from 1918), some with *Soloist* inlaid on peghead, some with *Olcott-Bickford Artist Model*
Production: 17.
Special model for performer/teacher Vahdah Olcott-Bickford, top and back binding like later (non-herringbone) Style 28.

0-45 *1904–39*
Pearl top borders, pearl side borders.
▪ Brazilian rosewood back and sides.
▪ Pearl soundhole ring, pearl top borders, pearl border around fingerboard on top, pearl around sides, ivory-bound top and back (ivoroid from 1918), tortoise pickguard from 1932, ivory bridge (ebony from 1918), zipper-pattern (row of horizontal inlays between 2 diagonal lines) backstripe.
▪ Ivory-bound ebony fingerboard (ivoroid from 1918), snowflake inlay at 5 frets beginning at fret 5 (at 8 frets beginning at fret 1 from 1914), ivory-bound peghead (ivoroid from 1918), 'torch' peghead inlay (vertical *CF Martin* logo from 1934).
Production: 158.

0-55 *1935*
▪ Same specs as 00-17.
Production: 12.
These are actually 00-17s special ordered by Rudick's of Akron, Ohio, and stamped 0-55, presumably the dealer's model number.

SIZE 00

00 scale is 24.9in except where noted. All rosewood-body Size 00 models have 12-fret neck and slotted peghead throughout production. All mahogany body models have 12-fret neck and

slotted peghead until 1934, 14-fret neck and solid peghead thereafter (except where noted).

00-16C *1962–82, 1988*
Classical, mahogany body, satin finish
▪ Mahogany back and sides, fan bracing, satin (low-gloss) finish.
▪ Soundhole rings in 1-9-1 grouping, dark outer binding on top only, no pickguard, no back binding, black backstripe, black bridgepins with white dots.
▪ Unbound rosewood fingerboard, no inlay, 12-fret neck, slotted peghead, 26.44in scale.
Production: 1962–82: 4,204; 1988: 1.
00-16AC, 1988, ash back and sides, X-bracing, soundhole rings in 5-9-5 grouping, black binding, tortoise pickguard, black bridgepins with white dots, 25.4in scale.
00-16CM, 1988, soundhole rings in 5-9-5 grouping, X-bracing, tortoise pickguard, 25.4in scale.
00-16M, 1988, soundhole rings in 5-9-5 grouping, X-bracing, tortoise pickguard, 24.9in scale.

00-17, 1st version *1908–17*
Only Size 00 model with mahogany back and sides during first run.
▪ Mahogany back and sides, spruce top.
▪ 3 black soundhole rings, 3-ply top binding with rosewood outer layer, rosewood-bound back.
▪ Unbound ebony fingerboard.
Production: 54.

00-17, 2nd version *1930–60, 1982–88*
All-mahogany body, double-dots at 7th fret.
▪ Mahogany top, back and sides.
▪ Soundhole ring of 3 thin white-black-white lines, unbound top and back, tortoise pickguard optional from 1932 (standard from 1934, black from 1982), rectangular (non-belly) bridge, thin black backstripe.
▪ Rosewood fingerboard, double-dot inlays at 7th fret.
Production: 1930–60: 13,360; 1982–88: 47.
Style 17 is almost identical to Style 15, except that Style 17 has a glossier finish

in the years when both styles were produced) and fingerboard inlays with two dots at the 5th fret.

0-55, 1935, special-ordered 00-17 by Rudick's of Akron, Ohio, stamped 0-55 by request, production: 12.

00-17H, 1934–35, Hawaiian, flat fingerboard, high nut, flush frets, non-slanted saddle, production: 20.

00-17P, 1941, plectrum neck, production:1.

00-18 *1898–current*
Dark outer binding.
■ Rosewood back and sides (mahogany from 1917).
■ Soundhole rings in 1-9-1 grouping (colored-wood rope-pattern until 1902, 'white' lines in 1-9-1 not actually inlaid until mid 1930s, 5-9-5 grouping from 1988), 5-ply top binding and 1-ply back binding with rosewood outer layer, (black from 1932, tortoise from 1936, then black from 1966), tortoise pickguard from 1932 (black from 1966), rectangular (non-belly) bridge, black backstrip.
■ Unbound ebony fingerboard (rosewood, some examples from 1935, all from 1940), no dot inlay until 1902. Production: 21,997.

00-18C, 1962–92, classical, fan bracing, loop bridge with rounded ends, 12-fret neck, slotted peghead, 26.44in scale, production: 4,351.

00-18E, 1959–64, electric, production: 593.

00-18G, 1936–62, gut-string, examples with X-bracing and fan-pattern, with pin bridge and with loop bridge, production: 5,140.

00-18H, 1935–41, Hawaiian, flat fingerboard, high nut, flush frets, non-slanted saddle, production: 255.

00-18K, 1918–34, koa top, back and sides, production: 61.

00-18S, 1932, earliest examples of R-18 archtop, production: 9

00-18T, 1931–40, tenor neck, production: 6.

00-18V, October 1984 Guitar of the Month, aging toner on top, tortoise outer binding, tortoise pickguard, ebony fingerboard, V-neck, gold tuners, 25.4in scale, production: 9.

00-21 *1898–current*
Rosewood body, dark outer binding.
■ Brazilian rosewood back and sides (Indian from 1970).
■ Herringbone soundhole ring between 2 groups of 5 rings (non-herringbone 1-9-1 ring grouping from 1947), 5-ply top binding and 2-ply back binding with rosewood outer layer (black from 1932, tortoise from 1936, then black from 1966), tortoise pickguard from 1932 (black from 1966), herringbone backstrip (deleted 1948).
■ Unbound ebony fingerboard (rosewood 1947), slotted-diamond inlays (dots from 1944), 12-fret neck throughout production. Production: 4,328.

00-21B, 1985, Brazilian rosewood, production: 1.

00-21G, 1937–38, gut-string, examples with X-bracing and fan-pattern, with pin bridge and with loop bridge, production: 3.

00-21H, 1914, 1952, 1955, Hawaiian, flat fingerboard, high nut, flush frets, non-slanted saddle, production: 3.

00-21LE, Sept. 1987 Guitar of the Month, aging toner on top, scalloped braces, herringbone soundhole ring, tortoise binding, tortoise pickguard, black bridgepins with white dots, ebony fingerboard, 14-fret neck without diamond on back of peghead, slotted peghead, chrome 3-on-a-plate tuners, production: 19.

00-21NY, 1961–65, wide fingerboard, no fingerboard inlay, production: 906.

00-21T, 1934, tenor neck, production: 2.

00-25K *1980, 1985 , 1988*
Koa back and sides, spruce top.
■ Koa back and sides, aging toner on top.
■ Soundhole rings in 5-9-5 grouping, 5-ply top binding with black outer layer, black back binding, tortoise pickguard, black bridgepins with white dot, chainlink backstrip.
■ Unbound rosewood fingerboard, chrome tuners.
Production: 1980: 125; 1985: 2; 1988: 1.

00-25K2 ,1980–89, koa top, black pickguard, production: 54.

00-28 *1898–1941, 1958, 1977, 1984*
Herringbone top borders through 1941, white binding and unbound fingerboard thereafter.
■ Brazilian rosewood back and sides (Indian in 1977 and '84).
■ Soundhole rings in 5-9-5 grouping, ivory-bound top (ivoroid from 1918 binding, non-grained white from 1966), herringbone top purfling (6-ply with white outer layer from 1947), tortoise pickguard from 1932 (black from 1966), 3-ply back binding with ivory outer layer (ivoroid from 1918 non-grained white from 1966), zigzag backstrip (chainlink from 1947).
■ Unbound ebony fingerboard, slotted-diamond inlays (no inlays before 1901, dots from 1944).
Production: 1898–1942: 754; 1958: 1; 1977: 1; 1984: 2.

00-28C, 1966–92, fan bracing, slotted peghead, 12-fret neck, 26.44in scale, no pickguard, production: 1,411.

00-28G, 1936–62, gut string, examples with X-bracing and fan-pattern, with pin bridge and with loop bridge, production: 1,531.

00-28K, 1919–33, koa back and sides, Hawaiian, flat fingerboard, high nut, flush frets, non-slanted saddle, production: 40.

00-28T, 1931, 1940, tenor neck, production: 2.

00-30 *1899–1921*
Pearl soundhole ring, wood bridge.
■ Brazilian rosewood back and sides.
■ Pearl soundhole ring, ivory-bound top and back (ivoroid from 1918, herringbone top purfling.
■ Ivory-bound ebony fingerboard (ivoroid from 1918).
Production: 101.

00-34 *1898–99*
Pearl soundhole ring, ivory bridge.
■ Brazilian rosewood back and sides.
■ Pearl soundhole ring, ivory-bound top and back, herringbone top purfling, ivory bridge.
■ Ivory-bound ebony fingerboard, slotted diamond inlay at frets 5 and 9, Maltese cross inlay at fret 7, ivory-bound peghead.
Production: 6.

94

0012-35 *1973*
12-string, 3-piece back.
■ Indian rosewood back and sides, 3-piece back.
■ Soundhole rings in 5-9-5 grouping, 6-ply top binding, with white outer layer, side binding with 2 black lines, black pickguard, white bridgepins with black dot, 3-ply back binding with white outer layer, 3-ply white-black-white backstripes.
■ White-bound ebony fingerboard, unbound peghead.
Production: 1.

00-40 *1913*
Pearl top borders, no pearl around fingerboard on top.
■ Brazilian rosewood back and sides.
■ Pearl soundhole ring, pearl top borders, ivory-bound top and back, ivory bridge.
■ Unbound ebony fingerboard, snowflake inlay at 5 frets beginning at fret 5.
Production: 1 (plus 3 with koa body in 1917).
00-40H, 1928–39, Hawaiian, flat fingerboard, high nut, flush frets, non-slanted saddle, production: 244.
00-40 koa, 1917–18, 1930, koa top, back and sides, production: 1917: 3 (stamped 00-40); 1918: 1; 1930: 5.

00-41 *1972–75*
Hexagonal inlays, no inlay at fret 1.
■ Indian rosewood back and sides.
■ Pearl soundhole ring, pearl borders around top, white-bound top and back, black pickguard, zipper-pattern (row of horizontal inlays between 2 diagonal lines) backstripe.
■ White-bound ebony fingerboard, hexagonal inlays beginning at fret 3, white-bound peghead, vertical *CF Martin* logo.
Production: 5.

00-42 *1898–42, 1973*
Pearl top borders, pearl around fingerboard on top.
■ Brazilian rosewood back and sides (Indian, 1973).
■ Pearl soundhole ring, pearl top borders, pearl border around fingerboard on top, ivory-bound top

and back (ivoroid from 1918), tortoise pickguard from 1932 (black, 1973), ivory bridge (ebony from 1918), zipper-pattern (row of horizontal inlays between 2 diagonal lines) backstripe.
■ Ivory-bound ebony fingerboard (ivoroid from 1918), snowflake inlay beginning at 3 frets beginning at fret 5 (at 5 frets from 1901), 12-fret neck throughout production, ivory-bound peghead (ivoroid from 1918).
Production: 1898–42: 502; 1973: 1. *Currently offered (1994) with tortoise outer binding.*
00-42G, 1936–39, gut-string, may have X-bracing or fan-pattern, pin bridge or loop bridge, production: 3.
00-42K, 1919, koa back and sides, koa top, production: 1.

00-44 *1913–22*
■ Brazilian rosewood back and sides.
■ Soundhole rings in 5-9-5 grouping, 6-ply top binding (white alternating with brown and/or black) with ivory outer layer (ivoroid from 1918), 3-ply back binding with ivory outer layer (ivoroid from 1918), backstripe of black and white lines with wide white line in center.
■ Ivory-bound ebony fingerboard (ivoroid from 1918), ivory-bound peghead (ivoroid from 1918), some with *Soloist* inlaid on peghead, some with *Olcott-Bickford Artist Model*
Production: 6.
Special model for performer/teacher Vahdah Olcott-Bickford, top and back binding like later (non-herringbone) Style 28.
00-44G, 1938, gut-string, may have X or fan bracing, pin bridge or loop bridge, production: 2.

00-45 *1904–38, 1970–current*
■ Brazilian rosewood back and sides (Indian from 1970).
■ Pearl soundhole ring, pearl top borders, pearl border around fingerboard on top, pearl around sides, ivory-bound top and back (ivoroid from 1918), tortoise pickguard from 1932 (black from 1970), ivory bridge (ebony from 1918), zipper-pattern (row of horizontal inlays between 2 diagonal lines) backstripe.

■ Ivory-bound ebony fingerboard (ivoroid from 1918, white from 1970), snowflake inlay at 5 frets beginning at fret 5 (at 8 frets beginning at fret 1 from 1914, hexagonal from 1970), 12-fret neck (14-fret from 1934; 12-fret from 1970), 24.9in scale (25.4in from 1970), slotted peghead (solid from 1934; slotted from 1970), ivory-bound peghead (ivoroid from 1918, white from 1970), 'torch' peghead inlay (vertical *CF Martin* logo from 1934).
Production: 1904–38: 167; 1970–current: 122.
00-45B, 1985, Brazilian rosewood, production: 2.
00-45K, 1919, koa top, back and sides, production: 1.
00-45N, 1989–current, non-scalloped braces, 25.4in scale.

SIZE 000

All have 24.9in scale unless otherwise noted (a few with 25.4in scale in 1934). All have 12-fret neck and slotted peghead until 1934, 14-fret neck with solid peghead thereafter.

000-16 *1989–current*
Single layer of dark binding.
■ Mahogany back and sides, scalloped braces, satin (non-gloss) finish.
■ Soundhole rings in 5-9-5 grouping, tortoise-bound top and back, tortoise pickguard, black bridgepins with white dots, black backstripe.
■ Unbound rosewood fingerboard, 25.4in scale, slotted diamond fingerboard inlay, chrome tuners. *Stamped **000-16M** in first year.*
000-C16, 1990–current, cutaway, gloss finish, oval soundhole, 9-ply soundhole ring, small dot inlay.
000-16M, see main entry above.

000-17, 1st version *1911*
Only Size 000 model with mahogany back and sides during production run.
■ Mahogany back and sides, spruce top.
■ 3 black soundhole rings, 3-ply top binding with rosewood outer layer, rosewood-bound back.
■ Unbound ebony fingerboard.
Production: 1

000-17, 2nd version *1952*
All-mahogany body, double-dots at 7th fret.
▍ Mahogany top, back and sides.
▍ Soundhole ring of 3 thin white-black-white lines, unbound top and back, tortoise pickguard, rectangular (non-belly) bridge, thin black backstripe.
▍ Rosewood fingerboard, double-dot inlays at 7th fret.
Production: 25.

000-18 *1911–current*
Dark outer binding.
▍ Rosewood back and sides (mahogany from 1917).
▍ Soundhole rings in 1-9-1 grouping ('white' lines in 1-9-1 not actually inlaid until mid 1930s, 5-9-5 grouping from 1988), 5-ply top binding and 1-ply back binding with rosewood outer layer, (black from 1932, tortoise from 1936, then black from 1966), tortoise pickguard from 1932 (black from 1966), rectangular (non-belly) bridge, black backstripe.
▍ Unbound ebony fingerboard (rosewood, some examples in 1935, all from 1940).
Production: 1906: 1 maple back and sides; 1911-31 (12-fret): 1,037; 1934–93 (14-fret): 16,852.
000-18 12-string,1913, production: 1.
000-18G, 1955, gut-string, production: 1.
000-18H, 1938, Hawaiian, flat fingerboard, high nut, flush frets, non-slanted saddle, production: 1.
000-18Q, 1986–current, retains non-adjustable truss rod, production: 32 (included in 000-18 totals).
000-18P, 1930, plectrum neck, production: 46.
000-18S, 1976–77, 12-fret neck, production: 3.
000-18T, 1930–41, tenor neck, production: 5.

000-21 *1902–79*
Rosewood body, dark outer binding.
▍ Brazilian rosewood back and sides (Indian from 1970).
▍ Herringbone soundhole ring between 2 groups of 5 rings (non-herringbone 1-9-1 ring grouping from 1947), 5-ply top binding and 2-ply back binding with

rosewood outer layer (black from 1932, tortoise from 1936, then black from 1966), tortoise pickguard from 1932 (black from 1966), herringbone backstripe (deleted 1948).
▍ Unbound ebony fingerboard (rosewood 1947), slotted-diamond inlays (dots from 1944).
Production: 1902–31 (12-fret): 450; 1934–54 (14-fret): 8,542; 1965: 1; 1979: 12.
000-21 10-string, 1902, production: 2.
000-21 12-string, 1921, production: 1.
000-21 harp guitar, 1902–09, extra sub-bass strings, production: 4.
000-21S, 1977, 12-fret neck, production: 1.

000-28 *1902–current*
Herringbone top borders through 1941, white binding and unbound fingerboard thereafter.
▍ Brazilian rosewood back and sides (Indian from 1970).
▍ Soundhole rings in 5-9-5 grouping, ivory-bound top (ivoroid from 1918 binding, non-grained white from 1966), herringbone top purfling (6-ply with white outer layer from 1947), tortoise pickguard from 1932 (black from 1966), 3-ply back binding with ivory outer layer (ivoroid from 1918 binding, non-grained white from 1966), zigzag backstripe (chainlink from 1947).
▍ Unbound ebony fingerboard, slotted-diamond inlays (no inlays before 1901, dots from 1944).
Production: 1902–32 (12-fret): 349; 1931–46 (14-fret, herringbone): 1,193; 1947–93 (non-herringbone): 4,458.
000-28 10-string, 1902, production: 1.
000-28 12-string, 1936, production: 1.
000-28-45, 1938–39, 000-28 body, Style 45 neck, production: 2.
000-28B, 1985, Brazilian rosewood, production: 6.
000-28C, 1962–69, classical, fan bracing, production: 560.
000-28E, 1970, electric, production: 1.
000-28F, 1964–67, specs unavailable, 12-fret neck, production: 10.
000-28G, 1937–55, gut-string, examples with X-bracing and fan-pattern, with pin bridge and with loop bridge, production: 17.
000-28H, 1949, Hawaiian, flat

fingerboard, high nut, flush frets, non-slanted saddle, production: 1.
000-28 harp guitar, 1906, extra sub-bass strings, production: 1.
000-28HX, 1965, specs unavailable, production: 2.
000-28K, 1921, koa top, back and sides, production: 1.
000-28NY, 1962, wide fingerboard, 12-fret neck, slotted peghead, production: 2.
000-28P, plectrum neck 1930, production: 3.
000-28Q, 1986–current, retains non-adjustable truss rod, production: 128 (included in 000-28 total).
000-28S, 1974–77, 12-fret neck, production: 31.
000-28T, 1929, tenor neck, production: 1.
000-28V, 1983–84, Brazilian rosewood, scalloped braces, aging toner on top, ivoroid binding, herringbone trim, zigzag backstripe, V-neck, white bridgepins with red dots, tortoise pickguard, chrome tuners, production: 17.

000-30 *1919*
Pearl soundhole ring, wood bridge.
▍ Brazilian rosewood back and sides.
▍ Pearl soundhole ring, ivoroid-bound top and back, herringbone top purfling.
▍ Ivoroid-bound ebony fingerboard, ivoroid-bound peghead.
Production: 1.

000-40 *1909*
Pearl top borders, no pearl around fingerboard on top.
▍ Brazilian rosewood back and sides.
▍ Pearl soundhole ring, pearl top borders, ivory-bound top and back, ivory bridge.
▍ Unbound ebony fingerboard, snowflake inlay pattern at 5 frets beginning at fret 5.
Production: 1.
000-40H, 1933, Hawaiian, flat fingerboard, high nut, flush frets, non-slanted saddle, production: 1.

000-41 *1975*
Hexagonal inlays, no inlay at fret 1.
▍ Indian rosewood back and sides.
▍ Pearl soundhole ring, pearl borders around top, white-bound top and back,

96

black pickguard, zipper-pattern (line of horizontal inlays between 2 diagonal lines) backstripe.
▪ White-bound ebony fingerboard, hexagonal inlays beginning at fret 3, white-bound peghead, vertical *CF Martin* logo.
Production: 2.

000-42 *1918–48*
Pearl top borders, pearl around fingerboard on top.
▪ Brazilian rosewood back and sides.
▪ Pearl soundhole ring, pearl top borders, pearl border around fingerboard on top, ivoroid-bound top and back, tortoise pickguard from 1932, zipper-pattern (row of horizontal inlays between 2 diagonal lines) backstripe.
▪ Ivoroid-bound ebony fingerboard, snowflake inlay at 5 frets beginning at fret 5, ivoroid-bound peghead.
Production: 127.

000-44 *1917–19*
▪ Brazilian rosewood back and sides.
▪ Soundhole rings in 5-9-5 grouping, 6-ply top binding (white alternating with brown and/or black) with ivory outer layer (ivoroid from 1918), 3-ply back binding with ivory outer layer (ivoroid from 1918), backstripe of black and white lines with wide white line in center.
▪ Ivory-bound ebony fingerboard (ivoroid from 1918), ivory-bound peghead (ivoroid from 1918), some with *Soloist* inlaid on peghead, some with *Olcott-Bickford Artist Model*
Production: 3.
Special model for performer/teacher Vahdah Olcott-Bickford, top and back binding like later (non-herringbone) Style 28.

000-45 *1907–42, 1970–85*
Pearl top borders, pearl side borders.
▪ Brazilian rosewood back and sides (Indian from 1970).
▪ Pearl soundhole ring, pearl top borders, pearl border around fingerboard on top, pearl around sides, ivory-bound top and back (ivoroid from 1918), tortoise pickguard from 1932 (black from 1970), ivory bridge (ebony

from 1918), zipper-pattern (row of horizontal inlays between 2 diagonal lines) backstripe.
▪ Ivory-bound ebony fingerboard (ivoroid from 1918, white from 1970), snowflake inlay at 5 frets beginning at fret 5 (at 8 frets beginning at fret 1 from 1914, hexagonal from 1970), low-profile neck from c.1988, ivory-bound peghead (ivoroid from 1918, white from 1970), 'torch' peghead inlay (vertical *CF Martin* logo from 1934).
Production: 1907–31 (12-fret): 142; 1934–42 (14-fret): 123; 1970 (12-fret): 7; 1971–93: 55.
000-45 7-string, 1911–31, production: 3.
000-45B, 1985, Brazilian rosewood, production: 2.
000-45H, 1937, Hawaiian, flat fingerboard, high nut, flush frets, non-slanted saddle, production: 2.
000-45 lyre head, 1914, production: 1.
000-45N, 1989–current, non-scalloped braces, standard-profile neck.
000-45S, 1974–76, 12-fret neck, production: 11.
000-45 vine fingerboard, 1912, production: 1.
S-000-45, 1975, 12-fret neck, production: 1 (plus 7 stamped 000-45 in 1970).

SIZE 1

1-17, 1st version *1906–17*
The only Size 1 with mahogany back and sides during production run.
▪ Mahogany back and sides, spruce top.
▪ 3 black soundhole rings, 3-ply top binding with rosewood outer layer, rectangular (non-belly) bridge, rosewood-bound back.
▪ Unbound ebony fingerboard, 2 dots at 7th fret.
Production: 145.

1-17, 2nd version *1931–34*
The only all-mahogany Size 1 during production run.
▪ Mahogany back, sides and top, flat natural finish.
▪ Soundhole ring of 3 thin white-black-white lines, no body binding, tortoise pickguard optional from 1932,

rectangular (non-belly) bridge.
▪ Unbound rosewood fingerboard, 2 dots at 7th fret
Production: 1,130
1-17P, 1928–31, plectrum neck, production: 272.
1-17P 5-string, 1939, production: 1.

1-18 *1899–1927*
Mahogany body, dark outer binding.
▪ Rosewood back and sides (mahogany from 1917).
▪ Soundhole rings in 1-9-1 grouping (colored-wood rope-pattern until 1902, 'white' rings in 1-9-1 are not actually inlaid), 5-ply top binding and 1-ply back binding with rosewood outer layer, black backstripe.
▪ Unbound ebony fingerboard, no dot inlay until 1902.
Production: 964.
1-18H, 1918, Hawaiian, flat fingerboard, high nut, flush frets, non-slanted saddle, production: 3.
1-18K, 1917–19, production: 46.
1-18P 5-string, 1930, production: 1.
1-18T, 1927, tenor neck, production: 3.

1-21 *1898–1926*
Herringbone soundhole ring.
▪ Rosewood back and sides.
▪ Herringbone soundhole ring between 2 groups of 5 rings, 5-ply top binding with rosewood outer layer, 2-ply back binding with rosewood outer layer, herringbone backstripe.
▪ Unbound ebony fingerboard, slotted-diamond inlays.
Production: 575.
1-21P, 1931, plectrum, production: 1.

1-27 *1898–1907*
Pearl ring, colored wood purfling.
▪ Brazilian rosewood back and sides.
▪ Soundhole rings of 4 groups of 5 rings with pearl ring in center, ivory-bound top, top purfling of green and brown wood in long diagonal pattern, 3-ply back binding with ivory outer layer, zigzag backstripe
▪ Ivory-bound ebony fingerboard, ivory-bound peghead.
Production: 13.

1-28 *1898–1923*
Herringbone top borders.

▮ Brazilian rosewood back and sides.
▮ Soundhole rings in 5-9-5 grouping, ivory binding (ivoroid from 1918), herringbone top purfling, 3-ply back binding with ivory outer layer (ivoroid from 1918), zigzag backstripe.
▮ Unbound ebony fingerboard, slotted diamond inlays from 1901.
Production: 238.
1-28P, 1928–30, plectrum neck, production: 19.

1-30 *1898–1919*
Pearl soundhole ring, wood bridge.
▮ Brazilian rosewood back and sides.
▮ Pearl soundhole ring, herringbone top purfling.
▮ Ivory-bound ebony fingerboard and peghead (ivoroid from 1918).
Production: 78.

1-34 *1898–1904*
Pearl soundhole ring, ivory bridge.
▮ Brazilian rosewood back and sides.
▮ Pearl soundhole ring, herringbone top purfling, ivory-bound top and back, ivory bridge.
▮ Ivory-bound ebony fingerboard, ivory-bound peghead.
Production: 11.

1-42 *1898–1919*
Pearl top borders, pearl around fingerboard on top.
▮ Brazilian rosewood back and sides.
▮ Pearl soundhole ring, pearl top borders, pearl border around fingerboard on top, ivory-bound top and back (ivoroid from 1918), ivory bridge (ebony from 1918).
▮ Ivory-bound ebony fingerboard (ivoroid from 1918), snowflake inlay at 3 frets beginning at fret 5 (at 5 frets from 1901), ivory-bound peghead (ivoroid from 1918).
Production: 44.

1-45 *1904–1919*
Pearl top borders, pearl side borders.
▮ Brazilian rosewood back and sides.
▮ Pearl soundhole ring, pearl top borders, pearl border around fingerboard on top, pearl around sides, ivory-bound top and back (ivoroid from 1918), ivory bridge (ebony from 1918), zipper-pattern (row of horizontal inlays

between 2 diagonal lines) backstripe.
▮ Ivory-bound ebony fingerboard (ivoroid from 1918), snowflake inlay at 5 frets beginning at fret 5 (at 8 frets beginning at fret 1 from 1914), ivory-bound peghead (ivoroid from 1918).
Production: 6.

SIZE 2

2-17, 1st version *1910*
The only Size 2 with mahogany back and sides in 1910.
▮ Mahogany back and sides, spruce top.
▮ 3 black soundhole rings, 3-ply top binding with rosewood outer layer, rectangular (non-belly) bridge, rosewood-bound back.
▮ Unbound ebony fingerboard, 2 dots at 7th fret.
Production: 6.

2-17, 2nd version, 'old style' *1922–30*
The only all-mahogany Size 2 during production run.
▮ Mahogany top, back and sides.
▮ Soundhole ring of 3 thin white-black-white lines, 3-ply top binding with rosewood outer layer, tortoise pickguard from 1932, rectangular (non-belly) bridge, rosewood-bound back (unbound from 1930), thin black backstripe.
▮ Rosewood fingerboard, double-dot inlays at 7th fret.
Production: 6,044.
2-17H, 1927–31, Hawaiian, flat fingerboard, flush frets, non-slanted saddle, production: 551.
2-17T, 1927–28, tenor neck, production: 45.

2-17, 3rd version, 'new style' *1930–38*
The only all-mahogany Size 2 during production run.
▮ Mahogany back, sides and top, flat natural finish (dark stain from 1935, gloss finish from 1936).
▮ Soundhole ring of 3 thin white-black-white lines, no body binding, tortoise pickguard optional from 1932 (standard from 1934), rectangular (non-belly) bridge.
▮ Unbound rosewood fingerboard, 2

dots inlaid at 7th fret
Production: 612.
#25, 1929–30, same as 2-17 new style (bindings were dropped from the 2-17 in 1929 so that price could be dropped to $25; the new style was called #25 for a short period before reverting to 2-17), production: 775.

2-18 *1898–1938*
Dark outer binding.
▮ Rosewood back and sides (mahogany from 1917).
▮ Soundhole rings in 1-9-1 grouping (colored-wood rope-pattern until 1902, 'white' rings in 1-9-1 are not actually inlaid until mid 1930s), 5-ply top binding and 1-ply back binding with rosewood outer layer (black from 1932, tortoise from 1936), black backstripe.
▮ Unbound ebony fingerboard (rosewood, some examples from 1935), no dot inlay until 1902.
Production: 100.
2-18G, 1954, gut-string, production: 1.
2-18T, 1928–30, tenor neck, production: 345.

2-21 *1898–1929*
Herringbone soundhole ring.
▮ Rosewood back and sides.
▮ Herringbone soundhole ring between 2 groups of 5 rings, 5-ply top binding with rosewood outer layer, 2-ply back binding with rosewood outer layer, herringbone backstripe.
▮ Unbound ebony fingerboard, slotted diamond inlays.
Production: 12.
2-21T, 1928, tenor neck, production: 1.

#25, see 2-17 new style.

2-27 *1898–1907*
Pearl ring, colored-wood purfling.
▮ Brazilian rosewood back and sides.
▮ Soundhole rings of 4 groups of 5 rings with pearl ring in center, ivory-bound top, top purfling of green and brown wood in long diagonal pattern, 3-ply back binding with ivory outer layer, zigzag backstripe.
▮ Ivory-bound ebony fingerboard, ivory-bound peghead.
Production: 8.

98

2-28T *1929–30*
Herringbone top purfling.
▪ Brazilian rosewood back and sides.
▪ Soundhole rings in 5-9-5 grouping, ivoroid-bound top, herringbone purfling, 3-ply back binding with ivoroid outer layer, zigzag backstripe.
▪ Tenor neck, unbound ebony fingerboard, slotted-diamond inlays.
Production: 35.

2-30 *1902–21*
Pearl soundhole ring, wood bridge.
▪ Brazilian rosewood back and sides.
▪ Pearl soundhole ring, herringbone top purfling.
▪ Ivory-bound fingerboard and peghead (ivoroid from 1918).
Production: 7.

2-34 *1898*
Pearl soundhole ring, ivory bridge.
▪ Brazilian rosewood back and sides.
▪ Pearl soundhole ring, herringbone top purfling, ivory-bound top and back, ivory bridge.
▪ Ivory-bound ebony fingerboard, ivory-bound peghead.
Production: 2.

2-40 *1909*
Pearl top borders, no pearl around fingerboard on top.
▪ Brazilian rosewood back and sides.
▪ Pearl soundhole ring, pearl top borders, ivoroid-bound top and back, ivory bridge.
▪ Snowflake inlay at 5 frets beginning at fret 5, unbound fingerboard and peghead.
Production: 1.

2-42 *1900*
Pearl top borders, pearl around fingerboard on top.
▪ Brazilian rosewood back and sides.
▪ Pearl soundhole ring, pearl top borders, pearl border around fingerboard on top, ivory-bound top and back.
▪ Ivory-bound ebony fingerboard, snowflake inlay at 3 frets beginning at fret 5, ivory-bound peghead.
Production: 2.

2-44 *1930*
▪ Brazilian rosewood back and sides.
▪ Soundhole rings in 5-9-5 grouping, 6-ply top binding (white alternating with brown and/or black) with ivoroid outer layer, 3-ply back binding with ivoroid outer layer, backstripe of black and white lines with wide white line in center.
▪ Ivoroid-bound ebony fingerboard, no inlay, ivoroid-bound peghead, some with *Soloist* inlaid on peghead, some with *Olcott-Bickford Artist Model*
Production: 4.
Special model for performer/teacher Vahdah Olcott-Bickford, top and back binding like later (non-herringbone) Style 28.

2-45 *1925–27*
Pearl top borders, pearl side borders.
▪ Brazilian rosewood back and sides.
▪ Pearl soundhole ring, pearl top borders, pearl border around fingerboard on top, pearl borders around sides, ivoroid-bound top and back, zipper-pattern (row of horizontal inlays between 2 diagonal lines) backstripe.
▪ Ivoroid-bound ebony fingerboard, snowflake inlay at 8 frets beginning at fret 1, ivoroid-bound peghead.
Production: 4.
2-45T ,*1927–28*, tenor neck, production: 2.

SIZE 2 ½

2½-17 *1909–14*
Only Size 2½ with mahogany back and sides.
▪ Mahogany back and sides, spruce top (mahogany top from 1927).
▪ 3 black soundhole rings, 3-ply top binding with rosewood outer layer, rosewood-bound back
▪ Unbound ebony fingerboard.
Production: 38.

2½-18 *1898–1923*
Mahogany body, dark outer binding.
▪ Rosewood back and sides (mahogany from 1917).
▪ Colored-wood rope pattern soundhole ring, (black and white rings in 1-9-1 grouping from 1902, 'white' rings are not actually inlaid but are the natural color of the top wood), 5-ply top binding with rosewood outer layer, rosewood-bound back, black backstripe.
▪ Unbound ebony fingerboard, no dot inlay until 1902.
Production: 58.

2½-21 *1910–21*
Rosewood body, dark outer binding.
▪ Rosewood back and sides.
▪ Herringbone soundhole ring between 2 groups of 5 rings, 5-ply top binding with rosewood outer layer, 2-ply back binding with rosewood outer layer, herringbone backstripe.
▪ Unbound ebony fingerboard, slotted diamond inlays.
Production: 29.

2½-28 *1909–23*
Herringbone top border.
▪ Brazilian rosewood back and sides.
▪ Soundhole rings in 5-9-5 grouping, ivory binding (ivoroid from 1918), herringbone top purfling, 3-ply back binding with ivory outer layer (ivoroid from 1918), zigzag backstripe.
▪ Unbound ebony fingerboard, slotted diamond inlays.
Production: 18.

2½-30 *1901–14*
Pearl soundhole ring, wood bridge.
▪ Brazilian rosewood back and sides.
▪ Pearl soundhole ring, herringbone top purfling, ivory-bound top and back.
▪ Ivory-bound ebony fingerboard, ivory-bound peghead.
Production: 5.

2½-42 *1911*
Pearl top borders, pearl around fingerboard on top.
▪ Brazilian rosewood back and sides.
▪ Pearl soundhole ring, pearl top borders, pearl border around fingerboard on top, ivory bridge.
▪ Ivory-bound ebony fingerboard, snowflake inlay pattern at 5 frets beginning at fret 5, ivory-bound peghead.
Production: 1.

SIZE 3

3-17 *1908*
Only Size 3 with mahogany body.
■ Mahogany back and sides, spruce top (mahogany top from 1927).
■ 3 soundhole rings, 3-ply top binding with rosewood outer layer, rosewood-bound back
■ Unbound ebony fingerboard.
Production: 1.

SIZE 5

Scale length is 21.4in prior to 1924, 22in from 1924 onward.

5-15T *1949–63*
All-mahogany, no double-dot fingerboard inlays.
■ Mahogany back, sides and top, non-gloss finish.
■ Soundhole ring of thin white-black-white lines, unbound top and back, rectangular (non-belly) bridge, black bridgepins.
■ Unbound rosewood fingerboard, tenor neck, 22in scale, single-dot inlays.
Production: 1,325.
Style 15 is almost identical to Style 17, with gloss or non-gloss finishes very hard to differentiate, but production of 5-15T does not overlap with 5-17T.

5-16 *1962–63*
■ Mahogany back and sides.
■ Soundhole rings in 1-9-1 grouping, black outer binding, tortoise pickguard, rectangular (non-belly) bridge.
■ Unbound rosewood fingerboard
Production: 127.

5-17, 1st version *1912–16*
Only mahogany-body Size 5 during production run.
■ Mahogany back and sides, spruce top.
■ 3 black soundhole rings, 3-ply top binding with rosewood outer layer, rosewood-bound back.
■ Unbound ebony fingerboard.
Production: 14.

5-17, 2nd version *1927–43*
Only all-mahogany Size 5 during production run.

■ Mahogany top, back and sides.
■ Soundhole ring of 3 thin white-black-white lines, 3-ply top binding with rosewood outer layer (unbound from 1930), tortoise pickguard optional from 1932 (standard from 1934), rectangular (non-belly) bridge, rosewood-bound back (unbound from 1930), thin black backstripe.
■ Rosewood fingerboard, double-dot inlays at 7th fret.
Production: 218.
5-17T, 1927–49, tenor neck, 22in scale, production: 3,666.

5-18 *1898–1989*
Dark outer binding.
■ Rosewood back and sides (mahogany from 1917).
■ Soundhole rings in 1-9-1 grouping (colored-wood rope-pattern until 1902, 'white' lines in 1-9-1 not actually inlaid until mid 1930s, 5-9-5 grouping from 1988), 5-ply top binding and 1-ply back binding with rosewood outer layer, (black from 1932, tortoise from 1936, then black from 1966), rectangular (non-belly) bridge, black backstripe.
■ Unbound ebony fingerboard (rosewood, some examples from 1935, all from 1940), no dot inlay until 1902.
Production: 2,774.
5-18G, 1954, 1956, gut-string, production: 2.
5-18K, 1921, 1937, koa back, sides and top, production: 3.
5-18T, 1940, 1954, 1961, 1962, tenor neck, production: 4.

5-21 *1902–27, 1977*
Rosewood body, dark outer binding (1977 example has same trim as 1977 5-18).
■ Rosewood back and sides.
■ Herringbone soundhole ring between 2 groupings of 5 rings, 5-ply top binding with rosewood outer layer, 2-ply back binding with rosewood outer layer, herringbone backstripe.
■ Unbound ebony fingerboard, slotted diamond inlays.
Production: 1920–27: 117; 1977: 1.
5-21T, 1927–28, tenor neck, production: 312.

5-28 *1901–39, 1968–81, 1988*

Herringbone top borders during first run, white binding and unbound fingerboard during later runs.
■ Brazilian rosewood back and sides (Indian from 1970).
■ Soundhole rings in 5-9-5 grouping, ivory-bound top (ivoroid from 1918, white from 1968), herringbone top purfling (6-ply with white outer layer from 1968), 3-ply back binding with ivory outer layer (ivoroid from 1918, white from 1968), zigzag backstripe (chainlink from 1968).
■ Unbound ebony fingerboard, slotted-diamond inlays (dots from 1968).
Production: 1901–39: 15; 1968–81: 10; 1988: 1.
5-28G, 1939, gut string, production: 1.
5-28T, 1939, tenor neck, production: 1.

5-30 *1900-02*
Pearl soundhole ring, wood bridge.
■ Brazilian rosewood back and sides.
■ Pearl soundhole ring, ivory-bound top and back, herringbone top purfling.
■ Ivory-bound ebony fingerboard, ivory-bound peghead.
Production: 3.

5-34 *1899*
Pearl soundhole ring, ivory bridge.
■ Brazilian rosewood back and sides.
■ Pearl soundhole ring, ivory-bound top and back, herringbone top purfling, ivory bridge.
■ Ivory-bound ebony fingerboard, ivory-bound peghead.
Production: 1.

5-35 *1971*
3-piece back.
■ Indian rosewood back and sides, 3-piece back.
■ Soundhole rings in 5-9-5 grouping, 6-ply top binding with white outer layer, black pickguard, 3-ply back binding with white outer layer, 2 black lines on side binding.
■ Bound ebony fingerboard, unbound peghead.
Production: 1.

5-42 *1921–22*
Pearl top borders, pearl around fingerboard on top.
■ Brazilian rosewood back and sides.

■ Pearl soundhole ring, pearl top borders, pearl border around fingerboard on top.
■ Ivoroid-bound ebony fingerboard, snowflake inlay pattern beginning at fret 5, ivoroid-bound peghead.
Production: 2.

5-45 *1922*
Pearl top borders, pearl side borders
■ Brazilian rosewood back and sides.
■ Pearl soundhole ring, pearl top borders, pearl border around fingerboard on top, pearl side borders.
■ Ivoroid-bound ebony fingerboard, snowflake inlay pattern beginning at fret 1, ivoroid-bound peghead.
Production: 1.

SIZE 7

7-28 *1980–current*
7/8 dreadnought size, rosewood body.
■ Indian rosewood back and sides.
■ Soundhole rings in 5-9-5 grouping with two larger white center rings, 6-ply top binding with white outer layer, black pickguard, 3-ply back binding with white outer layer, chainlink backstripe.
■ Unbound ebony fingerboard.
Production: 206.

7-37K *1980–87*
7/8 dreadnought size, koa body.
■ Koa back and sides.
■ Pearl soundhole ring, white outer binding on top and back, tortoise pickguard.
■ Unbound ebony fingerboard, slotted-diamond inlays at frets 5 and 9.
Production: 95.

MARTIN ACOUSTIC ARCHTOPS

Layout of entries as for flat-tops, explained on page 84.

SIZE C

C-1 *1931–42*
000-size mahogany body.
■ Mahogany back and sides, carved spruce top, arched back, round hole (f-holes appear in 1932, round hole examples continue into 1933), darkened top finish (shaded from 1934).
■ Black outer binding on top and back (3-ply with ivoroid outer layer from 1935), elevated plastic pickguard.
■ Unbound rosewood fingerboard (ebony from 1934), unbound peghead with vertical pearl *Martin* logo (*CF Martin* from 1932, decal from 1934).
Production: round hole (1931–33): 449; f-hole (1932–42): 786.
C-1 12-string, 1932, round hole, production: 1.
C-1P, plectrum neck, production: round hole (1931–33): 9; f-hole (1939): 1.
C-1T, tenor neck, production: round hole (1931–33): 71; f-hole (1933–38): 83

C-2 *1931–42*
000-size rosewood body.
■ Brazilian rosewood back and sides, carved spruce top, arched back, round hole (f-holes appear in 1932, round hole examples continue into 1933), darkened top finish (shaded from 1934).
■ 3-ply top and back binding with ivoroid outer layer, unbound elevated plastic pickguard (ivoroid-bound from 1935), zigzag backstripe.
■ Unbound ebony fingerboard (ivoroid-bound from 1935), slotted diamond inlay (hexagonal beginning at fret 3 from 1939), unbound peghead with vertical *CF Martin* logo.
Production: round hole (1931–33): 269; f-hole (1932–42): 439 plus 1 maple body in 1939.
C-2 12 string, 1932, f-hole, production: 1.
C-2 mandocello, 1932, round hole production: 2.
C-2P, 1931, plectrum neck, round hole, production: 2.
C-2T, tenor neck, production: roundhole (1931–34): 15; f-hole (1934, 1936): 2.

C-3 *1931–34*
000-size rosewood body, snowflake inlay.
■ Brazilian rosewood back and sides, carved spruce top, arched back, round hole (f-hole from 1933), darkened top finish.

■ 5-ply top binding with ivoroid outer layer, elevated plastic pickguard with inlaid pearl borders (black and white plastic borders from 1933), gold-plated tailpiece, zipper-pattern (horizontal row between 2 diagonal lines) backstripe.
■ Ivoroid-bound ebony fingerboard, snowflake inlay beginning at fret 1, ivoroid-bound peghead with vertical *CF Martin* logo, gold tuners.
Production: round hole (1931–33); 53; f-hole (1933–34): 58.
C-3T, 1934, tenor neck, f-holes, production: 1.

SIZE F

F-1 *1940–42*
Large mahogany body.
■ Mahogany back and sides, carved spruce top, arched back, f-holes, shaded top finish.
■ 3-ply top and back binding with ivoroid outer layer, unbound elevated plastic pickguard.
■ Unbound ebony fingerboard, unbound peghead.
Production: 91.
F-1S 12-string, 1941, production: 1.

F-2 *1940–42*
Large rosewood body, 3-ply top binding.
■ Brazilian rosewood back and sides, carved spruce top, arched back, f-holes, shaded top finish.
■ 3-ply top and back binding with ivoroid outer layer, ivoroid-bound elevated plastic pickguard, zigzag backstripe.
■ Ivoroid-bound ebony fingerboard, hexagonal inlay beginning at fret 3, unbound peghead with vertical *CF Martin* logo.
Production: 46 plus 1 maple body in 1941.

F-5 *1940*
Large maple body.
■ Maple back and sides, carved spruce top, arched back, natural finish.
■ Elevated plastic pickguard with white-black-white binding.
■ Ebony fingerboard with hexagonal inlay beginning at fret 3, maple

neck and peghead (light finish).
Production: 2

F-7 *1935–42*
Large rosewood body, hexagonal inlay beginning at fret 3.
▮ Rosewood back and sides, f-holes, carved spruce top, arched back, shaded top finish.
▮ 7-ply top binding with ivoroid outer layer, ivoroid-bound elevated plastic pickguard, zipper-pattern (row of horizontal inlays between 2 diagonal rows) backstripe.
▮ Ivoroid-bound ebony fingerboard with white line inlaid near edge, ivoroid hexagonal inlays beginning at fret 3 (pearloid from 1937), 3-ply peghead binding with ivoroid outer layer, vertical *CF Martin* peghead logo, chrome-plated tuner buttons
Production: 187.
F-7S, 1936, round hole, production: 1.

F-9 *1935–42*
Large rosewood body, hexagonal inlay beginning at fret 1.
▮ Rosewood back and sides, f-holes, carved spruce top, arched back, shaded top finish.
▮ 7-ply top binding with ivoroid outer layer, elevated plastic pickguard with white-black-white binding, zipper-pattern (row of horizontal inlays between 2 diagonal rows) backstripe.
▮ Ivoroid-bound ebony fingerboard with white-black-white line inlaid near edge, pearl or pearloid hexagonal inlays beginning at fret 1, 3-ply peghead binding with ivoroid outer layer, vertical *CF Martin* peghead logo, engraved gold-plated tuner buttons
Production: 72.

102

SIZE R

R-15 *1934*
▮ Maple or birch back and sides, 3-segment f-holes, sunburst top finish.
▮ Raised plastic pickguard.
▮ Rosewood fingerboard.
Production: 2
Prototypes, never in production.

R-17 *1934–42*
Mahogany top.
▮ Mahogany top, back and sides, arched (bent) top, arched back, 3-segment f-holes (1-segment from 1937), 12-fret body size, sunburst top finish.
▮ 14-fret neck.
Production: 940

R-18 *1933–42*
Small mahogany body.
▮ Mahogany back and sides, arched (bent) spruce top (carved from 1937), arched back, round hole (3-segment f-holes from late 1933, 1-segment f-holes from 1937), 12-fret body size, sunburst top finish.
▮ 4-ply top binding with black outer layer.
▮ 14-fret neck.
Production: 1,927 (includes estimated 400 round holes in 1933).
First 9 examples stamped 00-18S, 1932.
R-18P, 1934–36, plectrum neck, production: 4.
R-18T, 1934–41, tenor neck, production: 133.

R-21 *1938*
Small rosewood body
▮ Rosewood back and sides, carved spruce top, arched back, f-holes, 12-fret body size, sunburst top finish.
▮ 4-ply top binding with black outer layer.
▮ 14-fret neck.
Production: 1

MARTIN ELECTRIC ARCHTOPS

Layout of entries as for flat-tops, explained on page 84.

SIZE F

F-50 *1961–65*
Standard square-cornered peghead, 1 pickup.
▮ Thin hollow archtop, f-holes, single cutaway, shaded top finish.
▮ 1 pickup, 2 knobs, elevated pickguard of dark plastic, plexiglass (clear plastic) bridge.

▮ Unbound fingerboard, square-cornered peghead.
Production: 519.

F-55 *1961–65*
Standard square-cornered peghead, single cutaway, 2 pickups.
▮ Thin hollow archtop, f-holes, single cutaway, shaded top finish.
▮ 2 pickups, 4 knobs, 1 selector switch, elevated pickguard of dark plastic, plexiglass (clear plastic) bridge.
▮ Unbound fingerboard, square-cornered peghead.
Production: 675

F-65 *1961–65*
Standard square-cornered peghead, double cutaway, 2 pickups.
▮ Thin hollow archtop, f-holes, double cutaway, shaded top finish.
▮ 2 pickups, 4 knobs, 1 selector switch, elevated pickguard of dark plastic, plexiglass (clear plastic) bridge, vibrato tailpiece.
▮ Unbound fingerboard, square-cornered peghead.
Production: 566

SIZE GT

GT-70 *1965–66*
Single cutaway, 2 pickups.
▮ Thin hollow archtop, single cutaway, burgundy or black finish.
▮ 2 pickups, 4 knobs and selector switch, white elevated pickguard, vibrato tailpiece.
▮ Bound fingerboard and peghead, wide peghead with pointed corners, adjustable truss rod with cover on peghead.
Production: 453
XTE-70, 1965, prototype of GT-70, production: 3

GT-75 *1965–67*
Wide peghead, double cutaway.
▮ Thin hollow archtop, double cutaway, burgundy or black finish.
▮ 2 pickups, 4 knobs and selector switch, white elevated pickguard, vibrato tailpiece.
▮ Bound fingerboard and peghead, wide peghead with pointed corners,

adjustable truss rod with cover on peghead.
Production: 751
GT-7512, 1966, 12-string, no vibrato, peghead tapers, production: 3.
GT-75R, 1965, specs unavailable, production: 1.
XTE-75, 1965, prototype for GT-75, production: 3

XGT-85 1967
Prototype for GT-style guitar, specs unavailable.
Production: 1

Layout of entries as for flat-tops, explained on page 84.

SIZE E/EM

E-18 *1979–83*
Maple solidbody, laminate stripes, pickup covers.
❚ Maple solidbody with laminate stripes of rosewood, mahogany and/or walnut, double cutaway.
❚ 2 DiMarzio pickups with white covers and 1 row of poles visible, 4 knobs, 1 selector switch on upper bass horn, 1 mini-switch for phasing near knobs.
❚ Unbound rosewood fingerboard, adjustable truss rod with cover on peghead, modified scroll-shaped peghead with *CFM* script inlay.
Production: 341.

EM-18 *1979–83*
Maple solidbody, laminate stripes, uncovered pickups.
❚ Maple solidbody with laminate stripes of rosewood, mahogany and/or walnut, double cutaway.
❚ 2 uncovered humbucking pickups with white coils (2 rows of polepieces visible), 4 knobs, 1 selector switch on upper bass horn, 2 mini-switches for phasing and coil-tap near knobs.
❚ Unbound rosewood fingerboard, adjustable truss rod with cover on peghead, modified scroll-shaped peghead with *CFM* script inlay.
Production: 1,375.

E-28 *1980–83*
Mahogany solidbody, contoured top.
❚ Solid mahogany body with contoured edges, neck-through-body construction, shaded finish.
❚ 2 uncovered Seymour Duncan humbucking pickups with black coils, 4 knobs, active electronics, 1 selector switch above knobs, 2 switches for phasing and active-bypass below knobs.
❚ Unbound ebony fingerboard, adjustable truss rod with cover on peghead, modified scroll-shaped peghead with *CFM* script inlay.
Production: 194.

SCHOENBERG/MARTIN OM MODELS

Schoenberg guitars are a cooperative effort between Eric Schoenberg of Concord, Massachusetts, and the Martin Guitar Co. that began in 1987. Schoenberg supplies various components; assembly is done by Martin; then back to Schoenberg's shop for voicing and inlay. Schoenberg/Martin models say *Schoenberg* on the peghead. Inside is a Martin serial number and the notice: "Made expressly for Schoenberg Guitars by the C.F. Martin Co."
Soloist, modeled on OM-18, non-cutaway or cutaway (cutaway has round soundhole and shallower cutaway than Martin's 000 cutaway body), variety of woods including Indian rosewood, Brazilian rosewood, maple and koa, outer soundhole rings of 5 layers, Brazilian rosewood outer body binding, all wood binding layers (some early examples with plastic black and white lines), more binding layers than Style 18, side binding.

Concert (CM) Vintage, replica of 1930 OM-28, including open-end saddle slot, ebony bar in neck, bar frets, banjo tuners, no decal, brand/stamp on back of peghead.

Concert (CM) Standard, modernized version of 1930 OM-28, with closed-end saddle, T-frets, truss-rod.

OM-45 Deluxe, replica of original Martin OM-45 Deluxe.

SHENANDOAH MODELS

Martin Shenandoah guitars were produced from 1983 to 1993. Bodies and necks were made in Japan and shipped unfinished to Nazareth, where they were assembled and finished. Shenandoahs have model names similar to their Martin equivalents but with 32 added after the style number, e.g. the Shenandoah D-1832 is similar to a Martin D-18—unless otherwise noted. A CS prefix denotes a Custom model, which is fancier than its standard equivalent; these were made in a limited run of 25 each. The Shenandoah brand was revived in 1994 on guitars made entirely in Japan.

Most Shenandoahs have a *C.F. Martin & Co.* peghead decal with *SHENANDOAH* underneath.

All Shenandoahs with 000 or D body Size have the following:
❚ Laminated back and sides.
❚ Tortoise pickguard.
❚ Martin Thinline pickup.

Acoustics

000-2832, 1984–93, pearl torch peghead inlay.

D-1832, 1984–92
D-1832SF, 1989–92, satin finish.
CS-18, 1986, ebony fingerboard, slotted-diamond fingerboard inlays, tortoise binding and pickguard, low-profile V-neck.

D-1932, 1989–92, figured mahogany scalloped bracing, tortoise binding, tortoise-bound fingerboard and peghead with black-white purfling, gold tuners with ebony buttons, dot inlay, fancy inlay on 12th fret.
D12-1932, 1989–92.

D-2832, 1984–92.
D-2832L, 1989–92, lefthanded.

D12-2832, 1983–92.
HD-2832, 1983–93.
CS-28, 1986, tortoise pickguard, diamond on back of neck, snowflake inlay, low-profile V-neck.
CS-28H, 1986, tortoise pickguard, diamond on back of neck, snowflake inlay, low-profile V-neck.
HD-2832B, 1992, Brazilian rosewood.

D-3532, 1984–93.
CS-35, 1986, diamond on back of neck, snowflake inlay, low-profile V-neck.

D-4132, 1990–92.

D-6032, 1988–92.

D-6732, 1989–92, quilted ash back and sides, gold tuners with ebony buttons.

SE models

Shenandoah SE models have installed three-band EQ and volume controls in addition to the Martin Thinline pickup.

All have the following:
■ Body shape similar to an M but with a slightly narrower waist.
■ No pickguard.
■ Diamond fingerboard inlays.

SE-2832, 1992, natural of sunburst finish.

SE-6032, 1992, optional finishes: natural, sunburst, translucent black or translucent blue finish.

104

DATING MARTINS
■ Any Martin guitar made in 1898 or after can be dated by the serial number. Prior to 1898 Martins do not have serial numbers. The pre-1898 guitars can only be dated to general periods by characteristics, including the following.

DATING FEATURES BEFORE 1898
■ Stauffer features, especially the scrolled peghead with six-on-a-side tuner assembly: **1833–1840s**.
■ Slotted peghead (some solid with ivory friction pegs): **1840s onward**.
■ Pyramid-end bridge: **late 1840s onward**.
■ Brand stamp on back seam inside body, seen through soundhole: C.F. MARTIN, NEW YORK: **1833–1867**
■ Brand stamp: C.F. MARTIN & CO, NEW YORK: **1867-1898**
■ Brand stamp: C.F. MARTIN & CO NAZARETH, PA., and serial number on neck-block: **1898 onward**

DATING FEATURES AFTER 1898
■ Serial number present (but no model-name stamp): **1898–1930**
■ Model name stamp on neck-block: **1930-current**
■ Pickguards appear in **1929**, and they are tortoiseshell-colored until **1966**, after which they are black (except for some special issues with vintage specs).
■ Martin logo – C.F. MARTIN & CO decal or C.F. MARTIN inlaid vertically – on the headstock: from **1932**.
■ Top trim of colored wood purfling around the edge goes out by about **1902**. Elephant ivory binding goes out (replaced by "ivoroid" grained white plastic) in **1918**. Rosewood binding goes out about **1931**.
■ Necks with 14 frets clear of body appear in **1929** on OMs, then on most models by **1934** (but 12-fret continues on a few models).

BODY MATERIAL
The wood used for the back, sides and top can be a useful general dating criterion.
■ *Mahogany* (brown, quite plain) doesn't appear in a Martin guitar body until **1906** and doesn't appear as a top until **1922**. Practically all Martins before **1906** have rosewood (brown, usually figured) back and sides. The Style number of a mahogany guitar will not be higher than 20 (except for the limited-run HD-28M in **1988**).
■ *Koa* (tan, often figured) appears on either a small guitar (Size 0 or smaller, except for a very few 00s) from **1917** to **1935** or else a large bodied model (M or D) from **1980** onward. All of the small-bodied koas have a koa top; large-bodied koas may have a koa or spruce top.
■ *Maple* (yellowish brown) bodies appear on very small and very, very early examples (**1830s**) or else on large guitars (J, M or D) made in **1986** and after.
■ *Ash* (pale brown, often figured) and *walnut* (very dark brown, usually figured) first appears in **1987**.

GENERAL CHRONOLOGY
1833-39 Martin arrives in New York in 1833 and sets up shop. Guitars show **Stauffer** characteristics: scrolled peghead, six-on-a-side tuners, **clock-key** neck attachment, '**ice cream cone**' heel. Guitars have various **paper labels.**

1839-50 Martin moves to Nazareth, Pa., in 1839 but instruments still known as 'New York Martins' until 1898. **Brand stamp** reads: **C.F. Martin, New York**. Development of new American-style guitar. By 1850 the typical Martin has Brazilian rosewood back and sides, upper bout narrower than lower, X-pattern top bracing, binding of rosewood or elephant ivory, ebony or ivory bridge with ornamental **pyramids** at each end, dove-tail neck joint (clock-key and ice-cream cone heel still appear occasionally until about 1900), ebony fingerboard with no inlay, cedar neck with grafted-on slotted peghead. The X-bracing varies considerably from guitar to guitar, and some smaller examples do not yet have it. Some bodies have a line of binding wood around the middle of the side; some have a thin body lining of spruce.

1852 First record of standardized **body Sizes**.

1856 First record of standardized **decorative Styles**. Labels with body Size, Style number and price are attached to cases.

1867 **Brand stamp** reads: **C.F. Martin & Co., New York**.

1898 **Brand stamp** reads: **C.F. Martin & Co., Nazareth, Pa**. First catalog appearance of fingerboard inlays. **Serial number** stamped into neck-block.

1906 Style 17 is first model with **mahogany back and sides**, first with **rosewood fingerboard**.

1916 One-piece **mahogany neck** replaces cedar neck with grafted peghead. First dreadnought-shaped guitars (available in several sizes) made for the **Ditson** company of Boston and New York, but none with Martin brand.

1918 **Ivoroid** (off-white celluloid with ivorylike grain) replaces elephant ivory binding on Styles 28 and higher. **Ebony bridges** replace ivory on Styles 34 and higher.

1922 Style 17 is revived in Size 2 with mahogany top, back and sides – the first model made for **steel strings** and first with mahogany top. Styles 18 and 28 are braced for steel strings in 1923, all models by 1928.

1929 OM models introduce **14-fret neck**, solid peghead (as a standard model feature) and tortoiseshell plastic **pickguard**. Pyramid bridge is replaced by a **'belly' bridge** (Style 17 retains rectangular bridge) with open-ended saddle slot.

1930 **Model name** stamped into neck-block.

1931 First **archtops**, first use of **vertical logo** on peghead. First Martin-brand **dreadnoughts**. First appearance of curved **C.F. Martin & Co.** peghead logo, silkscreened in gold with black border.

1932 Gold peghead decal replaces silkscreened logo. **Black plastic binding** replaces rosewood on Styles 18 and 21. Models 0-17 and 0-18 are the first non-OMs to get a 14-fret neck.

1934 Tortoiseshell plastic **pickguard** standard. All models except rosewood 0s and 00s change to **14-fret neck** with solid peghead. **'T' frets** (cross-section looks like a T) replace older 'bar' frets. Neck reinforcement changes from ebony bar to metal, non-adjustable **T-bar**.

1935 **X-brace moved** away from soundhole toward bridge on 000 and smaller models.

1936 Some Style 18s (no D-18s) have rosewood fingerboards and bridges. **Tortoiseshell plastic binding** replaces black on Styles 18 and 21.

1939 **X-brace moved** away from soundhole toward bridge on dreadnought models.

1944 Braces no longer **scalloped**.

1947 **Herringbone trim discontinued** on Style 28 and from soundhole ring on Style 21. Herringbone backstripe on Style 21 discontinued in 1948.

1954 First 12-fret dreadnoughts (since earliest version) made for E.U. **Wurlitzer** of Boston.

1965 **Bridge saddle slot** no longer with open ends.

1966 **Black plastic pickguard** replaces tortoise. **Black plastic binding** replaces tortoiseshell binding on Styles 18 and 21. **White plastic binding** (non-grained) replaces ivoroid and Styles 28 and higher.

1967 **Square steel tube** replaces T-bar in neck.

1969 **Indian rosewood** replaces Brazilian on dreadnoughts, and on all other models in 1970.

1976 HD-28 introduced, signaling a return to **vintage features**. Subsequent models may have: scalloped braces, X brace within 1in of soundhole herringbone purfling, tortoise pickguard, tortoise binding, slotted-diamond inlays, snowflake inlays, V-shaped neck.

1981 First models with body **cutaway**.

1984 **Guitar of the Month** program inaugurated.

1985 **Adjustable truss rod** introduced.

1986 **Low profile neck** introduced.

1988 All non-cutaway models without pearl soundhole trim fitted with **Style 28 soundhole ring** (rings in 5-9-5 grouping).

1993 All models **scalloped braces** except standard-issue D-18, D-28 and D-35.

SERIAL NUMBERS

All Martin guitars (except solidbody electrics from the 1970s), basses, and tiples made since 1898 are numbered in one consecutive series. Beginning in mid-1991, mandolins (which previously had their own series) were numbered in the guitar series. A few early ukes have their own number series. Solidbody electrics, ukuleles, and many instruments made for sale under other brands do not have Martin numbers. On flat-top guitars the serial number is stamped on the neck block (look right inside the soundhole, toward the neck) except for some very early examples · which have the number stamped on the top of the peghead. On archtops the number is stamped on the center back seam.

The guitar series begins with #8000, which was Martin's estimate of the total number of instruments made before 1898.

Up to	Year	Up to	Year	Up to	Year
8349	1898	45317	1930	187384	1962
8716	1899	49589	1931	193327	1963
9128	1900	52590	1932	199626	1964
9310	1901	55084	1933	207030	1965
9528	1902	58679	1934	217215	1966
9810	1903	61947	1935	230095	1967
9988	1904	65176	1936	241925	1968
10120	1905	68865	1937	256003	1969
10329	1906	71866	1938	271633	1970
10727	1907	74061	1939	294270	1971
10883	1908	76734	1940	313302	1972
11018	1909	80013	1941	333873	1973
11203	1910	83107	1942	353387	1974
11413	1911	86724	1943	371828	1975
11565	1912	90149	1944	388800	1976
11821	1913	93623	1945	399625	1977
12047	1914	98158	1946	407800	1978
12209	1915	103468	1947	419900	1979
12390	1916	108269	1948	430300	1980
12988	1917	112961	1948	436474	1981
13450	1918	117961	1950	439627	1982
14512	1919	122799	1951	446101	1983
15848	1920	128436	1952	453300	1984
16758	1921	134501	1953	460575	1985
17839	1922	141345	1954	468175	1986
19891	1923	147328	1955	476216	1987
22008	1924	152775	1956	483952	1988
24116	1925	159061	1957	493279	1989
28689	1926	165576	1958	503309	1990
34435	1927	171047	1959	512487	1991 *
37568	1928	175689	1960	522655	1992
40843	1929	181297	1961	535223	1993 **

*Includes 11 mandolins
**Includes 6 mandolins

OWNERS' CREDITS

Guitars photographed came from the following individuals' collections, and we are most grateful for their help.

The owners are listed here in the alphabetical order of the code used to identify their guitars in the Key To Guitar Photographs below.

AC The Acoustic Centre; **AHR** Alan Hardtke; **AHY** Alan Hayward; **AR** Alan Russell; **CC** The Chinery Collection; **CM** Chris Martin IV; **DM** David Musselwhite; **GG** Gruhn Guitars; **HM** Henry Milner; **HR** Hank Risan (Washington Street Music); **IA** Ian Anderson; **LW** Larry Wexer; **MB** Mandolin Brothers; **MC** Mike Carey; **MG** The Martin Guitar Company; **PD** Paul Day; **SH** Steve Howe; **VH** Vince Hockey; **WC** Walter Carter.

KEY TO GUITAR PHOTOGRAPHS

The following key is designed to identify who owned which guitars when they were photographed for this book. After the relevant page number (*in italic type*) we list: the model number or other identifier, followed by the owner's initials in **bold type** (see Owners' Credits above). For example, '2/3: D-45 custom 1983 **CC**' means that the 1983 D-45 custom guitar shown across pages 2 and 3 was owned by The Chinery Collection.

Jacket front: D-28 'Special 1935' 1993 **AC**; D-45 1940 **HR**. *2/3:* D-45 custom 1983 **CC**. *2:* DC-28 1990 **MG**. *6:* 2-42 c1890s **CC**; *10/11:* Stauffer-style **CC**. *10:* Attributed to Stauffer **CC**. *11:* Stauffer-style **MG**. *14/15:* Late 1830s **AH**; Stauffer-style c1830s **CC**. *15:* Stauffer-style c1850s **CC**; Stauffer-style c1840s **GG** *18:* both **CC**. *19:* Martin & Schatz **MG**; Zoebisch **MC**. *22/23:* 2-27 **CC**; 1-40 **IA**. *22:* 2-24 **WC**. *23:* 1-28 **MG**; 0-28 **SH**. *25:* c1860s **CC**; 2-40 **MG**; 2-42 **CC**. *26:* 0-42 **HR**; 00-42 **MG**. *27/28/29:* 000-45 1926 **HR**. *28/29:* 00-45 **CC**. *29:* 000-45 1931 **MB**. *32/33:* 000-28 **DM**; 2-44 **CC**. *33:* both 00-21s **MB**. *36/37:* harp guitar **MG**. *36:* 5K uke **MG**; 3K uke **CC**. *37:* 00-18T **SH**. *40:* 00-28K **VH**. *41:* D-28H **HR**; 00-40H **CC**; 2-17 **IA**. *44:* OM-28 **HR**; OM-18 **LW**. *45:* OM-45 **MG**. *47/48:* Ditson **CC**. *48:* D-28 **MG**; D-18 1937 **HR**; D-18 1939 **CC**. *49/50/51:* 1938 D-45 **HR**. *50/51:* 1940 D-45 **MG**. *51:* Ditson **CC**. *54:* both **CC**. *55:* F-5 **HR**; F-1S **CC**. *58/59:* D12-45 **CC**; D-35 **HM**. *59:* D-28 **AR**; 5-16 **MB**. *62/63:* GT-75 **MG**; EM-18 **PD**. *63:* both **GG**. *66/67:* D-76 **MG**. *66:* M-36 **GG**. *67:* N20 **MB**. *70/71:* MC-28 **SH**; OM-45 custom **CC**. *71:* JC-40 **MG**; J12-65M **SH**; D-42LE **AH**. *74:* both **MG**. *75:* CHD-28 **MG**; D-45 Deluxe **CM**; D-45 Gene Autry **MG**. *Jacket back:* OM-21L 1994 **AC**.

The majority of guitar photography was by Nigel Bradley of Visuel 7. The exceptions are: 1840s Stauffer-style (p15), 2-24 (p22) and 00-18E (p63) by Walter Carter; F-55 (p63) by Dan Loftin; 0-28 (p23), 00-18T (p37), MC-28 (p70/71) and J12-65M (p71) by Miki Slingsby.

MEMORABILIA illustrated in this book, including catalogs, brochures, magazines, documents and photographs, came from the collections of Tony Bacon, Alan Hardtke, and The Martin Guitar Company. These exquisite items were photographed by Nigel Bradley and Will Taylor of Visuel 7.

THE AUTHOR AND PUBLISHER would like to thank The Martin Guitar Company for enthusiastically cooperating with the creation of this book. Special thanks to: *Mike Longworth* for his hospitality in Nazareth, his guidance through the Martin archives and instrument collection, and his history of the Martin company which was a valuable source of information and upon which the production summaries in this book were based; *Chris Martin* for candid comments about himself, his family and his company; *Dick Boak* for an entertaining tour of the Martin factory, for supplying model specs on disk, and for a unique insider's view of the company; and *John Wettlaufer* for magically producing all the things we really thought we'd brought with us.

IN ADDITION to those named in OWNERS' CREDITS the author and publisher would like to thank:
Douglas Adams; Gene Autry; Seamus Brady (The Acoustic Centre); Scott Chinery; George Gruhn (Gruhn Guitars); Fred Hellerman; Stan Jay (Mandolin Bros); Bob Johnson; Barry Moorhouse (The Bass Centre); Hans Moust; Tom Paxton; John Peden; John Reynolds (Mandolin Bros); Pres Rishaw; Jim Roberts (Bass Player); Eric Schoenberg; Bob Shane; Mark Silber; Matt Umanov; Larry Wexer (Mandolin Bros).

SPECIAL THANKS to Scott Chinery and Mike Carey for their care and attention in helping us to photograph items from The Chinery Collection for this book.

BIBLIOGRAPHY

Walter Carter *Gibson: 100 Years of an American Icon* (General Publishing Corp 1994); George Gruhn & Walter Carter *Gruhn's Guide To Vintage Guitars* (Miller Freeman 1991), *Acoustic Guitars and Other Fretted Instruments* (Miller Freeman 1993), *Electric Guitars and Basses* (Miller Freeman 1994); Mike Longworth *Martin Guitars – a History*; A P Sharpe *The Story of the Spanish Guitar* (Clifford Essex 1968); Harvey Turnbull *The Guitar: from the Renaissance to the Present Day* (Batsford 1974).